LOVE LESSONS

"You are afraid of me, Ranald Kincairn!" Enya said.

"I, afraid of a Lowland traitress, who in the bargain, I might remind you, is my captive and in chains? You jest, mistress!"

"Then kiss me."

"Nae." Ranald stood, gazing down at her, his dark eyes musing. "Should I teach ye the rudiments of lovemaking, do ye still think ye can make me love ye?"

"I will yet do it." She stood on tiptoe and kissed his hard mouth.

When he did not respond, Enya moved back a step and stared at him with an unnamed fear. "'Tis your blood that runs cold."

"Then heat it. Tonight. I tire of empty promises."

Other *Leisure Books* by Parris Afton Bonds:
SWEET ENCHANTRESS
SPINSTER'S SONG
WIDOW WOMAN

PARRIS AFTON BONDS

LEISURE BOOKS NEW YORK CITY

A LEISURE BOOK®

September 1993

Published by

Dorchester Publishing Co., Inc.
276 Fifth Avenue
New York, NY 10001

Printed in the United States of America.

For Mary Afton Burns Davenport—
I love you, Mother.

For Jack Baxter, MD—
who embodies all that compassion is.

For George I. McDaniel—
for all the right reasons.

Celtic tradition has it that the soul of one who dies in battle will take the low, or easy, road to the place of his clan. Thus:

Ye'll take the high road
And I'll take the low road,
And I'll be in Scotland afore ye.
For me and my true love will never meet again
On the bonnie, bonnie banks of Loch Lomond.

Author's Note

Four generations ago, a woman emigrated to the United States from Scotland and raved to her neighbor about the beauty of the Afton River in the Scottish Lowlands. That neighbor, fascinated by the Afton, named her daughter Afton. Her daughter named her daughter Afton, and so on.

Having four sons, I had no daughters to whom I could pass on the Afton name. Running short on boys' names by the time our last was born, I bestowed on him the name Ted Afton. I would like to continue this Afton legacy with the story of *The Captive.*

"Flow Gently, Sweet Afton"

Flow gently, sweet Afton, among thy green braes;
Flow gently, I'll sing thee a song in thy praise;
My Mary's asleep by the murmuring stream,
Flow gently, sweet Afton, disturb not her dream.

—Robert Burns

The CAPTIVE

Chapter One

"It looks as though Enya isn't going to be a beauty."

Enya awoke, incredibly, without a thought of her wedding in mind. Without anything beyond a feeling of general good will and buoyancy. Not until old Elspeth parted the pale green bedhangings embroidered with gold did the phrase from childhood leap to the forefront with a force that cut short her languorous stretch.

"G'morning, m'lady Lazybones," the nearly toothless woman said, and draped Enya's morning gown of green gauze across the foot of the bed. "'Tis late awakening you are for such a day of import."

"'Tis not a day of jubilation for me. For my people, aye, but not for me."

She had reached the advanced age of three

and twenty without bending her head to the rights and privileges of a husband. If any man came close to claiming the rights of her heart, it would be Duncan Fraser.

Dared her childhood friend come to her wedding?

She shrugged, took up her morning gown, and headed for her bath. Her serving maid, a short, plump farm girl, took her satin robe from her. "G'morning, m'lady! T'day's finally come! Yer wedding day!"

Along with Elspeth, Mary Laurie was to accompany her to her new home in the Highlands. "I should be so eager, Mary Laurie." Enya tried to maintain a good humor about this, of all mornings. But it was the end of all she had known and the beginning of the unknown.

The bath was still in a state of chaos. With a little smirk mixed with deep love, Enya felt this was just like her mother. Kathryn could rule the Afton clan benevolently, but she was a riot on running a house. Enya's very controlled and very controlling mother didn't suffer fools lightly, but, dear God, when would her mother ever finish the house?

Blue tiles were stacked in a wooden box, awaiting a mason from Italy. A washbasin of speckled marble quarried in Connemara, Ireland, had yet to be inset in the wall. Glazed windows served until leaded ones arrived.

Situated on a gardened terrace above the sandy shores of the Firth of Clyde, the great red sandstone house still had many rooms that were unfinished. Three years before, her mother had hired William Adam and Sons to design Afton House. Fashioned in neoclassical taste, it replaced the baronial castle that for centuries had governed the Lowlands of Ayrshire and the Clan Afton.

Enya knew that before her birth years of warring weather and warring clans had worn away the granite castle. Overlooking Loch Doon and its rolling braes, the vacated seat of the Afton clan was more rubble than rooms.

Which was virtually the state of Afton House at the moment. Admittedly, the finished portions were marvelous. Ionic columns, Venetian chandeliers, a multitude of tall, arched windows and oakwood floors gave Afton House a light, airy interior.

This contrasted with the massive, more oppressively masculine castle, with its crests and family mottoes strewn about to remind Enya of the heavy legacy left by her ancestors.

With peace, at last, established with England and the Afton clan united under her mother's benevolent hand, impregnability was no longer an essential aspect. Battles now were waged on croquet and tennis lawns or at the lively conversational duels held at the frequent dinners her mother gave. Guests were a hodgepodge of Scotland's intellects and creative geniuses.

Enya's bath was scented with a dozen herbs that old Elspeth claimed were a secret concoction dating back to her forebears, the Picts, or painted people, as the invading Romans had called them.

Enya's own lineage was even more impressive. Tracing, as the Picts did, through the matriarchal line of her mother, she could count farther back to Druid priests as ancestors. Enya's mother preferred to think her reign over the Afton clan was a more enlightened one than that of her mystical Celtic ancestors.

"You are starting earlier than is your wont, daughter. The first light of day has not silvered the sea."

Enya half turned in the marble tub. Kathryn stood in the doorway. A mauve-patterned morning wrapper covered her trim figure. At forty-five, her mother was still as beautiful as the day Enya's father, the Black Lion, had captured Kathryn's father in battle and demanded her as ransom. Her wealth of black hair, caught in a loose braid at her nape, was streaked with gray. Lines of laughter and time girded her mouth, now curved in a wistful smile.

"Aye, that I am, Mother. 'Tis a deed that must be done anon, and the sooner I begin the better."

With a nod, Kathryn dismissed Mary Laurie and settled onto the low stool beside the tub. Dampening a face cloth in the heated water, she began washing Enya's freckled shoulders.

"I empathize with your struggle, daughter, but 'tis a good match I have made for you. Wife of the Lord Lieutenant of the Western Highlands is an honor not to be dismissed lightly. I understand Simon Murdock is good to look upon as well as ambitious. What's more, he is young enough at two and thirty to comfort you in your old age."

Neither woman voiced her thoughts of Malcolm Afton. Fifteen years older than Kathryn, her husband was now confined to a separate bedroom. Few ventured beyond those doors. Even the maid servants scurried in and out, heads averted, breath held.

"Alas, this marriage is more to Murdock's liking than mine. A giant of a woman with no brothers to inherit a barony's estates of fertile, rolling crofting land and the lucrative fishing port of Ayr."

Kathryn's hand paused. Enya looked up over her shoulder at her mother. Those wise eyes had misted over like the fog that rolled in off the sea. "Andrew and Gordon would have been giving you away today in your father's stead."

"Which is the reason for the marriage, is it not?" she reminded Kathryn softly, repenting her reference to her brothers. Both had been killed in the service of His Majesty King George II of Great Britain.

Five years earlier, in 1746, the Scottish youths met their deaths at the Battle of Culloden Moor. Hope for an independent Scotland had also met its death. England had suppressed the Highland uprising. As a reward for their loyalty to Great Britain, King George had bestowed the county seat of Ayrshire upon the Afton family.

"'Tis true," her mother said, rising. "Your marriage assures the Clan Afton and its estates continual security—and the opportunity to foster peace with those barbarous Highlanders. Is peace such a bad thing?"

Enya couldn't hold her tongue. "At the price of one's values, Mother? Aye. Ye would trade Scottish blood for English."

"Ye are a product of your father as well as me, Enya. Roman-British blood flowed through his ancestor's veins before that of the Scots. He sorely misses the wearing of the kilt and plaid, but he wisely chose peace with the British. Ye will go to him before the wedding for his blessing?"

With a sigh, Enya rose from the now-cool water and accepted the warmed towel her mother passed her. "Aye, that I will."

Donning her robe, Enya followed her mother from the bath, and told her she would hurry with her dressing as Kathryn left the room. Elspeth alone was allowed to assist Enya that morning with her clothes. The old woman had been maidservant to Kathryn when the Black Lion and his men had stormed Sweetheart Abbey, where she had taken refuge. Alistair, Elspeth's twin brother, was as devoted, and had become the family steward and master of the household.

Over camisole and stays and hoops, white silk stockings and garters, stomacher and quilted petticoat, was draped the white wedding dress of satin. The virginal gown was trimmed with silver lace and seeded with pearls.

Only then did Enya don the dusting cloth and submit her angry red hair to the powder dredger. Her rebellious curls needed no waving, as was the latest court fashion. Slowly the fiery sheen whitened with the sifted powder. A blessed thing on her wedding day, since redheads were considered unlucky.

The mask she held over her face muffled her voice. "Has anyone heard news of Duncan?"

"Nae, m'lady." Elspeth frowned, adding more wrinkles to the accumulation already furrowing the bridge of her large nose. "'Tis best you forget that one. Nothing but a common smuggler."

"Arrant nonsense, Elspeth! Duncan is a Free Trader." Enya slid a foot into one of the silver embroidered slippers with high French heels. She was already tall for a woman. Tall and big-boned, she nevertheless moved with an untutored grace.

Was she taller than her English bridegroom?

"Bah," Elspeth muttered. She stooped to slide the other slipper onto her mistress's foot. "Duncan and his likes are avoiding the tax on malt and wool by operating out of Ayr. The gallows will hoist the smuggler ahigh one day, mark me words. An auld woman like meself knows these things."

Enya lowered the mask. The heritage of superstition that could be traced back into the mists of time prompted her to ask in words almost inaudible, "What else do you know? The Lord Lieutenant—will he make of himself a goodly husband?"

Alistair's spinster sister cackled. "Not for the likes of ye. A firebrand, ye are."

With none of her mother's serenity. Nor her beauty, Enya mentally lamented.

When she was growing up she didn't like to see her mother work in the garden. Her hair would be in disarray and dirt smeared across her cheeks. Enya wanted her mother always to be dressed in bejeweled gowns. She loved her mother most at dinner, when, after a glass of wine, the color was high on her cheeks and she'd be laughing.

Her mother didn't laugh much anymore.

"Ye are a bonnie bride, m'lady," Elspeth said. "Take a look."

Enya took the silver-backed looking glass the old hag held for her approval. Intelligent eyes of an ordinary hazel color stared back at her in the looking glass. Stared beyond her reflection, so singular and richly imprinted with her life's experiences as a homely child, and a daughter at that. There she found a profile so strong that it had virtually compelled her to develop a character to match.

With Enya's coming of age there had also been a coming to terms with her unconventional looks. It had paralleled her emergence from the shadows of her mother and father and brothers.

For years she had refused to look at her reflection, to see her nose, though patrician, too large for her face. Her distinctly square jaw with her cleft chin was too severe to ever be considered feminine.

Now she saw that her face had grown into proportion to her nose. That, while not beautiful, the young woman staring back at her with that unnerving direct scrutiny possessed uncommon looks. Striking was perhaps a better description.

Her old litany, "I might not have the physical perfection, but I'm going to *think* myself into being beautiful," had almost come to pass.

Her father's room was normally kept dark; bright light hurt his eyes. Today, the heavy dusky pink velvet drapes had been drawn open. August's warming sunlight revealed the room's book-paneled walls. French doors that opened onto a flagstone terrace were flung wide. Far beyond, carriages could be seen approaching down the winding, oak-shaded drive.

Fresh air and floral fragrances from the well-tended gardens of rhododendron, chrysanthemum, and snapdragons whisked away the prevailing sour smell of rot. The tinkling sound of the terrace fountain reached the room. It was a place of perpetual banishment and slow, agonizing death. A place of no hope.

Enya bent over her father's chair and kissed his forehead, made even more high by the lack of hair on his brow and crown. "You slept well, Father?"

"Humph! I'll never die in me sleep. I sleep too well."

She had to smile at his attempt at humor in the face of his malady. Rotting stumps moved in agony where once the valiant soldier had scaled fortress walls and wielded a heavy claymore. Leprosy was eating away at the Black Lion.

Malcolm had contacted the ravaging disease while serving in France with the Black Watch troops of King George. Upon Malcolm's return, her parents' joy at being reunited gradually was blighted.

At first, there had only been the thickened

facial skin to indicate something was amiss. Next came the eruption of a few sores between fingers and toes, then the hobbling about the old castle on feet that had no toes. And, at last, the disease had progressed so far that her father could do little more than sit and await his fate, a most difficult task for a man accustomed to action.

Her mother had assumed the mantle of authority, ruling the Afton clan and its estates with the justice and wisdom of her ancestral Pictish princesses. Her court was rapidly becoming the hub for men of Enlightment; it was the Athens of Scotland.

Kathryn had summoned numerous learned doctors from Edinburgh Medical School, the best in Europe, to attend her husband, to no avail. Most shook their head and took their leave. Some offered suggested remedies that worked no magic. Old Elspeth's vile-tasting concoctions at least seemed to soothe Malcolm's tormented soul.

At first, Enya felt shamed by the revulsion she felt; gradually, the enforced company of her father disclosed a man she had never known. Beneath the formidable manner was a man with sentiment. Behind the hideous mask was a man of dry humor. He loved her mother above all else and wanted to set her free with his death.

This, her mother would not allow.

Kathryn, dressed in a court gown of green watered silk, entered the room by way of the terrace. Behind her followed a tall man in a peasant's jacket of Yorkshire serge and a red handkerchief around his neck. Today, Brother Archibald was disguised as an itinerant scribe with his knapsack of inkhorn, ledger, quill, and paper. His own unruly red locks, grizzled with gray, declared him as much a renegade as Enya in his own way. A gentle renegade, albeit an inveterate one.

When most of Scotland was of Protestant persuasion, he appeared like a will-o'-the-wisp first in a medieval burgh, next a seaport, then a mountain village. Was he an itinerant preacher, a medicant friar? Enya had never been sure. His mission appeared to be to restore the free-and-easy climate of the old Scottish Catholic Church—when the more rabid Protestant Coventers weren't hot on his heels.

The Catholic Church had been replaced by the strict teachings of Calvinist Protestantism. The result was as if a red-hot iron had been plunged into a staved barrel of icy water. For the Calvinists, there was no straightforward confession of sins: If a person repented on his deathbed, it was too late. You either lived a good life or you roasted in hell for all eternity.

This teaching did not cure the Scots of sin, but left them with an abiding sense that punishment automatically goes hand in hand with most kinds of enjoyment.

Enya distinctly recalled as a child the rickety-boned kirk minister chastising her after he had caught her swimming down at Loch Doon. His wrinkle-puckered mouth had compressed into a stringent line. "Ye've had the pleasure long enough to suffer."

The following Sunday, the eve of Samhain, the Celtic lord of death, a neep-o-lantern was found on the kirk's pulpit. Some said it was the displeasure of the Auld Folk at the banishment of music from the church services. A smug Enya knew better.

Perhaps that was why she enjoyed Brother Archibald. In his mid-forties, the lean, lazy priest possessed the ability to make people laugh regardless of the dire situation. "Ye ready for your blessing, lass?" he asked her. "Marriage is a tricky affair. Soon you'll swear to love, then later you'll love to swear."

She grinned. "Just bless me, Brother Archibald, before I set the good Reverend Macives on you."

"Ach, lassie, but ye have a tongue of nettle."

Kathryn knelt at Malcolm's side and took hold of his hand, which was missing three fingers. With a grim countenance, she examined it. "Ye have a new weeping sore. I'll tend to it after the blessing, dear one."

Malcolm tugged his hand from his wife's grasp. "Let's get on with this foolery. I tire."

Enya lowered her head, as much to avoid her father's mortified expression as to receive Brother Archibald's blessing. She understood the reason for her father's brusqueness and could do nothing to alleviate his emotional pain. Going down on her knees, she said, "Bless me, for I have sinned."

"Not nearly enough, I think." The priest placed his spindly fingers atop her powdered coiffure with its net of pearls. His lantern jaw lost its wry smile, and his nimble lips took on a serious cast. "The greatest sin is to abstain from the passions of life. Passions teach us lessons about compassion, joy, love, and finally self-surrender. I charge you to seek these as the knight seeks the Holy Grail."

His hand on her shoulder signaled her to rise. "Go with God, Enya."

She dipped a curtsy and, with her mother, left the room. They sought out the immense salon with its cream-colored walls, reminiscent of London's Assembly Rooms. Their heels clicked hollowly on the inlaid mahogany floor. Each woman was silent with her own thoughts.

Kathryn was a private person; no one ever knew her feelings. Enya's thoughts centered, quite naturally, on the imminent wedding. Her intended was detained at Westminster and would join her at his Highland headquarters, Fort William. As a direct result of the Rebellion of

'45 and the battle at Culloden, a nervous London government had ordered its recent reconstruction, still in progress. She could only imagine the disorder of sawdust and hammering she would preside over as wife of the Lord Lieutenant.

For the wedding ceremony, Simon Murdock was to be represented by proxy. Enya could not pick out his proxy from the multitude of guests assembled in the salon, which with its coffered ceiling was the full height of the two-story mansion. Sunlight poured though the big orangery windows. The double row of marbled pilasters, reflected tenfold in the gilt-framed mirrors.

Alistair had outdone himself in decorating for the occasion: crystal candlesticks, satin table coverings, silver tureens, porcelain vases. Kathryn stopped to confer with the thin, stiff-mannered old man. "Are the peeled prawns fresh?"

"Aye, with a dash of cream and dry vermouth sauce," he said with his soft brogue and rolling *r*s.

"You transferred the monies in the Edinburgh account to Glasgow for Enya?"

"Aye, m'lady." He allowed himself a rare smile. "More than a fortnight ago."

She touched his sleeve, the most affectionate gesture Enya had ever witnessed between her mother and others, with the exception of Malcolm. It was as if her mother didn't allow herself to feel emotion, only devotion and duty.

"What would I do without you, Alistair?"

His big nose sniffed. "You would, as always, suffer in silence, madam."

The guests represented the elite of Scottish society. Writers, lawyers, philosophers, doctors, scholars, scientists, and painters paid tribute today. Kathryn had encouraged these Scottish men of learning and letters to come to her court. She believed this was the only way to rescue for posterity the culture of what was once an independent nation.

Having grown up surrounded by the best minds in Scotland, Enya had assimilated her mother's creed. After struggling against the English for almost a thousand years, Scotland, Enya felt, needed to seek its identity through peaceful means.

For that reason, and that reason alone, she consented to be led to the marriage altar. The man giving her away was her mother's friend, the famed dramatist Allan Ramsay, who had opened the first circulating library in Scotland. Before an ornate marble-and-plaster fireplace, Reverend Macives awaited the bride and the groom's proxy. In the absence of wedding music, silence reigned.

Enya's gaze searched the faces of the guests. There he was, toward the back of the crowded room: Duncan Fraser. He was clothed in a shabby frock coat and trews. She smiled tremulously.

Below the disheveled fringe of yellow hair, his brown eyes reassured her. All was well, then.

Next, she searched among the unrecognizable faces closest to the parish minister. The stocky little man wearing a fringed waistcoat—was he Simon Murdock's proxy? He exuded an aura of self-import.

Old Allan Ramsay kissed her on the cheek and nudged her forward. At the same time, the man in the fringed waistcoat stepped forth. Lurched was a better word, she thought. Obviously, he had imbibed too well.

He introduced himself in an officious and quite British tone. Each word was elaborately pronounced. "I am Sir Oliver Wakefield, Secretary to the Ministry of War and proxy for Simon Murdock, Lord Lieutenant of the Western Highlands, at your service, my lady."

Enya blanked out all thought. From hereforth, she would be leaving the Lowlands and her childhood to become a wife in whatever foreign land her husband's position would take him.

And the hinterland of the Highlands was as much a foreign country as would be the Russian steppes.

Was any cause, even one as noble as the preservation of all that was distinctly Scottish, worth this terrible sacrifice? God, but what she wouldn't give for an opportunity to sneak away and smoke her pipe for a leisurely half hour.

The marriage ceremony was over barely before it had begun. She wouldn't wear the ring of the Lord Lieutenant until she exchanged vows with him in a more private ceremony, so she still didn't feel wedded.

The afternoon festivities were spent in toasting with brilliant clarets, dancing, and, later, a sampling of sumptuous dishes: salmon with prawn sauce, succulent lamb with mint jelly, and a sublime pigeon consommé.

She did not see Duncan again.

Too soon, Enya's luggage and that of her maidservants was being loaded atop the Lord Lieutenant's private traveling coach. The proxy, Wakefield, had drunk too much and so chose to remain behind. Or, at least, that was the gentle yet very effective suggestion of her mother.

Enya had changed into a copper-red jaconet traveling dress with a bonnet of matching copper-red ribbons. Balmy weather blessed her bridal journey. It was to take her to Glasgow, where she would board ship. From there, the ship would transport her up the Clyde River and through the inner islands to the entrance of the Great Glen. The last stage of travel to Fort William would be accomplished over a series of Roman and English roads paralleling the Highland lochs.

Standing beneath the airy wrought-iron porte

cochere, she blinked back tears and kissed her mother good-bye. "You will come to visit me?"

Her mother's eyes glistened with her own unshed tears. Kathryn and Enya had been more than mother and daughter: tutor and student, closest of friends, confidants. "The Butcher himself couldn't keep me from you."

They both managed a weak smile at the jest. The Butcher was William Augustus, Duke of Cumberland, the third son of George II. General Cumberland had become infamous for the atrocities committed by his men after the Battle of Culloden.

Mary Laurie dropped a curtsy to her cousin, a stern-looking farm wife who doubtlessly was glad to be relieved of another mouth to feed. Alistair gave his twin an old man's quick, embarrassed hug. Kathryn's embrace for the departing servants was as reserved but as heartfelt.

Enya swallowed her pain of separation and, turning from her mother, boarded the coach. She did not know how long it would be before she saw her mother again. But both knew her mother would remain with Malcolm, who needed her more, and would remain with him until his last wheezing breath.

Elspeth, Mary Laurie, and two green-coated liveried footmen accompanied her. A contingent of redcoats, serving as Enya's guard, rode ahead of and behind her coach. With a jerk, it and its team of six grays set out at a fast clip down the double row of oaks. Haste was needed if the bride was to reach Glasgow by nightfall. The ship was to sail with the tide.

The coach's three occupants were silent, each already missing Ayr and Afton House. Each was wondering what the future would bring. The sounds of horses' hooves, harnesses, and carriage wheels were the only noises as the coach traveled the byroads through glen and dale.

After they crossed the Brig o'Doon spanning the Ayr River, the countryside sped past the coach window: manicured hills with flocks of sheep, patches of daffodils and violets and the delicate lavender heather, stone dykes separating small tenant farms, and country estates lavish with ferns and flowers.

The splendid summer sunlight was waning, the high-piled clouds pink with sunset, when the galloping grays stopped at a coaching inn. An ostler came running out to tend the horses.

"M'lady, I have need of the . . . privy," Mary Laurie said. She was a priggish lass who nonetheless was desirous of finding herself a learned husband. God knew where she would find a learned man in the Highlands. Their Gaelic tongue was the rude speech of a barbarous people who had few thoughts to express.

"Ayrshire plowboys want only a wife to cook and clean the mud from their boots," she had complained often enough in her Scots Braid, akin to Old English.

Enya nodded her permission. "Elspeth, accompany Mary Laurie, will you? A posting inn's common room isn't always the safest place to pass through."

Rather than seek out the inn's private parlor, Enya elected to remain in the coach. As she understood, a pause of only a quarter of an hour was allotted before the bridal journey would be resumed.

What she didn't understand was the dark silhouette that swung suddenly inside the coach and clapped a callused hand over her mouth to stifle her startled "What—?"

Chapter Two

"Duncan!" Enya jerked away the hand covering her mouth. "I might have known it was you. What do you think you are doing?"

His grin momentarily broadened his narrow face. One of his front teeth slightly overlapped the other. "Servin' as yer escort for yer bridal journey, m'lady." He plopped down in the seat opposite her. "'Tis verra dangerous roads ye'll be a'takin'. And without that Wakefield to—"

Her eyes narrowed. "Sir Oliver Wakefield? You put something in the proxy's drink to make him drunk, didn't you?"

His expression was one of affronted innocence. "The old goat would have bored ye to tears."

She reached across and clasped his roughened hand. In the confines of the coach, the smell of the sea and salt spray emanated from him. "'Tis no good, Duncan. What we have belongs to our childhood."

In the gathering darkness, the shrug of his thin shoulders was almost imperceptible. "I dinna ken if I can let ye go 'til I see for meself that ye are in good hands, Enya."

The ache in his voice was an echo of her own at leaving all that was familiar and dear to her. Duncan had given her her first and only kiss. His father had been the castle blacksmith, but the hammer and forge and fire were not for Duncan. No, the open sea and freedom were his desire. And, of course, her.

He propped his booted feet next to her on the seat. The heels were run down and the leather cracked and reeking of a briny smell. "So, me darlin', if ye canna stomach yer husband, will ye summon me to your bed?"

She thumped his boot with her fan. "I have no taste for the English gallows, Duncan, and that's where ye'll be keeping company if ye continue to ply your smuggling trade." Too often, she found herself lapsing into the Scottish brogue when talking with Duncan, whose accent was as broad as the River Clyde. He pronounced his *r*s with a trill of the tongue that Scottish bards had practiced for centuries from medieval minstrel galleries.

"Ye've insulted me, Enya. I am but a simple fisherman, and—"

"And you smell like one in the bargain. Herring and mackerel, I'd swear. Dead herring and mackerel. Long dead."

"I hadna time to change. Me cockle put in too late to do more than unload—"

"A shipment of French muskets, no less?"

"Nae. Ye do me verra wrong, Enya. I had only time to unload yer wedding gift."

The coach door swung open on creaking hinges, and Elspeth toted her bony body up the folding coach steps. Mary Laurie followed behind, and neither woman, their vision accustomed to light, noticed Duncan until Mary Laurie almost sat on him.

At the feel of his hands clasping her ample hips, she yelped, jumped aside, and plopped down opposite him. "May God take—"

"You remember Duncan," Enya said, smiling. Duncan's easy, hedonistic approach to life might be just what the hard-working, priggish maid needed.

"Hhmmp!" Elspeth snorted. Beneath her brown serge traveling cloak, her arms folded, a clear gesture of her disapproval of the new guest.

"Unfortunately," Mary Laurie replied. In the dim coach, her cheeks burned a beet red.

Only then did Enya recall that Duncan had once tweaked Mary Laurie's bottom by mistake. It had happened nearly two years ago when she had come to Afton House to apply for the position as Enya's personal maid. Running up and down the stairs had been getting to be too much for Elspeth.

Duncan, thinking the girl bending over the terrace fountain one evening was Enya, had committed that unpardonable act and sent Mary Laurie fleeing into the house, howling all the way. Like most Scots, she was superstitious, and she had been convinced she had been accosted by an evil agent of a clan of Druid witches.

Enya shifted her attention back to Duncan. Her eyes narrowed. "My wedding gift, you say?" What was the smuggler up to now?

"Aye. But ye willna see it 'til ye give me a kiss. For auld lang syne."

"She'll na be doin' that, ye weasel!" Elspeth said. "Not as long as I draw breath."

A wheel hit a hole, and Enya swayed to the side and caught the coach strap for support. "I am no simpleton, Duncan Fraser. Let me see the gift first."

"Ye dinna trust me? Ach, Enya. The wedding gift be too heavy to bring with me."

"Then how can I see it?"

"Well, now, m'lady, I dinna tell ye *when* ye would be a'seein' it, did I? But 'tis grand, to be sure. Ye ha' me word on it."

She chuckled. Duncan's company had always

proved diverting. "As grand as the tadpole ye put in my bowl of leek soup?"

"That was but a wee thing, a tadpole. A grand thing, now, would be the leech you secreted in me underdrawers. Me bum will ne'er be forgettin' that one."

Mary Lauried gasped and put her plump hand over her o-shaped mouth. Elspeth sniffed with indignation.

Enya began to laugh. "It could have been much worse for you, Duncan Fraser. Your poke could have been shriveled to a—"

"Enya!" Elspeth reproved.

"And at a grand loss for all the Afton lassies, I tell ye now," Duncan said.

Talk of memories continued to flow between them. It had always been like that. The unabashed bluntness, the unhindered sharing, the unstoppable caring. Time and miles sped by quickly.

A little after midnight, Enya looked out the coach window as it rattled through Glasgow's streets. Glasgow was one of the world's greatest shipbuilding centers, and Enya admired the town residences of country noblemen that lined the Clyde.

Down at the quay, Enya noted activity was still afoot. By the light of oil lanterns, men unloaded sugar and tobacco off a large vessel, from one of the American colonies, most likely.

The Lord Lieutenant's sloop, the *HMS Pelican,* was not difficult to spot. For one thing, additional redcoats stood sentry before the boarding plank. From the *Pelican*'s mast the British Union flag stirred desultorily in the dark stillness. Below the British flag drooped a standard, exhibiting a red sword on a black ground and the words "Only War Brings Lasting Peace" emblazoned in gold. The personal standard of the Lord Lieutenant, so the story went at one of her mother's salons.

After the frantic day and the long hours of traveling, Enya was weary. At that moment, a cabin berth was more welcome than any bed she had ever slept in. The armed sentries did not challenge her or question Duncan's presence.

But Elspeth did. She fixed him with her evil eye. "Are ye daft, lad? The Lord Lieutenant will have yer head for compromising his bride!"

"My Lord Lieutenant will shortly ken that his bride is untried." Enya laughed and picked up her voluminous skirts to board the sloop.

Behind her, Mary Laurie let out an audible gasp of shock, though by now she should have been accustomed to Enya's frankness. To Elspeth's chagrin, her charge would never be a coy maiden of mystery.

The mounted escort trotted off with the empty coach. A third of Enya's journey was over. At the end of the last third waited her intended and her new life. At the thought, she felt for the first time pleasant anticipation.

Both maidservants hurried to catch up with her, as did the footmen toting her trunks. Half a dozen sailors in red stocking caps, smocked shirts, and trews readied the ship for sailing on the tide, scarce three hours hence. They scrubbed the planks with vinegar and holystone and hosed down the decks.

A man's booming voice challenged, "Halt there. Who goes?"

She and Duncan stopped, glancing off to their left, where a uniformed man approached them. Short and bewigged, he wore the insignia of a naval officer. In the faint light of a lantern, the stocky man looked as uncertain as she. His thick white brows lowered. "Ye, I trust, are the bride of the Lord Lieutenant of the Western Highlands?"

"That I am."

He bowed low over buckled shoes. However, his sharp blue-eyed gaze was cautious as he viewed the shabbily attired Duncan. "Yer escort, m'lady? Sir Oliver Wakefield?"

"Detained. Duncan is my personal escort. My quarters, sir? I am weary."

"My apologies." He clicked his heels and bowed once more. "This way, madam."

They followed him down the companionway stairwell. Her maids' cabin adjoined her own.

She ducked her head. Ship-cabin lintels were notoriously low, and many a good bump on her noggin had taught her to remember her height.

Her own cabin was masculinely appointed, which startled her. She had foolishly expected quarters furnished for a woman with a canopied bed, maybe a tapestried settle or stools and cushions to make more restful the middle portion of her journey.

Across a small desk were strewn papers and maps. Nautical instruments—a polished brass telescope, a glass barometer, a brass-bound sextant, an hourglass—graced a sideboard. Alongside them were a decanter filled with a dark amber liquid, two quaiches, and a wicker basket of fresh fruit.

"The captain sends his regrets at being unable to greet ye himself," the officer said, indicating the fruit and spirits.

She nodded and began to untie her bonnet strings. There was still Duncan to deal with. "Now that I am safely aboard my husband's ship, Duncan, I—"

"But not safely at yer destination, me darlin'." He faced her in a stubborn stance, his arms folded, his legs spread.

She could order him thrown off the ship, but, alas, her affection for the grinning jackanapes stopped her just short of the command. Her shoulder blades felt the officer's suspicious stare.

"Quite right, Duncan. I charge you to guard my doorway."

But once at Fort William, she thought with irritation, I will send your smuggler's hide packing.

With a curt "G'night," she dismissed him. After the door was closed she sighed and turned to the younger maidservant. "Unlace me, will ye, Mary Laurie?"

A grumbling Elspeth was already prying open the portmanteau carrying her nightclothes. "A ship is no place for a bride."

Privately, Enya agreed as she let Mary Laurie take down her hair and braid it for the night. The resinous scent of cedar filled the hot, stuffy cabin. Four days confined aboard ship. Could she endure the monotony? No books to read, no horses to ride, no thought-provoking conversations with savants down from Edinburgh.

At least her husband would have provided some stimulation. Because of his military genius, Simon Murdock had been selected for the task of subduing the rebellious Clan Cameron and its brutish warlord.

"G'night, me darlin'," Duncan called from the other side of the door.

She did have Duncan to divert her for the next four days. With that comforting thought in mind, Enya dismissed Elspeth and Mary Laurie and retired to a less than comforting bed. The stale smells of mildew and pipe smoke clung to the bunk's blanket. Already hot, she kicked it off. She was still awake when the ship slipped anchor. The gentle rocking of the boat and the groaning of its timbers put her to sleep, at last.

Light awoke her. Too quickly. She rolled to her stomach and buried her face in the crook of her arm. "Elspeth? Draw the drapes, I beg you. I've barely closed my eyes."

"An enticing posterior ye present, Lady Murdock. Albeit, a bit too broad for me taste," a male voice added with brutal frankness.

In an instant wide-awake shock replaced drowsiness. She pushed herself upright and hit the back of her head on the bunk top. Spurts of oranges and yellows and blues blinded her momentarily.

The hand clamped across the back of her waist prevented her from moving. "Do as ye are bid, me lady, and the experience willna be too unpleasant."

The baritone voice had a soft, musical Scottish brogue, with its rolling *r*s and its clipping manner of the final consonants. She tried to twist around, but the big hand constrained her. "My Lord Lieutenant?"

The unamused laugh prickled the hair at her nape. "What do you want with me? Who are you?"

"I am not your Lord Lieutenant. I am your laird, Lady Murdock. Laird of the Clan Cameron of the Western Highlands."

"Me laird? Are ye mad?" Her nervousness was splintering the years of hard-acquired English. If she wasn't careful, she would be gibbering helplessly.

She tried to turn her head to see the man behind her, but his grip on her loose braid held her head fast against the pillow. She strained to glimpse him from the corner of her eye. All she could see was a dark form. She got the impression of a massive man. It wasn't just the immense weight bearing down on her; it was the heat of a body, much larger than hers.

"That may well be."

Fear began to stir panic. Where was Duncan? Had he ventured into one of the dockside brothels and missed the sailing? The lout!

She drew a calming breath and tried reasoning with the man who was nearly crushing her. "Of the Cameron clan, you say. Then you cannot be my laird. I belong to the Afton clan."

"Ye are on Cameron territory," came the low reply at her ear, his whisky-scented breath rustling the tendrils that had escaped her braid.

Obviously, he was quite mad. A veritable lunatic. "I must disagree. My home has been the Afton estates of Ayrshire and will shortly be the town of Fort William, ruled over by His Majesty, King George."

"Ach, no, me lady. You are on Cameron property at this very moment. The ship belongs to me, you see. So that puts you in my service, *mo kinruadh?*"

Gaelic! That haunting accent wasn't the legacy of the Scottish mother tongue that had survived among ordinary folk but the unique bequest of the Gaelic culture of the Highland Scots. Gaelic was a beast that refused to die, though weakened by the British effort to exterminate all that was peculiarly Scottish.

"Your ship? I beg your pardon, but the . . ." She paused to draw another breath. The pillow was stifling her. "The ship flies the colors of the British Union."

"A mere ruse."

With the ease of a Highland warrior wielding a claymore, he flopped her over onto her back. She saw only light-colored eyes in a dark face framed by darker hair. "But my Lord Lieutenant's guards?"

"Neither the vessel nor the mounted guard who escorted you belong to your Lord Lieutenant. They belong to me, your laird. Let me introduce meself." Sarcasm crept into his Gaelic-inflected voice. "I am Chief Ranald Kincairn of the Clan Cameron. Now it is time for ye to pay homage to your laird, me lady."

Her breath stilled. Her heart pounded. She could smell him now. The scent of smoke, leather, blood, and unwashed male. "What do you mean?"

"Ach, me lady, have ye nae heard of the *droit du seigneur?*"

She gasped. The right of a lord to have sexual relations with a vassal's bride on her wedding night was only practiced in isolated areas still adhering to feudal customs. "You have no right—"

"'Tis me perogative, as unalienable as me pride and me poverty."

Highland chiefs, for the most part, had been well-traveled, well-educated men. She appealed to this. "You speak like a man of at least some education. You cannot act like a barbarian."

"Canna I?" In the dark, his teeth glowed an unearthly white. As the spirits of the Druid witches were said to do. "The Lord Lieutenant is an educated man, I am told. He also carries out Westminster's interest in sterilizing Highland women when it is his wish."

She had heard of this horrendous policy of the British government, but had not known General Cumberland had instructed it to be implemented.

In addition to sterilizing Highland women, the policy included the banishment of the wearing of the kilt, the playing of the bagpipes, and the carrying of weapons. Along with that banishment had been the outlawing of the very language itself, Gaelic. General Cumberland meant to stamp out everything relating to the rebellious Highlanders, including the people themselves.

With angry misery, she cried out, "You canna hold me responsible for the British parliament's policies."

"Ach, but I can for the Lord Lieutenant's. He is Cumberland's agent and takes the devil's delight in tormenting Highland women."

"I don't understand! Please, release me!" She tried to twist free, but his hand held her wrists fast above her head against the bunk. A beast of a man, he was.

"It would be fitting, *mo kinruadh,* for the wife of Simon Murdock, an English cur, to give birth to a Highland bairn."

She trembled. "Ye cannot mean what ye say! I am innocent of any misdeed against your clansmen."

His laughter was low, his breath hot against her cheek. "At first, me thought merely to ruin your bridegroom's pleasure in bedding his virginal wife. But now that I have given it further consideration . . . aye, what I have in mind would be quite fitting retribution."

"Retribution? For what? I have done nothing." She was babbling, she knew. Anything to stall until rescue. Or was she being utterly foolish to hope? "Surely something can be worked out to recompense you for—"

"Recompense?" His laughter was silky, but to her it roared against her ears. "Not all the gold in King George's treasury would recompense me for the Highland clans' death, dishonor, and degradation."

Obviously, his thoughts, like his language, were short, strong, and conclusive.

He paused, then added, "Aye, degradation would be a fitting recompense, I wager." He pressed his lower torso against her. She could feel his massive thighs crushing hers. The bulge of his genitals thrust insistently against the apex of her legs.

There was to be no escape, she saw. Abandon hope she might; yet, cower she would not. "Go ahead with your raping then. Prove yourself the savage your ancestors have always been! Aye, have they not raped and pillaged the Lowlands for centuries? Get it over with."

She closed her eyes and clenched her teeth, waiting for the first brutal assault. Instead, she heard a laugh of genuine amusement. "A perfect martyr, ye make. And I wager a real shrew of a wife. I have a much better notion. Let's play the degradation to the hilt."

"What?"

Once more, he pressed his pelvis against hers.

"I shall let me men take turns with ye. Once ye are fertilized, ye will be incarcerated until the birth of the we'an. Then the process will began anew."

His free hand slipped down to caress the curve of her hip, then moved up to cup her left breast. "Aye, I think ye are built well for childbearing. Wide of hip, though your breasts are somewhat meager. Ye will produce many fine Highland bairns."

She spat into the shadowy face. "Be damn to your black Highland soul!"

His low growl of response both frightened and pleased her. She had penetrated through that steely veneer and insulted him. That was a beginning.

For the plans he had for her degradation, she would find a way to retaliate tenfold. This she swore, even as his fingers, thick as musket barrels, stroked her breast with brazen familiarity.

"Mayhap ye are not a virgin." His words dripped into the darkness like hot wax onto the flesh. "Mayhap, that snapping puppy outside your door has sampled his mistress's wares."

"You foul—!" The thought of Duncan and his fate cut short her oath. "What have you done to my friend? I swear, if you—"

"Ach, merely a friend, *cinaed?* It beggars the

imagination what the Lord Lieutenant's lady might do for a friend."

She hated the sardonic amusement that colored his voice. His voice, the weight of his body, his callused hands . . . that was all she knew about him. That, and the fact that he was a demonic artist skilled at instilling fear in his captive.

"You are afraid of the dark, you are. Light exposes your ugliness. Your ugly face and your ugly soul."

She felt him flinch. Obviously, he was not a man to be charmed; but then, she was not the kind of woman to charm a man.

"So you come to me by night and do your dastardly work," she continued, taunting. She would not submit docilely to her defilement.

"I might tell ye I come by night because I cannot bear the loathsome sight of a Lowland traitor. The sight might tempt me to order for ye the same torture Murdock perpetrated on me family."

"You will regret this—"

"Me oldest brother was tortured by—"

"I do not want to hear this."

"At Murdock's command, three of his dratted Lobsterbacks went to work on me Davy. Their torture must have vastly amused them. Too late, they noticed the intruder in the dungeon cell and the dirk that ultimately slit their throats."

A pulse beat in her throat.

"As for me sister, Mhorag—I have yet to take me reprisal."

Surging blood threatened to burst the veins at her temples. The image was too grisly to contemplate. "What have you done with Duncan?"

"The puppy is learning to heel. As will ye, me lady." The bed creaked as he removed his weight. "Do not consider escape. Should ye be able to swim, there are nevertheless others to consider. They remain safe as long as ye cooperate with your laird."

"You are not my laird, and my cooperation is limited by the—"

"By the length of your tether," came his melodic reply. "Whether your tether remains invisible or becomes very real is up to ye. I trust you will choose wisely. G'day, *cinade.*"

When she heard the door close she sprang from the bunk, this time careful of the overhang. Naturally, the door was locked. She could scream, but it would be of no avail. Most likely, every hand on the vessel was a Cameron clansman.

Nay, she would have to use her intelligence, guile, and wit to delay her captor's machinations until rescue came. She would not allow herself to doubt it would.

Without the aid of Elspeth or Mary Laurie, she began to dress herself by the light of a candle stub. Considerable time was required, which presented no problem. Time was all she had. She didn't even know the hour.

She chose a simple sack gown of glazed, lavender-striped lawn with flounced lace ruffles at the elbow. A gauze handkerchief was secured by a breast knot, modestly covering the gown's low, lace-bordered decolletage. A small round cambric cap perched over a less-than-artfully arranged chignon.

Then she could only pace. And wait. The cabin grew hot and stuffy. How long had it been? How much longer? Perspiration dampened her clothes. From the heat—or from fear?

She spotted the hourglass and cursed her forgetfulness. Inverting it, she began to pace again. Her gaze flickered ever so often to the hourglass. The sands trickled so slowly!

She was hungry. Surely, the chief of the Cameron clan would see that she was fed.

An hour had passed. She inverted the hourglass once more. How long before it became obvious she had been abducted? And then how much time could elapse before a rescue party was mustered? Days? Weeks? More like months, if she was realistic about her predicament. The Highlands' hazardous geography, which helped the remaining Jacobites fight slowly back, would work against her and her servants.

Elspeth, Mary Laurie, Duncan—what had

become of them? God forbid that their lives had been taken!

Five more times she turned the hourglass over before apathy dulled her agitation. She sought the solace of sleep. Sometime much later, the opening and closing of the cabin door roused her. The candle had gutted out. She could not see her visitor, but she knew who it was. She was alone with her captor.

"G'evening, Madam Murdock. I imagine ye must be hungry."

So it was evening. She picked up the pillow and hurled it in the direction of that marvelous deep voice. "You are a simpleton, Ranald Kincairn. A starved captive will bring you no ransom."

His rich laughter infuriated her. "I never spoke of ransom. I spoke of retribution."

Fear smote her anew. "You willna get away with this! This outrage!"

The bed shifted beneath her. She smelled food: hot porridge. "A simple meal I have for ye, perforce one of the nuisances of voyages. Gratefully, ours shall not be a lengthy one. Open your mouth."

She could not credit what she was hearing! The man meant to feed her like a chained dog! She felt the spoon nudge her lips. With a backlash of her hand, she knocked the spoon from her lips.

A softly murmured Gaelic curse enhanced the darkness. "I take it ye are not hungry."

"I'm famished, you brute! You dolt! You blackguard!"

The bed creaked with the release of his weight.

"No! Wait! Come back!"

The cat-quiet tread, unusual for so big a man, halted. "Aye?"

"Please, my servants? Assure me they are alive and all right!"

"That they are. As for ye, I keep ye alive, me lady, not out of kindness. I do it for the perverse pleasure I shall take in observing your degeneration from highborn lady to a slut who inhabits closes and wends and whom none but the lowest of humanity deign to touch. I shall return tomorrow."

"Oh, God!" Tears stung her eyes. She swallowed back their salty taste. "What must I do?"

"I'm not God, so I canna answer as to His opinion," came the sardonic reply. "I, however, would suggest an apology for your crudeness. When last we talked I had thought ye spirited. Ye sink much faster to the dregs than I had anticipated. That shortens me pleasure."

A neat psychological trap he had prepared: surrender now and assure her own self-destruction; defy him and give him diversion.

Delay was the only prospect she had. "Then I proffer an apology." Her tone was flippant. Her brain raced. The words she next chose were of the King's finest English. She would not betray her cowardice to her captor again. "But if it is entertaining you I must, I would hope the same from yourself, sir."

"Ye are not in a position to hope for such."

Good. She heard the humor in his voice. "Alas. But you will feed me?"

"A pleasure." His voice, as smooth and potent as Scotch whisky, made her grit her teeth.

Once again, the bed shifted beneath her. As he fed Enya the less-than-appetizing porridge, she could detect his easy breathing. Detect, too, a fresh scent about him. "You have bathed since last you entertained me with your presence, Highlander."

He chuckled. "Not for your sake, *sassenach,*" he said, using the Gaelic term of contempt for all Saxons. "I had ridden hard and long to make the sailing of the sloop. I might add that ye could use a bath."

She couldn't help herself. Before she realized the costly gesture, she spat the mouthful of porridge at him. "You bloody oaf!"

"And I had thought you a bright lass. Or perhaps you weren't hungry after all. Tomorrow I shall bring you a bowl of leek soup. That may suit your palate better, eh?"

"Leave me, you cad!"

Again, that abominable laughter. "I look forward to your next apology, me lady. I trust your imagination will create a more amusing one on the morrow."

The door closed on her and her imagination. The horror of what awaited her was more than she wanted to contemplate, and she sought once more the oblivion of sleep.

Chapter Three

Sunlight, though mist-shrouded, nevertheless blinded Enya. She put up her palm to shield her eyes. The *Pelican* was putting into what appeared to be a wide bay. Bulbous fishing boats clustered at the far end.

Glancing around the plank deck, she saw a score or more of common sailors. A handful had scaled one of the sloop's masts and were hauling down a sail billowed by roguish winds. Others worked the shrouds or coiled heavy ropes. They worked silently, quickly; diligence combined with rapid movement for a purpose. But what?

The brisk, early-morning breeze felt wonderful on her sticky skin and sweat-snarled hair. How many days had she been locked in the cabin? The closest she could calculate was three.

The last time Ranald Kincairn had come to her in the cabin was yesterday morning. Since the old officer had let her out this morning she had not seen her abductor.

Enya turned to the bushy, white-browed officer who had received her that first night. Gone was the old man's wig, as well as his naval uniform. In its place were breeches and a stained linsey-woolsey shirt beneath an equally stained leather jerkin.

"Where is Ranald Kincairn?"

"On Highland soil, me lady." Beneath thinning white hair, his blue eyes beamed. "Aye, Highland soil and Highland sky. Nowhere the likes of them on all the earth."

"You aren't prejudiced, are you?"

His bushy white brows waggled. "Captain Knox is me tag. To be sure I'm prejudiced. I've yet to see the Indies and the American colonies. Watch yer step now. Yon hawser'll trip ye sure."

"My maidservants—and Duncan. Duncan Fraser. Where are they?"

"Oh, they will be brought topside to join ye shortly, Madam Murdock. Me laird has given his permission to ha' them wait on ye now."

"How gracious."

"I thought ye would enjoy yer first sight of the Highlands." He pointed a gnarled and stubby finger toward the ship's foreward. On the distant opposite shore of the oblong lake appeared to be a town, and perched above it a fortress. "Yon is Fort William."

Her heart jumped with joyous anticipation. "You are returning me to the English, then?"

"Ach, no." The white-fringed eyes looked sorely bedeviled. "Look ye, lass, this is the sealoch Linnhe. We're putting about to travel up Loch Leven. There, on the leeward side."

She followed the direction of his jabbing finger and saw, closer, another wide inlet bound by innumerable rifts and crags of steep slopes still laced with a slowly drifting web of mist. Even though late-summer sunlight filtered through the murky mist to warm the morning, she felt a chill. "Exactly where are we going?"

Beneath the white brows, the eyes shifted. "I'll leave it to me laird to talk to ye of such matters. There be yer companions, Madam Mudock."

"M'lady," Mary Laurie cried out. Tangled brown hair straggled from her mob cap, askew on her head. Her cheeks, normally apple red, were pale, and her bow-shaped mouth trembled. "We've been kept—"

"Take yer hands off me, ye knave," Elspeth told a startled Captain Knox, "or else ye'll sing like a choir boy!" Indignant, she tried to straighten shoulders that time would never permit to straighten again. After having been confined in the small cabin, she wobbled.

Immediately, he dropped the supporting hand he had offered. "A pox on ye, then, hag."

Her hooded eyes squinted at her charge's face, as if searching for some sign from heaven. "Ye are unhurt, me bairn?"

"I am unhurt. And you and Mary Laurie?"

"It would take more than Highland dolts to do me in. Yer breast knot is torn."

She avoided the sharp old eyes. The lace knot had been torn the fourth or fifth time—she couldn't remember—that the Cameron chieftain had come to her. He had proffered peas to her on his dirk.

Foolishly, he had cautioned her before her lips had touched its sharp edge.

Foolishly, she had seized the opportunity to drive the dirk into his chest.

With the ease of a man swatting a pesky fly, he had deflected the attempted stabbing. In the tussle for the dirk, he had won, and her breast knot had suffered.

"How close do you think I can come to cutting the knot before I prick your soft skin?" he had taunted.

She had dared not breathe. Without light to guide him, he might have done just that. The breast knot had yielded on his first attempt. Next, he had drawn off her lace handkerchief, and she had felt the knifepoint feathering the hollow of her throat. She had only to swallow to feel its painful prick.

She hadn't, and the seconds strung out into what seemed hours. She had heard his measured breathing. What had he been thinking? At last he had arisen and left the cabin without another word. She had almost welcomed his anger rather than a return to the maddening isolation in which he kept her.

"Where is your laird?" she demanded of Captain Knox.

"Gone ashore, he has." Once again the blue eyes twinkled. "Paying an unexpected visit on the English garrison quartered at Fort William."

Swiftly, her gaze inventoried her chances at escape. The sloop's seamen were busy enough. No weapons were in evidence. A nearby dinghy would provide the means to reach shore. The canny old captain should give her and Duncan little resistance.

"My escort, Duncan?"

"Below, me lady."

"Bring him to my cabin." Enya pointed a negligent finger in that direction and turned to her serving ladies. The fretful wind was teasing her skirts, revealing more of her ankles than was proper. For all she knew, the sloop's sailors could have been asea for months and sex-crazed, like their chief. "We'll repair inside."

Such was her habit at giving orders, so sure of her command was she, that Captain Knox almost tugged at his wispy forelock in acknowledgment, before he remembered himself. "The laird has forbidden that, madam."

She turned back. "Forbidden what?"

"Forbidden ye to be alone with a man. Any man but himself, that is."

She felt her color rising—and felt Elspeth's obelisk glance.

Mary Laurie whispered, "Oh, mistress!"

She collected herself. "Very well. Send Duncan to me here—on deck. Very little can happen before the eyes of these charming . . . gentlemen . . . can it now?" She made a sweeping motion to take in the sailors who look more like the dregs of a dock impressment.

Why had she not noticed earlier their untrimmed beards and flowing mustaches? Anyone with two eyes could see that they had not exhibited the spruced appearance of seasoned British seaman.

Captain Knox rubbed his stubbled chin. "Weel, I don't see how that could hurt anything."

Waiting for Duncan, Enya watched the passing countryside closely. She would need to know as much as possible about this far-flung land when the time for escape came. She saw a savage monotony of mountains. They rose steeply from the shores of the reed-rimmed loch and appeared to be crossed only by daredevil single-track roads.

She found the craggy Highlands disturbing,

lacking the harmony and proportion of the rolling, lush hills of the Lowlands. Here in the Highlands, the air was crisper, the light paler.

The surrounding countryside she viewed was a wild, timeless land where, no matter which direction she turned, she seemed to be lost. She knew that no cities and only a few towns managed to survive in the murderous mountain-shaped Highlands. Words like *desolate* and *inhospitable* came to her mind.

"M'lady, yon is Duncan," said Mary Laurie.

"Handcuffing is too lenient for a slick scoundrel like him," Elspeth said.

He was blinking. A scraggly growth of blond beard stubbled his lantern jaw. If possible, his clothing was even more rumpled and dirty than usual.

"Duncan," Enya called.

He hesitated, then lurched in the women's direction. Obviously, his quarters of confinement had been even smaller than hers. Two sailors guarding him did nothing to impede his detour, but merely looked on. Apparently, duty called Captain Knox elsewhere.

Hands held awkwardly before him, Duncan asked, "Ye fare well, Enya?"

"Aye. And you?" She reached up to touch his high forehead, where a fresh cut was haloed with a prominent purple bruise.

"Ach, got that from tussling with the crew here, I did."

"Took on all of them, did you now?"

With a judicious squint, Elspeth intervened to finger the wound. "A compress of lichen, egg, and spiderweb shouldna hurt ye too much."

Enya drew closer. "Duncan, what think you our chances of escape?"

His eyes, the brown of acorns, narrowed to scan the rifts and crags of the brooding massifs, dominated now by the sight of the hefty humpback of Ben Nevis, the highest mountain of the British Isles. Loch Leven's sandy shores were empty of human habitation. He looked down at his bound wrists and wiggled their chains. "Swimming is just what I had in me mind."

She chewed on her lower lip. "The longer we wait, the less chance we may have."

The warm wind whipped his butter-yellow hair. "The four of us be in no condition for flight. Do ye know if a ransom price has been asked?"

Enya shook her head, and her straggling hair brushed her shoulders. Doubtlessly, she looked like the slattern that the laird of the Cameron clan wanted her to be. "Not ransom, retribution. It seems that our illustrious captor has a distaste for Lowlanders and English alike, especially Simon Murdock."

Duncan's straw-colored brows lowered in a

scowl. "If not already, then soon, Simon Murdock will have discovered his escort, guards, and sailors were replaced by brigands. Help will be on the way. Better to wait it out."

He was right. But how long could she postpone what Ranald Kincairn had in mind for her? As if she could do anything about it!

As the day wore on, the sloop traveled farther up Leven, one of many glacier-gouged lochs. The capricious wind lapped the cold and haunted waters. Below the mountain peaks, capped in mist, was spread a rugged, heather-splashed glen. It was here that the sloop put in.

The dinghy was lowered, and Duncan was put ashore with half a dozen of the scruffy-looking crew. She didn't like being separated from him. As it turned out, she, Elspeth, and Mary Laurie were next rowed ashore, along with Captain Knox and three more of Ranald Kincairn's Highlanders.

Skirts lifted over the reeds, she picked her way to drier land. Beyond, an expanse of bog and dark pools and ocher grass stretched into the wildest of empty moorlands. "My trunks and baggage, Captain Knox?"

His expression was one of regret. "To be forwarded later, madam. If you will accompany me . . ."

Armed with dirks, matchlocks, and swords, her escort didn't appear likely to grant her leave.

She nodded, as if this was but the anticipated last stretch of her bridal journey. "Of course."

The sun seemed about to break through the clouds between the distant peaks as her bridal party set out. It had traveled no farther than a short distance over the soggy moors when a group of mounted men could be seen cantering toward them.

Hope took light within her. Even if it wasn't Simon Murdock and his men, the riders might be someone she could appeal to for help.

Closer, she could see the lead rider wore a kilt and tartan, the symbol of Scots pride. She felt like sobbing. These had to be more of the Cameron clan.

The man in the lead swung down from his bay mare and approached her captors. About her age, he was tall and handsome, with long, glossy auburn locks. Fear leaped anew in her heart. Was this her tormentor, Ranald?

He stopped to confer with Captain Knox. Almost immediately, she could see that this kilted man was not as brawny as the one who had come to her in the dark of the sloop's cabin. That man had to weigh close to twenty stone. Twenty stone of might and muscle.

This slighter man advanced toward her, his intelligent, dark blue eyes surveying her with minute curiosity. "Lady Murdock?"

Her gaze ran the length of him with the accustomed ease of a mistress to a minion. Closer, she could detect his plaid and kilt colors, interwoven red and hunter's green, with narrow yellow bands. She surmised the colors blended well for hiding in the heather. "Aye?"

He surprised her with a bow. "I am Jamie Cameron, here to welcome you." He waved a careless hand behind him. "I have brought mounts for you and your—"

"Fellow prisoners?" she suggested caustically.

He grinned. "—Traveling companions. The trek to the village of Lochaber is a rather rough one. Much of the countryside is penetrable only on foot."

Her glance took in the indicated mounts. "Ponies?"

"They are sturdier, Lady Murdock. Bred for carrying deer off the hill after a successful kill in the stalking season. You'll be quite safe in traversing the narrow mountain paths."

She eyed the little animals. "I think I trust my own footing more."

"The mountain's quick weather changes bring sudden hill mists and strong, chilling winds or heavy snows." He nodded toward the peak. "Buachaille Etive can be dangerous and the cause of many accidents, and warrants the use of Highland-bred horses."

There was little of the Scottish brogue to his accent, but definitely a foreign lilt colored it.

His eyes looked as if they revealed hurt easily. Nevertheless, she was prepared to dislike him. "My traveling companions and I are extremely grateful for your concern."

At her acerbic tone, his bird-bright blue eyes crinkled. "Then we'd best start. The eve promises a drizzle at best."

Gallantly, he helped her mount one of the little, shaggy white ponies. From behind, Duncan watched sullenly. His lanky legs dangled from his own mount.

Captain Knox bade her farewell. "Me bones belong on a boat, lass."

"Come snowmelt," Jamie told the peppery old man, "anchor in the loch again. By then Ranald will be ready to move out the reivers."

She was sorry to see Captain Knox go. He was her last link with civilization.

The ever-present overcast sky lent little beauty to a glen carpeted with tall, dark-purple Scottish thistle. "We go by way of the Hidden Valley Trail," Jamie said in a most conversational voice. "A glen near there is famous. In '92 Campbell clansmen massacred the MacDonalds."

She knew he was trying to distract her. "How very interesting," she said dryly.

That charming grin again.

She ignored it and turned her attention toward maintaining her seat. Enya was a proficient horsewoman, but the pony's gait was uneven.

Eventually, she adjusted to its peculiar rhythm.

The torturous climb through the mountains proved to be a dizzying experience. Spiraling pine with their high red limbs contrasted with the plummeting depths of granite glens. Thickets of birch and fir began to close in on the single-file party. At times, sheer walls of granite narrowed the pass. The air grew cooler.

Always, the jagged peak of Buachaille Etive spied upon them.

Nearer, a silvery stream tumbled over rocks and misted the area. Wild salmon leaped in the rushing water. Water, like whisky, flowed freely in the Highlands.

The cascade's thunderous echo made normal talk impossible. Not that anyone was talking by late afternoon. Enya hadn't eaten since the wee hours of the morning, the last time Ranald Kincairn had come to the cabin to feed her. Her stomach rumbled almost as loudly as the falls.

"How much longer?" she shouted to the leader, Jamie Cameron.

He dropped back to ride beside her. "Not that much longer. We enter Lochaber by the back way, up from the loch. One of the attractive features of the village—'tis hard for an enemy of any size to get to in winter. Leastways with cannon."

"Any longer wait," Elspeth grumbled, "and I will have calluses on me backside."

As hungry and tired as she was, Enya realized that the longer their journey took, the better. Duncan, Elspeth, Mary Laurie—they had been treated humanely enough and expected the treatment to continue.

For her, arrival could only mean further misfortune.

The steep, pinecone-strewn path entered into a dark forest, dripping with lichen-covered pines. The place had a melancholy air. At her side, Jamie said, "The romance of the road is enhanced by tales of a hidden hoard of Jacobite gold."

She slid him a sidewise glance. "You are my appointed entertainment for the journey?"

In the sunlight-siphoned gloom, his eyes twinkled like distant blue stars. "My cousin would never forgive me for being boorish."

"Your cousin?"

"Ranald. Ranald Kincairn."

"Him? That—that blackguard."

"He really isn't so bad. He's a good shot, a master of the claymore, and an accomplished golfer."

She sniffed. "He's inhuman."

Jamie grinned. "I assure you, he's mortal. As boys, we hunted and fished and studied together, whenever I came home from school on holidays."

"Where were you educated?"

"In London—at Winchester. From the time I was four, I spent more time in England than I did in Scotland. Ranald, now, is—"

"—is an ignorant lout."

"True, Ranald didn't finish examinations, but he is intelligent, I assure you. Clan chiefs are cosmopolitan. Most of our Jacobite leaders were polished men."

"I'd hardly call Ranald Kincairn polished."

"You have to understand that Ranald's the eighth child of a feckless father and was tutored by the village *dominie.*"

"Oh, then Ranald Kincairn is most truly cosmopolitan." Her praise was quenched with a sneer.

"Well, he did attend Winchester in London with me for a year. I continued my studies alone at the University of Aberdeen. Without him, it wasn't the same."

That explained Jamie's accent. Several centuries earlier, Flemish wool merchants had settled Scotland's east coast near Aberdeen, which was within as easy traveling distance of Norway and Sweden as it was London. The resulting new nobility spoke French. In France, the Scots aristocrats were accepted as equals.

Except the Cameron chieftain could hardly be called aristocratic. His manner was coarse and threatening. She recalled his volley of hot Gaelic oaths when she had literally bit the hand that had fed her. He was hardly comparable to his courtly cousin.

"You speak French?" she asked.

"Aye, French comes easily for me. As a randy young man, I loved my way through France, but grew bored and returned to the Cameron clan. What was left of it."

As they rode past crofts, Enya reviewed the surroundings. Small tenant farms were bordered by stone fences and hedges, and closer to the village were clusters of pink half-timbered houses, roofed with bluish slates and latticed by gardens and arbors. Smoke eddied from the chimney of a quaint tile-roofed, conical kiln.

"Your cousin—Ranald Kincairn," she said, seeking as much information as she could from Jamie, "is really a laird, then?"

"Actually, my father is hereditary chief, but he canna ride well anymore; arthritis. A man who canna ride a horse well canna be regarded as a true leader."

She nodded. "I understand, but why your cousin and not you? Are you not next in line?"

"Oh, I do not have the disposition toward warfare that Ranald does. Ahead is Lochaber. Its castle is just beyond where the road forks. The branch to the left is the main approach to Lochaber from the countryside below."

She saw an old dame glance up, startled, from the water she was drawing at a moss-laced mill standing beside a rushing spring-fed burn. It fed a loch bordered with red clover and blue bells and yellow wild irises.

A herd of hardy Highland cows trotted across the old wooden bridge leading into the village itself. The head cow man tugged at his forelock in deference to Jamie, who hailed him by name.

She spotted an ironforger, bellows in hand, who came out to watch the procession of riders, as did patrons of an alehouse, a linen shop, and a butcher's stall. The pungent odor of fried herring drifted from the low doorway of a shuttered house. Over the narrow, winding street, upper windows opened, and inhabitants gazed down with curiosity upon the captives.

The first drops of rain began to beat at the shop signs. Jamie gave a signal, and the horses were spurred ahead. Enya's pony's pace quickened, also. Steam rose from its smelly flanks.

At the marketplace, the road divided. The lead horses turned right sharply to ascend a precipitous incline and clattered across a drawbridge lowered over a moat. Hoisted iron portcullises that were badly rusted allowed access to twin gatehouses and the bailey.

Sudden sunlight shafted through the scudded clouds. Enya glanced up. Serrated parapets, slim pepperpot turrets, and spires of silver granite embedded with mica chips glinted like a million mirrors. Tall, lancet windows slitted the lower portion of the castle, while larger bowed ones look out from above.

Gargoyles snarled in silent menace from the battlements. Fluttering from the highest spire was the standard of an arm in armor holding a black dagger with the Gaelic words *Skean Dhu* inscribed at the bottom.

"A suitable place for ghosts and evil spirits," Duncan commented drily.

In the bailey below, stone rubble was piled as if the place were an ancient ruin. A blackened, skeletal wing of the castle's twelve-foot apron walls revealed that cannon bombardment had gutted it long ago, probably during the first Jacobite Rebellion of 1715.

So, this was the Cameron's temporary stronghold. Did Ranald Kincairn truly think to rid Scotland of the English? Then the brute was truly ignorant.

Enya felt a frisson of excitement. The prospect of dealing with the man offered unanticipated diversion. Surely she could keep the Highland chieftain at bay with her wits until she found a means of escape or help arrived. The clanking chains of the drawbridge rising behind her were not reassuring.

Within the keep, stablehands scurried to take the weary horses. The outbuildings were in shadow. Jamie came to assist her in dismounting, but she put out a halting palm. She would not present herself as some weak-kneed lassie, however tired, wet, and miserable she was.

With her maidservants and Duncan in tow, she followed Jamie up a flight of crumbling stone steps built into the wall. The cavernous hall was already lit with rush torches against the encroaching darkness. Shafts of dying sunlight sifted through the high window slits. Between the windows were hung weapons and shields. In the ceiling's exposed jousts, spoked beams radiating from a center post, nested birds twittered noisely.

A huge fireplace beckoned her to warm her hands, but noisy conversations from the room's far end drew her attention, as did the savory smell of food. She noted the greasy rushes strewn on the floor had not been changed in months. Probably not since Kincairn took possession of the castle.

Weaving his way through servants bearing trays and coming-and-going diners, Jamie advanced toward the head of the lengths of tables that formed a T-shape. Several men sat along the width of that table section. Her breath held, Enya waited to see who Jamie approached.

Incredibly, he stopped before a man who had to be as old as or older than her own father. Both the man's hair and beard were grizzled with gray. The stern set of his mouth betokened a man accustomed to authority.

As Jamie talked, she felt, rather than saw, the older man's eyes shift to her. With a curl of his finger, he beckoned her.

Ire rose like sour mash in her mouth. Who was he to summon her like a servant girl? Still, the better choice was to comply, at least, for the moment.

Picking up her skirts, she walked down the long aisle between the tables. A frowsy-looking servant girl in brown kersey cap and gown darted her a glance of curiosity before turning her attention back to the trencher of bread she set on one of the tables.

Head high, Enya paused beside Jamie, who introduced her. "Father, this is Lady Murdock. Ranald's . . . guest. Lady Murdock, my father, Ian Cameron."

Closer, she could see the deep furrows across the bridge of the man's nose and high forehead. His lids were lowered, as if he perpetually squinted against sunlight. His bird-claw hands clutched a haunch of venison.

"I trust you will find comfort here at Lochaber Castle," he said, his gravelly voice betraying a weariness that echoed her own.

She used a tone of authority reserved for minions. "How long am I to be held hostage?"

The brows rose like ladder rungs on his forehead. "My nephew hasn't informed you?"

She wasn't certain who was in high command

here. She hedged. "Ranald Kincairn discussed the, uhh, terms, not the length of my . . . stay."

He flicked a questioning glance at Jamie, who said, "Ranald took three men with him to scout out Fort William. He hasn't returned yet?"

Ian Cameron shook his head. "Ye hear no bagpipes, do ye?" He rubbed his temple with grotesquely gnarled fingers. "I could sorely use the comfort tonight."

"I'll install Lady Murdock in the undamaged wing."

It was more a question, and Jamie's father responded with a nod of his head. "Do that. I'll speak with Ranald when he returns."

Rush torches lit another staircase that spiraled up several flights. Following Jamie and two other kilted men, she inventoried her chances for escape. Even with access to the occasional cluster of weapons along the walls, flight from the castle would be nigh impossible tonight.

Perhaps tomorrow, with the aid of disguise . . . but that thought was banished by Elspeth's crusty admonishment to Mary Laurie, both of whom hurried to keep up with her. "Fall behind and ye'll find yeself the sport of some of the Highland churls."

The old woman spoke verily, for several armed men, dicing at one end of the hall, looked up with interest glinting in their eyes. They rose from where they knelt, but, at Jamie's negligent acknowledgment, resumed their gaming.

Not only did she have guards with which to contend, Enya realized, but she also had Mary Laurie and Elspeth to consider. And where had Duncan been taken?

They passed another room, the iron-studded door open. A big man sat at a desk hunched over a book. He nodded at Jamie, who returned the nod and continued on down the hallway. His spurs clinked against the stone floor.

The room in which she was to be incarcerated was chilly, with no tapestries to warm the stone walls and only a small window to let in the waning light. A steward scurried to light the candles. Shadows receded from the gray, sepulcherlike room, revealing little more than a bed with tattered curtains that would be little use against the coming winter's errant drafts. Rafters crisscrossed the room at a low height.

"It could be worse," she murmured.

"Did you expect a block and ax?" Jamie teased.

"I stay with milady, ye maggot of a—"

Enya whirled back to the doorway, where Elspeth and Mary Laurie were being hustled away by the kilted men.

"They will be given a room not far from this," Jamie said at her side.

Enya flashed him a withering look. "You

expect me to be pleased. The room is no larger than a monk's cell."

"We occupied the place less than a month ago. The best—and safest—winter accommodations Ranald could find at the last moment." His Friar-Tuck cheer gave way to a truly contrite expression. "When you are settled in it will be easier for all of you."

"I demand to see your cousin—Ranald Kincairn—when he arrives."

"You already have."

Chapter Four

How long, O Lord? Wilt Thou forget me forever?
How long wilt Thou hide Thy face from me?
How long shall I take counsel in my soul,
  having sorrow in my heart all the day?
How long will my enemy be exalted over me?

Ranald Kincairn closed the Bible, a translated version ordered centuries earlier by the Scottish king, James. He gave an utterance that was half groan, half sigh. It seemed to him that, like the biblical David, his success in battle, in the war he waged, ebbed and flowed according to his own doubts.

From his most recent visit to Fort William, appearances indicated that the bastion was being further fortified with each passing week. English troops were quartered in every house, store, and stable.

Were it not for Jamie's abiding friendship, support, and, aye, love, he could not have continued to lead the Cameron clan ere this long. Jamie was his biblical Aaron, supporting Moses's hands aloft so that the battle would continue to wax in the Israelites' favor.

At the foot of his chair, the old collie Thane snorted in its sleep. Ranald ruffled its shaggy coat, then shut his eyes and rested his head against the chair's high-paneled back.

Could he really expect to defeat the might of the English with only a handful of men? Some of his reivers followed him, not out of patriotism, but because of money, maintenance, or promise of loot. The scattered numbers of loyal clansmen amounted to a mere thousand, give or take a couple hundred, depending on the time of year: calving season, harvest, shearing time, the birth of a bairn, the death of a loved one.

Loved ones. He could not even protect his own loved ones. Images fleeted across the back of his lids of his mother, his aunt, his brothers, and other family members, all tortured and murdered by the English for no more reason than they were Highlanders.

Mhorag's haunted eyes followed him even into his dreams. He could not restore his sister's innocence, lost four years ago. But he could take vengeance on his sister's violator.

He thought of the woman who had just passed his study. Murdock's wife. For all that she was highborn, she was a scrapper, that one. She would scratch and hiss and hurl things.

Not wholly unlike Mhorag. But Mhorag contained her heart. And contained her hate. Mayhaps, if she would but loose the raging beast inside her that fed on her pent-up hate, the beast would run out of fuel eventually. Now, even here at Castle Lochaber, the beast was feeding on her from within.

The witches of auld would know what to do for her. He didn't. All he knew to do was fight. With his last breath he would fight, for all that it would gain him.

Outnumbered, he could not expect to hold the line. He could only vanish and reappear again with his men. He could not gather his forces for an Armageddon but for a slow wearing out by confrontation. The isolation of the Highlands' treacherous geography was on his side.

There, in the Bible, were laid out David's and Joshua's own strategy plans. The object was not to maintain territory but to dispirit the opposition. Make them pay a higher price than they were willing to pay.

Just how much would Simon Murdock pay for what was left of the spirited young woman now asleep only a few rooms farther down the hall?

Ranald opened his eyes and rubbed absently at the welting bruise on his shoulder. An injury not from some sword-wielding lobsterback, but from a bowl thrown by Lady Murdock.

In how many ways could he make her pay?

The eerie, mournful sound of bagpipes awoke Mhorag. She bolted upright in the bed. Fairy music, *port na bpucai,* her Gaelic ancestors called it. A wand of moonlight lay upon the floor. How long had she been asleep?

The bagpipes' skirl reached her once more. The piper played a reliquary air with its lilt and drone, tune and countertune. Ian Cameron was being comforted. Ranald Kincairn had returned.

She shivered and snuggled back under the coverlet. She could not sleep now. For four years her sleep had been sporadic. Riding with the Jacobite reivers, modern-day Rob Roys, she had slept rough in heather and in bothies. But then, growing up with seven brothers had made the transition to hunted criminal easier.

Hunted, haunted years. Of mounted Redcoats with stinking torches.

Five years before, in '45, when her brothers supported the Young Pretender, Bonnie Prince Charlie, and his claim to the Scottish throne, the nightmare, and nightmares, began.

With the defeat of Bonnie Prince Charlie, the Duke of Cumberland had ordered the glens to be ravaged, men shot or hanged, women raped, homes burnt, and valuables stolen. Thousands of head of cattle and flocks of goats and sheep were driven south. The castles of those who aided the prince were burned. Forty Jacobite chiefs lost their land.

Those Jacobite chiefs apprehended were beheaded or sent to the West Indies. Two of her brothers bent their head to the ax, another two met death in battle, Robby was sent to the West Indies, and Davy died in torture.

Her husband had died with a bullet in his back. The Redcoats had bashed her baby, rosy-cheeked Claire, against the wall until it was red. Red. Red like the Redcoats.

The Forty-five Rising had split families. Her childhood friend, Bryan Boyd, fought on the English side, while his father had stood loyally behind the Prince. The Chief of Clan Chisholm had sons fighting on both sides to avoid forfeiture.

In London, Parliament had suggested recolonizing the Highlands with "decent God-fearing people from the South" and sterilization of all Jacobite women. When she would not flee Scotland Ranald had no choice but to take her with him.

Her thoughts turned to the young woman she had sighted from the gallery. Simon Murdock's wife. Ranald's captive.

Perhaps there truly was justice in this cold, gray world.

At thirteen, Kathryn had married the man who had captured her father in an interbaronial battle. All these years, she had abetted her daughter's efforts to delay marriage. She had hoped that Enya would have the opportunity to make a marriage with someone who shared the same values and interests.

Not that Kathryn would erase these twenty-six years of marriage to Malcolm. How could she not help but come to love the gruff man who, after an argument, laid a posy of wild flowers on her pillow? What matter they were bruised and wilted? He loved her as fiercely as he loved soldiering.

She knelt at Malcolm's bedside. Did her husband realize the anguish he had set in motion the day he had captured her father? Now his own daughter was apparently a captive somewhere.

If not already dead.

This news Kathryn could not share with him. Such information might worsen his condition. Still, he had survived far longer than all the doctors had predicted. "Malcolm, I go below to receive Simon Murdock. It is said he has word of our Enya."

Which was truth enough.

"The mon should join our daughter. 'Tis nae good, this dallying."

She tried to make light of the statement. "All dallying isn't bad, husband of mine."

Malcolm's disfigured hand stole out to caress the thick, black plait of hair draped over her shoulder. A weak smile eased his permanent scowl lines. "Well said, me love. I miss our . . . dallying."

She took his hand. "You have only to touch me, and all is well." She kissed his brow and relinquished his hand to seek out her new son-in-law.

Simon Murdock waited for her in the Chinese Room. The salon's various shades of green were a foil for his black-figured silk coat and gold baroque satin vest. Froths of creamy lace dripped from his Mariner's cuffs. His black greatcoat was draped over the back of a jade-lacquered, latticework chair, his cocked hat on its chartreuse padded seat. A gold knobbed cane was tilted against the chair's arm.

"G'day, Lord Murdock."

He gestured languidly at the carved mirror framed with gilt gesso. "A lovely piece, Lady Afton."

She disliked him at once. She could have said it was because of the parsimonious mouth, the nose that was just a wee too pointed, the eyes that were set too close. But they were less than authentic reasons. "Thank you."

"I took the liberty of ordering my mount watered."

"Of course." It was said the man prized his white stallion above his own mother. And, Kathryn wondered, his wife, also?

"You have word of my daughter?" she asked crisply, going to stand at the hearth. Its cheerful fire eased the chill in her heart that had been there since the moment she had been informed that her daughter and her retinue had vanished en route to Fort William, two weeks ago to the day.

Murdock withdrew a pinch of snuff, not from any ornate box but from a rather curiously made pouch of wrinkled hide or something similar. Instead of placing the snuff in one nostril, he crumbled the tobacco between the beringed fingers of his left hand.

The action took a maddeningly long moment. "Well?" she prompted.

With that disarmingly boyish smile, he looked up at her. "My wife, according to army dispatches, is the hostage of one of the Highland rebels."

Her heart sank, but she reminded herself that, at least, her daughter was still alive. "What does this rebel want in exchange?"

"My head, most likely."

"Tell him he can have it." She regretted at once her reply. The glitter in those gray eyes told her he would not forget it.

His fingers sifted the crumbled tobacco into the opened tea poy. "I'll have his head, madam. You may count on that."

Her teeth gritted. "I don't want his head, I want my daughter safe!"

"My wife is my personal property, and I protect what is mine. For that reason, if not because it is my sworn duty, I shall take great delight in exterminating another clan from the face of Scotland."

His utterly boyish smile was chilling. Actually, Simon Murdock was deemed handsome by many. A trim physique, short-lashed gray eyes, hair as black as hers once had been, which he wore unpowdered and fully curled—these physical qualities attested to some of the reasons the man was celebrated in London's salons.

It was that other quality, eliciting warranted regard in London's political circles, that bothered her. The quality of the man was one she sensed as a negative aura rather than identified through any specific deed, though Simon Murdock was legendary for his absolute political and military conquests.

Two years earlier he had led troops of the East India Company in defeating the more numerous Indian forces, whose religion forbade them to eat pork. To illustrate the fate of those who opposed the English, he had ordered the blood of pigs poured into the mouths of all Indian soldiers taken alive. Their drownings had been made all the more effective by the manner.

His political victories were equally absolute. Returning home, he had campaigned for a seat in parliament and won by default of the incumbent. The man had chosen suicide by hanging rather than face exposure of his unsavory lifestyle. The source of the incriminating evidence leaked to the London newspapers was attributed to Simon Murdock. His reply had made even the *Edinburgh Times:* "My opponent was an expression of stupidity and cowardice."

Appointed the year before as Lord Lieutenant of the Western Highlands, Murdock had been brutally thorough in his efforts to subdue rebel Highlanders. His effective, however merciless, measures had elicited acclaim from the king himself.

Reluctantly, she had given in to Malcolm's insistence that she grant Murdock's request, by an envoy-delivered letter, for Enya's hand in marriage. After all, she herself had found a measure of contentment as a warrior's wife, decidedly not a role she would have chosen.

On the surface, the marriage between Murdock and Enya appeared a good match. Certainly, Kathryn could understand Malcolm's preference for a man with army experience and empathize with his desire to see his daughter's future settled before his death.

She couldn't resist the urge to prick his pride, when, in truth, she was all for the defeat of the Highland rebels, and for good reason.

Some clansmen had given monetary and manpower support for feudal reasons; others, Episcopalians and Roman Catholics, for religious reasons. A few took up arms because they believed in rebellion for political reasons. Mostly, it was for economical ones. The Highlanders saw the prince's campaign as a chance to revive on a grand scale the traditional rape of the Lowlands.
"'Tis been five years, and the Highlanders are still rebelling, Lord Murdock."

"I leave tomorrow for Fort William. It may have been five years since I last served in the Highlands, but once there, I shall smoke out all clan chieftains harboring secret sympathies for Jacobites. Neighborhood locals can be all too free with the secrets of these people when encouraged with reward or drink. I assure you, it will not take long to find the particular rebel I seek."

With foreboding, she watched him depart. If Enya was still alive, he would get her back; of that there was no doubt. Murdock never failed.

Yet, instinct told Kathryn that he would not suffer a tainted wife. Pride would demand that, if he so chose, he be the one to rid himself of his wife, not this Highland rebel.

Kathryn who had espoused peace and enlightenment during her rule in Malcolm's stead, had no soldiers to call upon in her time of need.

She turned to the only one who might be able to help her.

Brother Archibald saw Kathryn coming long before she spotted him. He set down on the rocky outcrop the quill he sharpened, along with his knife, and waited for her.

He had been waiting for her, it seemed, forever. Since the day she arrived, at age thirteen, at the baronial castle of Malcolm Afton. He himself had been not much older, a mere laddie at fifteen. The rest of his life was ever after changed. From being the son of a fisherman, he had hoped to become a fisherman of men.

But that was much later. After the dark night of his soul.

He rose, standing tall above her. The wind, warmed by the Gulf Stream, whipped the hem of her concealing cloak around his trousered legs.

The color on her cheeks was high. Because of the warm afternoon or this meeting?

In his mind's eye, she was still a lass of sixteen, her hair spread across the stable straw like a jeweler's black velvet backdrop.

Her dark blue eyes reflected the sunlight sparkling off the water. Yet, deep in them he saw a storm. "Aye, Kathryn?"

"You got my message then." It was a statement of relief rather than a question.

"A tinker brought it."

She sighed. "I never know where to find you or when you'll come."

He took her hand, slender and slightly veined. "Something is amiss. What is it?"

"'Tis Enya."

His heart seemed to lurch in his chest. "Let's walk." He collected his quill and knife—and collected his wits. Taking Kathryn's elbow, he turned their steps toward the burn below that emptied into the sea. He asked gently, "What has happened?"

Her eyes shimmered, her normally serene voice trembled. "She was abducted on her way to Fort William. Less than twenty-four hours after she left Afton House and her wedding reception."

His hand tightened over her entwined ones. "Do you know who did it?"

She shook her head, and wisps of her bound hair, silver-streaked, tumbled from the hood of her cloak. "No. I mean, aye. Some Highland rebel. Simon Murdock was here the day before yesterday. He doesn't know the full details yet, but says she is apparently being held hostage. He means to go after her."

He turned his face out to the Firth of Clyde. Its salty spray invigorated him. "The odds of defeating the Scottish rebels are on Murdock's side."

"Aye, but how long will that take, Arch? And, in the meantime, what will have happened to Enya?"

Seeing Kathryn's shudder, he didn't have to imagine what was on her mind. The same was on his. What kind and how much torture might Enya have to endure?

Murdock cared not a whit. Other than to salvage his pride, his main objective was to defeat the remaining Highlanders still in rebellion against British dominion a full five years after the Scottish defeat at the Battle of Culloden.

He squeezed Kathryn's hands with a reassurance he did not quite feel. He sometimes felt her unswerving faith in him was misplaced. "I have contacts. I'll return the day after tomorrow with the full story. When we know all there is to know, then we can plan accordingly."

The relief in her fair face was worth all those lonely nights of his adult life. Now the burden had shifted to him; so, after leaving Kathryn at the banks of the sluggish burn, he prepared for another journey. His destination was the trackless wilds of Midlothian and Rosslyn Chapel, the underground headquarters of the Knights Templar.

A contingent of Knights Templars had allegedly fought on Robert Bruce's side at the Battle of Bannockburn in 1314, in which Bruce defeated the English. Because the papal bull dissolving the Templars was never proclaimed in Scotland, the order of warrior-monks was never officially suppressed here.

The order began a clandestine existence, gradually secularizing itself and becoming associated with both the Scottish Rite Freemasons and the prevailing clan system. Indirectly, it had worked to support the cause of Bonnie Prince Charlie in '45.

After a hard ride that took all night and part of the next morning, Arch arrived exhausted at Rosslyn Chapel. Visitors to the site were not uncommon. The chapel was famous for the quality and variety of stone carving inside. Also inside was a secret passage known only to a select few.

In the guise of a wine merchant, Arch entered the chapel, dimly lit by wall sconces and sputtering candles at the altar. A few pilgrims either sat on the scarred benches or tiptoed around the circumference of the walls to better view the carvings. For a moment he idled, enjoying the coolness the interior afforded a tired and perspiring traveler.

A little-used staircase off one alcove descended to a wine cellar below. Unobtrusively, he went down its narrow, dank steps. Someone moved in the room, damp and chill, with mold growing on its walls.

Wary, he paused. A wayfarer, an artist by his pad and charcoal, wandered among the wine cellar's empty casks. Arch peered at the pad and ascertained that the young man had, indeed, been sketching. The drawing was of the cellar's high, vaulted stone roof.

Arch strolled forward. "G'day. Spooky place, isn't it?"

The young man nodded. "That it is."

"Anything left for our refreshment?"

"Not a drop," the artist said. "The English swigged it all." Soon thereafter, he took his leave.

Arch had to smile. The artist's eye was not that observant or he would have noted that the cellar's cobwebs did not adorn all the oak casks. At the back of the catacomblike cellar, one large vat in particular showed no trace of dust.

By simply pulling on what appeared to be a spigot, he swung open the vat's end to reveal a tunnel, lit by a sconce at the far end. Pins in well-greased hinges turned noiselessly as he closed the portal behind him. The cellar's stone floor ended here, and the tunnel's hard-packed dirt softened his footsteps. Just beyond the sconce, the tunnel veered and terminated with another door. Without knocking, he entered.

A bearded man wearing the Knights Templars' white robe with splayed red cross was perched on a stool before a counter. On it, the vials, flasks, mortars, and pestals indicated this anteroom also served as an alchemical laboratory. The man turned, head canted, and asked, "Archibald Armstrong?"

"You remember. 'Tis been almost fourteen years."

The owl-like eyes twinkled. "How could I forget someone who not only bested me at claymores but made me look like a laddie in the bargain?"

Arch smiled. He, too, remembered. Remembered not only Bernard, but the man's eccentric uncle, Isaac Newton, who had performed some of his clandestine research in this very laboratory. "I need help, Bernard. Information."

The Knight Templar nodded. "About Lady Enya?"

"Then word is already out?" He took a seat on another stool, which the Knight indicated. "Aye. Do you know who is holding her hostage?"

The Templar laid aside the beaker he held and wiped his hands on a cloth. "Reivers, no less. The fiercest of the raiders, in this case—Ranald's Reivers."

"Where can I find these reivers?"

"Their leader, Ranald Kincairn, is of the Clan

Cameron. Red Castle near Ballengarno used to be the power base of the Camerons. The Earls of Atholl of the Cameron branch could trace their clan back to the sacred origins of St. Columba and the royal house of Fife.

"These days, Ranald Kincairn abandons one base for another. He had the English troops quartered at Fort William chasing their tails. Murdock's arrival has changed all that."

Arch rubbed his chin. "Does anyone know where their present base is?"

"Some say the Trossack area. That is Gaelic for bristly country. Which should hint at how difficult your search will be." The Templar's owlish eyes hooded over in a secretive look. "Seek out first the keeper of the Templar graveyard in Argyll."

Arch knew he could learn no more. He thanked Bernard and left. He still had a return journey of fourteen hours of hard riding before him. Kathryn would want to know the news as soon as possible.

He reached Afton House just after four o'clock the following morning. The sky was still dark, without a hint of moon. His horse's flanks were steaming, his own labored breath frosty in the crisp early-morning air. Kathryn was still up. Her light shone in her bedroom on the second floor.

She could wait 'til sun-up, he reasoned. Nothing could be accomplished before then anyway. He cantered on to the stables. After unsaddling his weary horse he sought out a bed of straw, which was better than he often got.

When he awoke Kathryn was kneeling over him. For a moment he thought he was back again twenty-five years. His arms raised to embrace her. Then he recollected where he was, who he was. Instead, he pushed himself upright. "What time is it?"

"Just before matins. One of the stable boys found you. What news have you?"

He rubbed the sleep from his eyes. God, he ached all over. He was too old to be chasing around the countryside. He should have taken his vows to his order long ago, changed his vocation from brother to priest, and then taken his carcass out of Scotland for good.

"Enya is being held by Ranald Kincairn, acting chief of the Camerons."

"Do you ken where?"

He shook his head. "No."

Kathryn rose and began pacing before him. The hem of her skirts swished the dirt and straw. Dust particles filtered up in the shafts of early-morning sunlight. The odor of horse manure was powerful, and he realized he had fallen asleep with one elbow in a pile of it. "God's blood, but I smell rank!"

"I can be ready to ride by dawn tomorrow."

"What?" He bolted to his feet and hit his head on the stall's low lintel.

She halted, stared at him, and wrinkled her nose. "A bath wouldn't hurt you either before we leave."

Rubbing her palms together, she resumed pacing. "Malcolm mustn't ken of this. I'll tell him I am going to Edinburgh. That's it. I'll tell him Allan Ramsay wants to paint my portrait, and I'll need to stay a fortnight. Alistair is capable enough to run Afton House and care for Malcolm until I return."

"You're not going with me, Kathryn."

She whirled on him. "Enya is me daughter, too."

He took her hands in his. "Not only would you slow me down, but I would accomplish more without you. People don't question a scribe traveling on the back roads. A fine lady they would."

"I don't have to go as a fine lady."

His lips curled in a scoff. "You wouldn't know how to go as anything else. A life of nobility is all you've ever known. You'd slip up and betray us in less than an hour. We can't afford to alert this Ranald. He's expecting Murdock. But not me."

She put her hands on her hips, still slender even after childbirth and middle age. His mind's eye saw her again in that pose—a fetching lass who had often challenged him. "I can go places and get information that even a man can't, Arch."

"Like where?"

She raised a brow. "Think about it."

He could feel his big ears turning red with heat. "You'd go to the Highlands even if I said I wouldn't take you, wouldn't you?"

Her smile was gentle, guileless, serene, and noble. "A repentant prostitute on pilgrimage is an excellent disguise, don't you agree?"

Chapter Five

The reivers were eating haggis and neeps, jesting and quarreling and enjoying the comradely pleasures of the great hall. They conversed in that strange Gaelic language. Although there had to be more than fifty men tonight, more than usual, Enya knew at once which one was Ranald Kincairn before he even took up the bagpipe.

Her mother would claim she was daft, but Enya didn't know how else to explain her knowledge of the man, other than to describe it as second sight, like dreams or visions that Elspeth said some of the auld folk had.

From that distance, Enya could not really say the man was handsome. Rather ordinary, in fact, if she discounted his size.

The tall, brawny man left his place at the head

table to play the pipes for Ian Cameron. A collie that had been moping in the castle now perked up and padded behind the big man, who had taken up a hide-bound chair a short distance from her place at the end of the table. Unlike his kilted uncle and cousin, the appointed laird of the Cameron clan wore a hunting shirt and trousers of deerskin so worn and stained that the leather shined.

In the five days she had been held captive at Lochaber Castle, she had learned through questioning Jamie that Ranald Kincairn had come and gone and come again, like a will-o'-the-wisp. Clearly, he was in no hurry to carry out his expressed intentions in regard to her.

"'Tis a *ceilidh* tonight," Jamie said at her side.

"A what?" The wild-sounding, hard-to-pronounce Gaelic words spoken by Highlanders confounded her. Like *Eidiann* for Edinburgh and *Glaschu* for Glasglow. Gaelic was a completely separate tongue, with its own unique vocabulary and grammar, as different from English as were Greek or Polish.

"A *ceilidh* is a Highland-style evening of music, dance, and drinking. The villagers will find any excuse for a *ceilidh*."

"What is the celebration?" In all the time she had been at Lochaber, the days and evenings had passed in monotonous isolation. Tonight was the first time she had been allowed to leave her room, although she had been permitted the services of Elspeth and Mary Laurie.

She realized she had taken for granted the dancing classes, literary correspondences, debates, and flirtations that had enlivened her life at Afton House.

Jamie's dancing blue eyes didn't meet her own. "We are celebrating a victory of sorts. Ranald's men trounced a small English search party."

Her pewter tankard of ale stopped midway to her mouth, but the sudden wail of the bagpipe postponed her obvious question.

There was a quality to this music unlike any of her Lowland childhood experience. Until the English banned the bagpipe as a weapon of war because it had led the clans to battle at Culloden, many Lowland towns had employed a town piper. An honored citizen with a special uniform, the town piper's duty had been to pipe the town awake in the morning and pipe it to sleep at night.

This was no simple tune. It opened with a theme that developed over a sequence of variations into an eerie musical scheme of soulful depth. This music, once heard, was not to be forgotten. The instrument's piercing, haunting tone emerged from the sound of the drones like a needle sewing silver thread through coarse linen.

She shivered. Her gaze scrutinized with

aroused interest the man responsible—for both the music and her captivity.

His head was slightly tilted and lowered so that she got a glimpse of his queue, tied at his muscular nape by a leather thong. His hair was the color of hot tea marbled with cream.

He took a momentary breath, releasing the blow-pipe, and lifted his head. In that instant, she saw that, while not handsome, his face was arresting.

She couldn't take her eyes from it. The brow was broad, the light-colored eyes impassioned. High, craggy cheekbones created steep, bronzed walls into which a pleat had been carved at either side of a mouth etched with purpose.

There was nothing soft about his countenance. Shrewdness, determination, and a certain recklessness glinted there.

For a moment his gaze clashed with hers. Beneath the sharply angled brows, his eyes challenged her. She realized he wanted her to try to escape. He wanted an excuse to make her life more difficult than it already was.

His gaze relinquished hers, and she let out a breath she had not known she had been holding. He replaced his mouth over the blow-pipe. Nearby, his uncle leaned his head back against the great chair and closed his eyes. The tormented expression of his old-prophet's face eased into repose.

Between Ian and Ranald Kincairn's empty chair sat a young woman Enya had not noticed in the great hall the first time. Clad in men's trews and a too-large cambric shirt, she appeared to be approximately the same age as herself but of a diminutive build. The young woman's hair, unbound in the style of a maiden, reminded Enya of a lioness's tawny mane. In the heart-shaped face, her blue eyes had that look of the wild. She was definitely striking, but too gaunt to be considered attractive.

Enya realized the young woman was staring back at her. Such hate filled those ice-blue eyes that Enya had to steel herself against flinching. At last, the woman looked away, but not without first flicking her a smile that promised pain.

"The young woman there," she said to Jamie, "is she the laird's?"

"Ranald's wife? No, he has none. Mhorag is his sister."

Enya could almost have sworn she had heard the young woman snarl at her. Perhaps it was the final drone of the bagpipe.

Ranald Kincairn passed his sheepskin bag to a waiting lackey and resumed his seat. She watched him prop his high leather boots on the table and light his pipe. Such was her desire to smoke, that for one mad moment she thought about stealing his pipe the next time he deserted the table to play his bagpipe.

A fiddler put an end to the lull in music, if the screeching noise could be called such. Several couples in rustic homespun, most likely from the hamlet of Lochaber, forsook their tankards to dance to a reel. Entertained, she watched while her foot tapped—until she realized the name of the song, "Old Stewart's Back Again."

The elbow at her ribs recalled her attention. She followed Jamie's nod. Ranald Kincairn, pipe stem between his lips, curled a finger in her direction, beckoning her to come to him.

All conversation in the great hall ceased, as did the old fiddler his reel. The dancers eased back onto their benches.

She could feel all eyes upon her. She did not move. Irritation, indignation, and resentment threatened to undermine her attempt at civility, composure, and control. Badly, she wanted to tell the Highland heathen where he could put his pipe.

His expression never changed. He simply waited. The tension in the room was as thick as the steak-and-kidney pudding.

Her nerves tingled, but she remained seated. Behind his hand, Ian murmured something to his nephew.

"You had best comply with Ranald," Jamie said to her. "He is the laird, you know."

She managed a shrug. "And if I don't?"

"His patience is not infinite."

"I'll worry when that time comes."

"Well, you have a point there. I've only seen him lose it once."

For all her insouciant facade, she blurted beneath her breath, "What happened?"

"One of the grooms forgot to rub down Ranald's horse after a particularly hard ride. It was the second time the groom had forgotten. Ranald ordered the armorer to forge a permanent saddle on the back of the groom."

"You jest."

He shook his head solemnly, and his lustrous auburn curls rustled across the tortoiseshell brooch clasping his plaid to one shoulder. "No."

"How cruel!"

"If it was just Ranald, the groom's laxity wouldn't have required so great a penalty. But the safety of an entire clan was at stake. A chief without a horse canna lead his men effectively."

The finger curled again. In the light of a wax-sputtering candelabrum, the chief's mouth, clamped about his pipe stem, had a hard, relentless cast.

She drew a fortifying breath and chose her own safety above pride. Rising, she gathered her skirts and sauntered toward Ranald Kincairn. It seemed a collective sigh issued from the room's occupants.

She stood before him. She was so angry, she

could not speak. That close, she saw that his eyes were more green than blue. And very light. Like the center of bright-burning fires. His unwavering gaze held none of the friendliness of his collie, which eyed her with curiosity. His gaze was more that of a predatory animal. A wolf, a lynx, a falcon.

He set aside his pipe. "As you are now residing with the Cameron clan, you will be required to take an oath to me, its laird and chief."

In the silence of the great hall, she found her voice. "Even though I reside here not by my own will?"

"You reside here by my will."

His eyes had not flashed with fury, his mouth had not compressed in ire, his voice had not changed timbre. Nevertheless, it was obvious that she would be unwise to argue the point now. She shrugged her shoulders. "As you will."

"Aye, as I will. Tomorrow you swear your oath of allegiance in the Justice Room."

Justice? If there were such a thing as justice, she thought, you would be drawn and quartered.

"Ye . . . are prepared for . . . what happens. . . ."

Enya glanced back over her shoulder. "The ties are too binding, Mary Laurie. And say what it is you are thinking."

Mary Laurie loosened the stays' ties somewhat,

and Enya let out her breath. She knew she would never be willowy, nor ravishingly beautiful. Nor did she care any longer; that way there would be no longing for the years of youthful good looks that time stole.

"'Tis just that I was speaking with my lord Jamie Cameron, and he said that—"

She turned around completely this time. Perhaps there was, after all, hope for the maid's reticence with men after all. "You are interested in Jamie?"

Mary Laurie blushed. "Oh, nae. The mon is much too worldly for the likes of me. He merely asked me how long I had been in yer service, m'lady." She paused. "Then he said that yer service with the laird would begin after the oath-taking."

"I see." So the time of reckoning was drawing near. Well, she would not go to her fate with the compliancy of a lackey.

"Ye don't see at all," Elspeth said, entering Enya's room with a pair of freshly washed silk stockings. "Or else ye'd not treat this Ranald for a simple coof. That he is not."

"I never thought him a fool," she said, and took one of the proffered stockings. Spreading her skirts, she sat on the low stool and began easing the stocking's white silk up one bare leg. "But he is a warrior, ruled by aggressive tendencies. Give him no battle and he is lost."

She had had enough time to think through her predicament, and this course seemed the wisest. Delay would be to her advantage. Besides, she needed to find out what had become of Duncan. He appeared to have vanished once they reached the castle.

"Hhmp!" Elspeth said, and passed her a green satin garter. "That's a *wheen o'blethers.* I canna imagine ye bypassing a challenge anymore than ye could give up smoking."

Her head jerked up. "How did you find out?"

"I'm na coof either. Ye didna really think I believed the pipe or smoke was Duncan's all these years?"

"Well, the pipes were." She reached for another stocking and garter. "The smoke was mine. I could use one now."

"Ye could use some good sense. This man is nae Duncan or any coxcomb struttin' in yer mother's court. He will break yer will."

"That he canna—cannot—do." She pinned a saucer-sized lace cap atop her carefully coiffed hair, then picked up her red woolen shawl. The old castle's three-foot-thick stone walls might be hard to breech, but they also retained the autumn chill.

Or maybe it was just that her heart was chilled.

The Justice Room was warmed by a fire and the bodies of perhaps a hundred or so people. Enya listened to the men and women who presented petitions, lodged complaints, and complied with the justice dispensed. It was that time of year when, among other annual transactions, clan members paid their tithes to their laird. Crofters and burghers, caps in hand, girded walls made somber by their dark-colored arras.

Her eyes traveled to where Ranald sat in the Justice Chair. The collie lay beside the chair, guarding Ranald like Cerberus guarding the gates to the underworld. The chair's high-paneled wheel back supported an improvised canopy of the same Cameron plaid Ranald wore.

His tartan slanted across a broad chest clothed in a white linen shirt with ruffling at the wrist. An odd contrast with the scarred and sun-browned hands, she thought. Tight knee breeches accentuated his heavily muscled thighs, and an unruly forelock tumbled across his forehead as he scanned parchments Jamie passed to him.

Her glance shifted to where Ian sat, slightly behind Ranald, a pair of crutches propped against the arm of his chair. Whatever his thoughts, Ian's expression was buried beneath the full gray beard and thick, hoodlike brows. A veritable patriarch overviewing the scion, she mused wryly.

"There you are," Jamie said.

Enya turned. She had stationed herself, and Mary Laurie and Elspeth, in the seclusion of a window embrasure where she could watch the proceedings. She found it difficult to be put out with the man who had assisted in her abduction when he possessed such an elfin smile.

"Aye, Jamie?"

"I'm to be your escort for today's ceremony."

She inclined her head and raised a cynical brow. "Ceremony—or exhibition?"

That high forehead furrowed, and the astute eyes reproached her. "It won't be such a difficult thing to do, my lady, to swear allegiance to Ranald as your laird. Do you nae see, Ranald could make it much more difficult for you? He would have to imprison you. All he's asking is your word of obedience."

She sighed. With every turn, it seemed she was becoming more enmeshed in the gossamer chains of her captivity. "What does this ceremony involve?"

"'Tis a formal contract between a vassal and a noble by which the vassal agrees to become part of the noble's household."

"Why would me bairn want to do that?" Elspeth snapped with about as much ferociousness as a tiny terrier.

"Common sense," Jamie said. "I could tell you that by becoming part of the household a vassal is guaranteed a job for life, a homestead, and personal protection. But I think you know whereof I speak."

"And what does Ranald Kincairn proffer by this?" Enya asked.

"The earl's half of the bargain is called—"

"Ranald is an earl?"

"Aye. In his own right. The seventh Earl of Fife."

Her scornful gaze scanned the room. "And this heap is now his castle."

Mary Laurie touched her arm. "M'lady, careful."

Enya saw the patient pleading in the young woman's eyes. "Let's get this sideshow over with."

The next hour proved to be most interesting. Many of the transactions were conducted in Gaelic, which Jamie occasionally interpreted for her.

Later, his knowledge of French was demonstrated. Ranald called upon him to translate for a Parisian artillery expert who had been smuggled in by Captain Knox. The man displayed his gunworks, and Jamie conversed with him in fluent French.

She could not help but compare the cosmopolitan Jamie with his primitive cousin and think how much better suited Jamie was for the title of laird of the Clan Cameron.

A local would-be alchemist approached Ranald

about financing a project to turn base metals into gold. A widower, a village merchant, requested permission to marry his stepdaughter, and a shepherd accused a crofter of stealing an ewe.

Puffing occasionally on his pipe, Ranald listened to the various supplicants. Every so often he scratched the collie behind its ears. Several times he motioned to a one-eared man to make certain notes in a record book and twice conferred with Ian, but he said little himself. A veritable King Solomon.

Enya's attention was distracted by the entrance of Duncan, his hands bound in chains, as were his ankles. A scruffy growth of beard shadowed a mouth that normally laughed at the world.

Ranald called a wayward sheriff to hell before turning his attention to Duncan. "Ye are ready to take the Bond of Manrent? Or do ye wish to languish another fortnight in the gaol?"

Duncan flashed a lopsided grin. "What I wish, sire, is to take leave of yer hospitality. 'Tis not that I find yer accommodations appalling. 'Tis that my legs ache to stretch free."

A pleat just below one cheekbone twitched. "I'm certain we could find something to take the kink out of your leg muscles. Robert?"

The one-eared man, Robert of Macintosh, peeled off a rolled parchment and began reading in a polished though heavily accented voice: "Be it known to all men by these present letters

I, Duncan of Ayrshire and the Clan Afton, to be bound and obliged, and by these my letters and the faith and truth in my body bind and oblige me to a noble and potent lord Ranald, Earl of Fife, Laird of the Camerons of Scotland, and to his male heirs, that I shall be loyal, true, and faithful to them and to him because my said good laird and master has enfeifed me in his lands of Cameron for all the days of my service foresaid and all the days of my life."

Duncan grinned and held forth his bound hands. "A pen, me lord? To sign me name."

Pipe aglow, Ranald leaned a jaw on one fist. "Ye give your allegiance easily, Duncan of Ayrshire."

"More easily than I do me life."

When the quill pen was presented by Robert, Duncan said, "Alas, I canna write. Ye have a scribe whereby I can sign me *X*?"

"I shall write his name," a female voice said.

All eyes swiveled slightly to one side and behind the Justice Chair. Mhorag stepped forward. Beneath a soiled leather tunic she wore a man's smock shirt over baggy sailors' trews. Her wild, sun-scorched mane mocked feminine propriety.

Her brother eyed her askance. "You will be responsible for the vagrant?"

Her remote manner eased. "I shall see that he does me bidding, brother."

"Then you may take the Bond of Maintenance in me place," Ranald told his sister.

In a calm, cool voice, she recited the pledge read aloud by Robert. "Be it known to all men by these present letters . . . I, Lady Mhorag Ranald of the Clan Cameron . . . to be bound by these our letters and the faith and truth that binds and oblige me . . . to my loved vassal Duncan of Ayrshire and the Clan Afton . . . for as much as he is become special man to me . . . herefore I bind and oblige myself . . . that I shall supply and defend the said Duncan in all and sundry his rights."

When she finished reciting she motioned for him to follow her. Hands still chained, he tugged at his forelock and fell in step behind her. As they walked down the aisle cleared by the spectators, he passed Enya and darted her a mischievous grin. "They found me strolling back down Hidden Valley Trail."

Ranald's sister jerked on his chained hands. He staggered on and followed her out of the great hall.

"M'Lady Murdock," Robert of Macintosh announced, summoning her before the Justice Chair.

Her breath quickened and she lifted the hem of her skirts and walked toward Ranald Kincairn.

Her heavily embroidered underskirts rustled in the suddenly quiet hall. Closer to him, she could see that the plaid was pinned at his shoulder by a brooch in the form of a black dagger—and that the blue-green of his pupils were rimmed with black.

"You witnessed the exchange of Bonds, mistress."

He was patently ignoring her rank or title and addressing her as a common maid. Her mouth compressed. "I did."

"'Tis a lifetime guarantee from both parties on behalf of one another," he continued. "Do ye wish to submit your will in this?"

Disdain curled her lips. "Do I have any alternative?"

"Aye." He fixed her with those oddly colored eyes that were fringed by black lashes longer than a woman's. "Ye will be treated with the same courtesy as Edward I of England treated one of our countesses. Ye will be imprisoned in a cage suspended over the city walls, wherein ye will be given your meals and wherein ye will perform all bodily functions without the benefit of privacy."

Her breath hissed out. "What?"

"Ye heard me, mistress."

She stood as stiff as Lot's wife. Behind Ranald, a sober Jamie nodded, encouraging her to comply.

Her captor was not to be trusted, despite Jamie's assurance that integrity was central to the code of the Highlander, that a written contract was not needed when he gave his word. Had her captor not warned her he kept her alive only to witness her degradation? Yet, her best recourse—her only recourse—was to delay. "Very well. Since the alternative is not to my liking, I agree to the Bond of Manrent."

He leaned forward, one forearm braced on a muscle-striated length of thigh, pipe bowl in hand. "Ye understand this is a lifetime guarantee on both your part and that of your ruler?"

She could barely keep from spitting. Her teeth ground together. "Aye, I do."

"'Aye, I do, me laird,'" he prompted.

Her hands knotted. The image of looking out from between bars upon gawkers staring up at her goaded from her an "Aye, I do, my laird."

He blew an ever-widening circle of smoke. "Well said. I think some time spent in honest work would benefit thy temperament. What say ye, Ian?"

The uncle hobbled forward a step, one arm propped on his crutch. "What had you in mind? Something not too harsh for a lady, me lad."

"The women of the castle could use her help. Too, she could learn Gaelic. I grow weary trying to converse with an unschooled lass."

Wax candles could not have sputtered more. "I'll have you know that I read Latin, as well as—"

"Ye are a prideful cat, mistress. What I have in mind for ye should cure that sin."

"A scurvy dog, ye are, Duncan of Ayrshire!" Mhorag spun from the window seat and slashed at his thigh with the riding crop she still carried from this morning's ride. "I had set ye to cleaning my boots."

The man's eyes flared at the smarting rap, then the hangdog brows drooped even farther at the outer ends. He retrieved from the tartan carpet the letter she had held and, backing away, dropped it on a kidney-shaped table, donated by some luckless English sympathizer, she remembered not who.

When she had arrived at the castle only a few pieces of furniture remained among its ruins. Even those pieces were not in the best of condition.

The same could be said of her life now . . . not in the best of condition. A life spent quartered in castle ruins, on an abandoned farm, in the houses of villagers still loyal to the Jacobite cause and the restoration of an independent Scotland.

"Ach now, me lady," Duncan said with that

mocking smile. " 'T'was merely admiration that prompted me to watch ye dry yer hair instead of cleaning your boots."

The thudding in her heart slowed but did not stop. That always took time. And solitude. "Hie ye back to your duty, knave."

He retreated and returned to the fireplace, where her muddy boots slumped against each other for support. She turned back to the leaded window. She had been reading Murdock's purloined letter greeting his new wife by the morning's wan sunlight.

The sunlight did not penetrate the mist that capped the formidable peak of Buachaille Etive. Trees on its exposed heights leaned permanently to the northeast. Moisture-heavy southwest winds tortured the trees, rendering them grotesque weather vanes.

She felt grotesque, though her mirror showed a normal, well-formed woman. She felt angry, too. Her anger had driven her to ride through the mist and rain like a demon spurred by the de'il himself, lashing the world for being there.

So the Lowland woman was wife to Simon Murdock. And the oaf cleaning the riding boots was in her retinue.

Mhorag closed her eyes. Her hand twisted at her crop's leather quirt. She must, indeed, be stone mad to guarantee the man's safety.

Or deviously sane.

How long before the remnants of the convivial girl she had once been lost the struggle for sanity?

She wasn't even aware of the banshee wail peeling from her lips until Duncan's hands shaking her shoulders snapped her back to awful, unalterable reality.

With her maidservants sent packing back to their quarters that morning, Enya was assigned to Jamie, who escorted her out into the inner bailey. Following him into its spinning house and loom shed, she heard a powerful thudding, accompanied by women's voices lifted in song.

In the spinning house's outer room she was introduced to spindly Dame Margaret, " . . . who will teach ye what ye need to ken," he finished lamely, backing out rather hurriedly.

The dame was a stringent string bean of a woman, with a mouth pursed like a prune. "I'll put idle hands to work. Join the women at yon table."

As if on an inspection tour of Afton's crofts, Enya strolled through a low-linteled door. Their heads bound in scarves, a dozen or so village women of all ages sat round a long, narrow table. They were cleaning and thickening a band of newly woven cloth with their hands to make it ready for use. The thump as they banged the tweed on the table in unison gave the "waulking songs" a steady, stalwart beat.

"Seat yeself and lend ye hands to honest work, m'lady," the old dame said, her arms crossed, her scarf-wreathed face set in wrinkled lines of satisfaction.

Enya eyed the ruddy-skinned young woman on her left. Molly's reddened hands deftly kneaded the coarse, tweedy material. Shrugging, Enya plowed her hands into the work. For seven hours she crunched and thumped and rolled and twisted. Having to learn Gaelic at Ranald's insistence had turned out to be easier than the chore assigned her.

At one point, a fat, mustachioed woman to Enya's right jammed her thumb and muttered what could only be a Gaelic curse.

For just a moment Enya rejoiced that she was not the only one suffering—though she did so silently.

The tormented, deafening keening of the women set off a throbbing pain at her temples. She felt like screaming at them to shut up. Her spine and upper arms ached unbearably. So this was her reward for having taken the oath a scant three weeks ago. Well, so be it. With grim determination, she kept her hands moving in unison with the women and their God-awful singing.

The monotonous work became sheer torture

for her. Every woven piece she touched she snarled.

Dame Margaret rolled her eyes in despair.

At one point Enya swore in English, but somehow the English no longer yielded the satisfaction of the good Gaelic curse that she tried next. *"Mo Dia!"*

Next to her, the fat, mustachioed woman winked.

Enya began laughing, but tears of fatigue lurked behind her lids.

Later that day the old dame deserted the table. Through the partially opened door, Enya spotted her conversing with Jamie. Reporting on her poor work?

At last, Dame Margaret dismissed the women for the day, or evening as it turned out to be when Enya left, remembering to duck her head to avoid the spinning house's low doorway.

She barely found the energy to climb the stairway to the keep. Others, mostly Ranald's warriors, sought out the great hall also. Dinnertime was nearing. She could have cared less. She wanted only a bed. And a back rub.

"Milady."

She half turned at the staircase, her hand on the scrolled newel post to support her sagging body. It was Jamie. "Aye?"

"I have orders from my laird." He paused. His slender, elegant hands rubbed together. "You are to be in the kitchens at dawn."

"At dawn? Is the man *dirled*? I need rest. You tell him that, Jamie. And tell him I said he could—" She thought better of what she had been about to tell Ranald he could do with himself.

She could outlast his persecution. She had to.

Chapter Six

"The laird wants ye to serve the council this morning," said Flora, the cook. The homely, sparsely haired matron smelled as foul as the kedgeree she set on the dimpled copper tray. "Now dinna dally. Ye know how men muck about. Me own mon was a monster at that. Mind ye, when ye return the kitchen needs to be redd up."

From its bed of rice with hard-boiled eggs, butter, cream, and parsley, the smoked herring seemed to fix an accusing eyeless socket on Enya. If the Highlanders could eat this, they were indeed heathen souls.

At the moment her mouth salivated for thick clotted cream with scones—always her downfall, and doubtlessly accountable for her less than lithsome form.

She swallowed back her distaste for the unappetizing fish and accepted the tray of kedgeree, porridge, cream, and steaming tea.

"I can carry the tray," Annie Dubh said. Annie, whose cleavage was as deep as Loch Ness, was none too pleased with Enya's presence in the castle. Enya suspected the fetching scullery wench had her sultry brown eyes set on her new laird.

"I'll have yer head if ye don't fetch yon platter and more butter," Flora said without looking up from the sweetbread she basted with great globs of melting butter. Garrulous and gossipy, Flora was doubtlessly interested in how the Lowland captive would contend with the Highland laird.

Enya would have loved to pass the duty off to Annie, and not just because she had no desire to remind Ranald Kincairn of her presence. Since four that morning she had been at work in the large room with its chopping table, myriad cauldrons, and turnspit in an immense fireplace that could roast an entire ox.

It was not even the sixth hour, and she looked as if she had been at work a full day. The kitchen's heat and steam had wilted her naturally curly red locks to limp strands snaking down her neck. Sweat stained her dress. Lack of sleep had left her eye sockets looking as empty as that of the herring's.

Leaving a fuming Annie to bring more cream

up from the buttery, she climbed a back staircase spiraling up a window-slit turret to the third floor. Already the days were noticeably cooler, and her sweaty dress chilled her flesh. The backs of her legs began to hurt, and her arms ached from carrying the heavy tray. The tea sloshed with each step she climbed.

Wakening birds in the surrounding forests chirped a hymn to the new day, even though the sky was still faintly smeared with stars. In the predawn darkness, the village bell tolled the hour dolorously.

Exactly her sentiment. For the past fortnight, since her debacle at the loom shed, she had been reduced to working as a scullery maid, of all things.

She knew the servants were wary of her. They hadn't decided what status to accord her just yet: that of a titled lady, a prisoner, or another servant.

A routine had begun to take form. Mary Laurie was given the duty of chambermaid; Elspeth was put to work wielding both needle and spinning wheel; and Duncan had been commandeered by Mhorag as a Jack of all trades.

Enya followed the sound of men's voices. " . . . Glenfinnan . . . fortnight . . ."

A long, narrow hall led to a room that had to be an armory. Muskets, claymores, dirks, bayonets, and powder horns ribbed three walls. On the fourth, a window, with the shutters thrown back, funneled into the room air scented with wild thyme, fir, and pine. Outside, an owl hooted eerily.

In the room's center was a table lit with two candles whose flames flickered with the morning breeze. The table, rubbed to a satin finish by the hands of centuries of diners, was bordered by more than half a dozen men of the Cameron council. She recognized four: Jamie, Ian, Robert of Macintosh—and Ranald.

The last sat at the head of the table, leafing through a list of some sorts, and barely afforded her a glance. She had seen him only three times in the past fortnight, and that had been when she served him at mealtimes.

"Put the tray on the sideboard," the nearest, Ian, told her. His crutch was propped against the arm of his chair.

"Then come here," Ranald said.

The memory of his vivid threats to degrade and defile her still smote her with apprehension, but Enya sauntered toward him. "Aye?"

"You should know we canna breakfast without platters and utensils."

She strived for an attitude of indifference. "I only brought what I was told to."

"You have a brain. I suggest ye use it."

She heeded not Jamie's warning look. Her hands knotted into fists on her hips. "I suggest ye eat with your fingers like the pig ye are."

He laid aside the papers—a list of male names, she saw—and regarded her with a blinking stare, as if he didn't quite credit her audacity. "I think the time has come to bring ye to heel, to take the retribution I promised. I have other pressing matters, but I shall deal with ye anon."

The insouciance of his tone chilled her to the bone. She had no actual authority here. She had behaved like the fool she was taken for. "Then demonstrate the brute you are. Take me by force, as you threatened."

His dark brows angled to a peak. "Take ye? Look at yourself. Besides, I have no desire for a Lowland traitoress. But breed ye I will." His forefinger flicked the pages with its list of names. "All dead, these men are. The English are killing our men and raping or sterilizing our women."

"The English, not I, are doing this."

"Ye are our Lord Lieutenant's wife. Ye will give birth to children to be brought up as Highlanders. Then me Lord Lieutenant can have ye back, if he should still live . . . and should still want you."

He glanced at the other men sitting around the table. "Weel," he asked in his thick, musical Scots accent, "which of ye wishes to bed her first?"

"Ranald!" said Jamie.

"Lift your skirts, mistress," Ranald ordered. "Show what you bring to the man who is bold enough to bed ye first."

"I will!" a young man volunteered. His jaw was heavily bearded and uncombed, and his eyes were glazed with sexual desire.

"Nae, Colin," said a squat-sized man, looking uglier than any fabled troll. "The wench is mine by right of lineage."

Farther along the table, two burly men offered to arm wrestle for her. Three other men were loudly arguing. "Ye already ha'—ha'—a woman, Macdonald!" one stuttered, a fair-haired man who looked to be about her age.

"That's 'cause—'cause I ken how—how—to keep her, Patric," the pot-bellied Macdonald mimicked.

A riot was threatening to break out among them. The scene might have been comical but for the awful reality of it. At that moment no compassion was to be found in those faces, only lust and violence.

Despite the early morning's cold, sweat beaded at her temples. Was she to be ravaged there on the table before one and all?

Ian thumped his crutch on the floor. "Enough, Ranald. This is dividing the men. Select one for her and get it over with."

Ranald rubbed his jaw, his eyes passing over the avid faces of his council. "Select one, Ian?

If each had a turn, the Lowland lass would be certain to breed."

His words pierced her like a bayonet. "You couldn't mean it!"

"Why not? Me sister fared no better."

"Would your revenge bring back her innocence? Would your revenge gain you anything but a corrupted heart?"

"On the contrary, mistress, revenge would gain me release of me heart's ache, if you will."

She spun back to the others. "Then which of ye will behave as the lowliest of men?"

She raised her skirts, exposing her scarlet stockings of coarse worsted all the way to her gartered thighs. "Come on! Which of you is lower than even the English you so despise? Which of you would rape a Scotswoman? Come now, speak up. Here I am. Unarmed. Yours for rutting with like a beast of the field!"

Silence. Shamed silence.

Pipe in mouth, Ranald studied the scene. Watched, waited, and listened.

"I suppose you are vastly entertained by this—" she flung out a hand "—this demonstration of depravity!"

"I'll take ye," said the troll. "Me name's Nob. I'll see that ye are filled with a Highland bairn and care for ye both afterwards."

By force of will she kept herself from shrinking against the wall.

Ranald cocked a questioning brow at her.

Shoving back her panic, she tried to think. Nob seemed gentle enough. She could steel herself to endure his taking of her until such time as she found a way to escape. Dear God, what if Nob got her with child first? Escape would be made more difficult.

And what if the child looked like Nob?

She swallowed a nervous giggle, dropped the ugly little man a curtsy, and said in a most formal voice, "I thank you, Nob, but as I already am married I could not accept your offer. You understand, I'm sure?"

Dumbly, he nodded.

"Then I shall make ye, too, a widow," Ranald told her in the hush of the room.

Her breath eased out of her. That particular threat would take time.

"But I shall not wait 'til that time to see that ye are with child. Go on with ye, mistress. I shall summon ye when I am ready for—" He paused, smiled, and amended his words. "Me thinks an appropriate time to get ye with child would be All Hallow's Eve."

"The fact that I have contacts within the Knights Templar Order doesn't mean they will give me the information we seek," Arch shouted.

Kathryn pulled her fur-lined hood against her

cheek. The harsh, sea-ladened winds frosted her lips and plowed the tiny fishing boat up over another spumy crest.

Maybe this was a punishment for her lie to Malcolm. Yet the truth behind her journey might have wrought his end.

Indeed, it was a pilgrimage of sorts. The first stage of the journey was to yon island of Iona, the burial place of Scottish kings until the eleventh century and the site of a monastery chosen by the Irish monk Columba from whence to spread Christianity.

Her leather gloves did little to keep out the unseasonable cold that made her fingers ache. Another sign that she was too old to be chasing off on an adventure that did not promise anything. That was, if she discounted this intimate time spent with Arch.

He gave her solace in these agonizing weeks when she wasn't sure what had become of Enya. He was actively helping her in the search, as well he should. Most of all, his presence reminded her of the simple pleasure of being with someone who knew her as she had been. Of being with someone who had loved that girl . . . and loved the woman she had become.

She grabbed the railing as the skiff dipped into another trough, then lurched drunkenly to the starboard side. Arch's hand shot around her waist to steady her. For just a minute they were as one, the length of them from shoulder to their knee. Her eyes locked with his. She saw there that same longing for all that might have been and now was too late to ever be.

He was the one to break the spell. "Look. There is the lighthouse. Soon we'll put into port."

The westerlies were piling up high breakers against the rocky ridges of Machir Bay on the Argyle island of Islay. The seascape was bleak, and gannets dove through the bare branches of wind-twisted trees. Below the rock-rooted lighthouse, the boat's hull skidded onto a beach, shingled with ground granite washed down from the island's glacial interior.

Arch dropped over the side to help the old fisherman pull the skiff ashore. The empty land, the Icelandic winds, the clear water, and the coldness of the air made her feel isolated from all that was warm and human. She was grateful for the reassurance of Arch's large hands, spanning her waist to help her alight from the boat.

He thanked the weather-wrinkled fisherman in Gaelic, passed him a handful of forty crowns and a portion of their goat cheese, then took her elbow. "I asked the old man to return here this evening when the tide is in," he told her. "That should give us enough time to accomplish what we came for."

They set out walking, she trying to keep stride with his longer legs. Her skirts dragged across sand and salty grass draped with strands of seaweed. At last, she and Arch reached a more solid support of pebbles, rocks, and boulders. "Where do we go from here?" she asked.

He pulled his cloak's hood up over his wind-lashed red locks. "Beyond. Past the sea caves. In yon dense oakwood."

The coastal trek led by barnacle geese who, in conjunction with a multitude of seals, provided an unexpected, noisy background. One old, asthmatic bull protested their presence. They skirted his domain and tramped past King's Cave. It was almost concealed by plumes and fans of white spray rising from hidden reefs.

Here, so Arch told her, was where a disheartened Robert the Bruce was inspired by the patience and determination of a web-spinning spider.

Kathryn's determination to find Enya was infinite. But the distant woodland, with the tallest trees in Scotland, remained just that.

Her suede boots were wet, her feet cold, her teeth chattering. There was no shelter from the whistling, whipping wind. She halted in a midst of brown bracken. Her blue lips were compressed so as not to betray her quivering jaw. "How . . . much farther?"

He wrapped an arm around her shoulders and tucked her into the hollow of his body. His hunter's-green cloak of thick, soft wool enveloped her. "According to my source of information, not more than an hour or more."

"Well, I hope your source is reliable."

"The Knights Templar are the most reliable source on the face of this earth. At their zenith they were the most powerful and influential organization in the whole of Christendom, with the single possible exception of the papacy."

She knew he talked to keep her mind off her misery. Pausing to help her negotiate a tiny burn flowing from rounded, tree-crowned hills above, he then resumed his discourse. "With the power to make or break monarchs, they were bankers for Europe's kings and advisers to Eastern potentates. There are those who claim the warrior-monks, knight-mystics are custodians of an arcane wisdom that transcends Christianity."

She knew that this part of Scotland was pagan to the point of superstition. Belief in things unseen—along with the mountainous geography—had left it straggling behind in ignorance.

When she and Arch reached high moors, grassed with marram, the journey became easier. She almost took the ancient monument for a random arrangement of boulders. Small, rounded granite-boulder circles and much taller red-sandstone monoliths formed chambered cairns.

A wraithlike mist had descended over the

stone, and their looming shapes seemed to come alive. It was not difficult to imagine strange rituals taking place here in the misty past of the Celtics.

Arch ushered her through the maze and into a thicket of mossy oaks that cloaked a derelict kirk of crumbled gray stone and fallen timbers. In the kirkyard were some grave slabs and a wealth of stone carvings bearing Masonic motifs: the Celtic cross, the ankh, the cross pattée, the crescent moon of the Mother Goddess with stars.

From the corner of her eye, a shadow moved. Her imagination? When it coalesced into another shape within the kirk's fallen doorway, she almost screamed. A scraggly bearded man in a dirty, tattered brown coat with a ragged tartan wrapped around his neck stepped forward with a spriteliness that belied his advanced age. A merlin perched on his shoulder. "Ye be lost?"

"We're looking for directions," Arch said.

The wrinkle-enfolded eyes narrowed so that the old man resembled his pigeon falcon. "Who be ye?"

"I come by the recommendation of Bernard of Rosslyn Chapel."

Like a magpie, the man's frosty gray head canted. "Directions, ye say? Now where is it ye wish to go?"

"I seek the abducted daughter of milady here."

"And the daughter? Her name?"

"Enya Afton of Ayrshire," she said.

It seemed the rheumy eyes flared. "Aye, there is one who knows of her whereabouts."

She was losing patience. "Arch, I thought you said he would—"

"Sssh," Arch said, holding up a silencing palm. "Could we talk with that one?"

"He will meet with ye at the Bellochant Inn in Oban. 'Tis on the mainland, where the Firth of Lorne enters Loche Linnhe."

"When?"

The wings of the merlin flapped with impatience. "Day after the morrow. As to the hour, he'll contact ye, of that ye can be sure. Ask him about Ranald's Reivers."

Like ghosts, the old man and his merlin faded back into the murk.

Bewildered, she looked at Arch. "That's all?"

He spread his palms in a helpless gesture. "At least 'til the day after the morrow." He gave her a consoling grin. "I suggest we repair to Oban and the Bellochant Inn to warm our tootsies."

She closed her eyes. "That sounds absolutely heavenly."

The Bellochant Inn was heaven and more. A converted hunting lodge, it had a sitting room with a flagstone floor and a toasty log fire rather than a peat-burning hearth. The bedroom—one of twelve—to which the rotund host showed them was within earshot of the sea. Here the water, leaving the deep, narrow loch, foamed and fought with the sea tide, creating turbulence and curious cascades that lulled one to sleep.

All but Kathryn.

Arch slept in the adjoining room. The memory of his strong arms encircling her young body and his gentle touch was old yet ever new. How many nights that memory had sustained her during Malcolm's groping worship of her body, followed by his quick subjugation of it! Since he contracted the hideous disease, her body had not known a man's touch.

Argyllshire was characterized by long, dark winters. Though only autumn, this night might have been her longest.

"There is no point in sitting and waiting," Arch told her over steaming tea and marmalade and scones the next morning. "Nothing can be done until this contact shows up. Let's explore, find out what we can on our own."

The idea appealed to her. Throughout the morning she and Arch scoured Oban from waterfront to foothills for information on Ranald's Reivers.

"Of the half a dozen people we've questioned," she complained at midmorning, "no one knows anything. And this Gaelic. 'Tis unintelligible!"

"Oban is a fishing fraternity. We're foreigners, to their way of thinking."

"These people aren't going to answer any questions about Ranald's Reivers."

"Probably not. They stand to lose as much as they gain. Repeated sweeps by the English armies have left lawless wakes in which raid and counterraid have became a way of life here. The Highlander clans survive by communal ventures, including cattle raids. I imagine that Ranald's Reivers are, in these people's minds, heroes."

By midday, failure to ferret out information combined with hunger coaxed them to abandon their search for a couple of hours. Like the youths they had once been, they climbed the hills above the inn. Nippy air pinked their cheeks. Sheltering firs dripped the wetness of a fine mist. Below, the coast was riven with a crinkly fretwork of deep inlets, where the sea probed far inland.

On a bed of bell heather, they lunched on tiny, bittersweet blaeberries bordering a spring-fed burn. Without touching, they reclined close to one other; he on his back, her on one side.

"Arch," she asked, propping herself up on one elbow, "what happens after this? If . . . after we find Enya . . . do you go back to spreading the word of your God?"

He reached across and wiped a smear of blue from the corner of her mouth. She trembled at his touch. "That's always a part of me, Kathryn. But I have another side. A side that strives for changes. Changes for the better. You really know so little of me. Despite what . . . we've been to each other."

"Oh, look!" A red deer darted from the underbrush, startling them. The diversion was a blessing. All these years of keeping her emotions tamped. They had become numbed, so that now she rarely felt anything. At least, not until Enya's abduction.

He rose and held out his hand for hers. "Time to go. The more information we can find out about Ranald's Reivers, the better."

The waterfront of Oban was less than savory, but it was legitimate. Enough fishing boats plied the river that Kathryn could have crossed the jammed harbor from deck to deck on the moored boats without wetting her feet.

In the guise of a woman of the streets—rouged cheeks and tight bodice—she easily entered the Stag's Head Pub with Arch. The pub was located at the end of a cobbled wend. Smoke-darkened beams, a wall paneled with nautical charts, and a peat fire gave the place a warmth that the proprietor and patrons lacked.

Near the fire, three sailors played shove-hal'penny on a slab of slate. Their weather-beaten visages were less than friendly.

She pulled her black woolen scarf farther up

over her head. "Surely we don't look any less couth than our cohorts," she whispered to Arch and nodded to her left, where a man with an eye patch, no less, hunkered over his tankard of ale.

Arch slid onto the bench opposite her. "I'm sure word is probably out by now that we've been asking about Ranald's Reivers."

Now that she was warmed, she pushed back the hood of her cloak. "Wouldn't a reward open someone's lips?"

He shrugged with an easy grace. She loved that about him, how mobile his body was. His readily smiling lips, his quick mind. "The code of the Highland supposedly governs all conduct, including hospitality."

"Their hospitality leaves a lot to be desired," she said, accepting one of the mugs their taciturn host brought them.

Arch leaned toward her, forearms braced on the table, and lowered his voice. "You have to remember that every Highland family has a Ranald somewhere. 'Tis common enough a name. Tracing him won't be that easy."

The ale she swallowed was certainly stronger and heavier than that of Ayrshire. What she really could use was a bottle of strong port. "I'm not giving up so easily. Maybe this contact we're—"

"Couldn't help but overhear ye," the patch-eyed man said. He leaned on one arm and fixed them with his good eye. "Ye're looking for Ranald's Reivers?"

Arch flicked her a warning glance. "We've heard of them. What do you know of their leader?"

The coarse-looking man took another quaff of his beer, then wiped his mouth with his sleeve before answering. "He is no hero. He uses what he and his reivers take."

Her heart flinched. "Have you heard anything about a young woman he captured recently?"

"That Lowland lass? Enya of the Afton clan?"

"Aye!" she gasped.

"What do you know of her whereabouts?" Arch asked.

"Ye might as well count that one as lost. Ranald uses first one place as base, then another."

"If we could contact him," Arch asked, "do you think we could negotiate for her return?"

Like a parrot, the man cocked his head. "I think he might give her up. In return for Simon Murdock's testicles."

A muscle in Arch's cheek flickered. "If that canna be arranged?"

The man rose from his bench and staggered slightly. "If I were the lass, I would rather face the dragon of Loch Ness."

With a weeping heart, Kathryn watched the man lurch through the maze of tables to the arched door and fling it open. A cold wind whipped at his soiled coat. "Maybe the man who is supposed to contact us can give us more information." She wanted desperately to believe in hope.

"I think that was our contact," Arch said. The expression on his face destroyed that last vestige of her hope.

Ranald peeled off the band and its eye patch. It was barely three o'clock. He was weary and wet and chilled. Every muscle in his body ached. With the receipt of the merlin's message tied about its leg, he had ridden hard to reach Oban. Locating a man and woman asking questions about him hadn't been that difficult. Restraining his pity, a deadly weakness, had been.

His thoughts went to the Lowland wench the couple sought. She should be entering the kitchens soon to start the fires. Like the breakfast fires, her tresses blazed a fiery *roy*.

Alas, the breakfast porridge she cooked tasted like reekin' sheep offal.

Chapter Seven

In the castle's outer bailey men mended saddles or cleaned muskets, the guard drilled, a cat stalked a frantically clucking hen, a stray blackface sheep bleated for its flock, and a handful of village children played prisoners' base.

The game reminded Enya of her status at the castle. A reluctant October sun peeked through gray-fringed clouds. Her dark-blue velvet cloak was lightweight, barely warm enough for the nippy day. She strolled at a vigorous clip and with purpose.

Beside her, Annie Dubh pattered on. "Look at 'oo now! The way 'oo speak and walk. 'Tis clear 'oo were born to it!"

"Dias Muire!" Enya said, unconsciously resorting to the common Gaelic expletive of "God and Mary." "If you but used your brain, Annie

Dubh, half as much as you use your bum, you could pass yourself off as a lady with but little practice."

Annie halted. "'Oo mean that? 'Oo would make a lady of me?"

A half step ahead, Enya half-turned to eye the slatternly wench. Sloe eyes the color of hot molasses, a complexion like whipped cream, and an hourglass figure were Annie's assets. Frowsy hair that had been badly hennaed, nails bitten to the quick, and stained teeth were to be listed on the debit side. Those, and dirty elbows and neck, but a good bath could correct the latter.

"I didn't say I would do it. Such an undertaking could take years."

Annie, cheeks rosy with the brisk air, flashed her a good-natured grin. Enya suspected that Annie no longer worried about her setting her sights on the Reiver himself. "'Oo'r not going anywhere."

God's blood, but she hoped Annie was wrong. More than six weeks had passed, and she was still a captive. Surely by now her mother and Simon Murdock had been informed she was missing.

"I'm going to the smokehouse, that's where." She set off again, with Annie trotting at her heels like Kincairn's faithful collie.

"'Oo could teach me to read, 'oo could."

Enya stopped again, and her dove-gray gown of Italian silk swished about the clogs she had taken to wearing against the ever-damp ground. Already her overskirts, hitched at her left side by a tassel in the French fashion, were frayed at the hem. She had brought with her no sturdy, working clothing. Of course, she had never thought she would be doing menial tasks. "You can't read?"

The Lowlands' near-obsession with education had resulted in at least one school in every parish. Certainly all of Afton House's servants read.

"Me da's a ploughman."

"That's no excuse. Hornbooks are easy enough to come by."

"Weel, will 'oo? Will 'oo make a lady out of me? Mind ye, I'm not asking to be a grand lady. Just a lady."

She rounded on the scullery maid. "Annie, I don't plan on staying here. Understand?"

Her stained-toothed smile was confident. "If'n the laird says 'oo are, then 'oo are."

"G'day, milady—mistress," said Jamie, joining them. He wore a matching tartan plaid and a hunting kilt and gaily checked knee-high woolen stockings.

Annie turned a saucy eye on him. "G'day, sire."

His blue eyes alighted on her. Head to one side like a kestrel, he said, "You're Annie Dubh, aren't you?"

Pleasure heightened the rosy color of her cheeks. "Aye, that I am."

At that instant Enya realized her suspicions had been in error. It was Jamie, not Ranald, in whom the illiterate maid was interested.

"Well," he said, "tell Flora I am abducting her newest scullery maid."

"I've already been abducted," Enya said after a pouting Annie set off to do his bidding.

"Ever see a goldcrest?"

"A what?"

"Scotland's smallest bird. Found right here in the Highlands." He took her arm. "Come along."

"But Flora—she sent me for—"

"Fie on Flora. Should the old hag's tongue lash you, she will have her hands full with your Elspeth."

"Right you are. Then show me this fascinating bird."

The outing was an opportunity to explore afoot the wooded countryside beyond the castle walls and their spying, grim windows.

If she and her companions had to escape on their own, any villager who observed them would report their flight. The forest offered concealment—but, also, the risk of getting lost.

Indeed, voluble Flora had said the quick weather changes had been the cause of many an accident and death. "Me niece's husband went out one sunny afternoon to herd sheep. Found him the next morning sitting beneath a tree—frozen solid as yon loch, we did."

Enya and Jamie strolled along paths layered with leaf mold and trimmed with spindly saplings of fir and yellowing larch. Jamie talked of the wildlife.

"The increase in human habitation has all but made extinct most of Europe's wildlife. Even in England once common animals such as bear and lynx and fox are disappearing."

"So will the hart and the hind, with hunters like Ranald Kincairn scouring the forest."

"On the contrary," Jamie said, ignoring her spite, "the Highlands is their last refuge."

"The Highlands is not my refuge but my prison," she snapped, then regretted her ill temper.

A prickly gorse bush snagged her overskirts hem, and Jamie knelt to free her. "You're not properly attired for an outing, milady."

"Well now," she chided, "I did not know I would be held captive in the mountain wilds of the Highlands."

"An incident I most sorely lament."

She stared down at his wavy auburn hair. Perhaps she should have been cautious about walking in the woods alone with him, but she trusted him instinctively. There was something in his manner—the eagerness of a jaded youth just beginning to appreciate life fully.

They resumed walking, and she said, "With your enthusiasm, Jamie, *you* should have been the Cameron chieftain."

He did not miss her bitterness, but he continued to smile. "Alas, it seems I am not a leader of men. I don't have a warrior's heart."

"This warrior has no heart."

He eyed her speculatively. "I gather your attitude has not softened toward him?"

"If there is one spark of warmth in the great stone face, it is for that collie."

"He cares for his sister, for—"

"You can't see it. He rarely shows her or anyone else affection. Even an embrace would be some demonstration of emotion. After all, you are family."

"Actually, my cousin is much more the family man than I. You see, at Winchester the other boys made fun of his Scottish ancestry and accent. He came home over the holidays and never went back. He was content riding, skating, fishing, and playing cards by the peat fire of the cottage.

"I, on the other, hand, prefer frequenting coffeehouses, bookshops, and taverns."

She smiled. "'Tis obvious; you are well-read. And equally well-traveled."

"Aye. When Bonnie Prince Charlie decided to reclaim the Scottish throne I was in Europe taking the Grand Tour. I had been trying to make up my mind whether to read Divinity at St. Andrew's University or look to law as a career."

They reached the bank of the stream whose rapid current took it through the village. "That was in '45. What of the past five years?"

He smiled. "As you said, I am well-traveled. I know more about the Continent than I do Scotland. The money ran out, and I came home. To this." He spread his hands. "A land whose burns run red with the blood of reivers and Redcoats."

Looking at the burn, she glimpsed salmon hurtling their speckled bodies against the current. She was reminded of Ranald Kincairn's penchant for fishing. "So your cousin preferred fishing to facts?"

His smile broadened. "Ranald secreted one of those lovely pink salmons into a professor's bed."

"So the chieftain has a sense of humor. Warped."

"Ranald was but sixteen at the time and thoroughly detested schooling, you understand. And he—look, there! In the nearest bough of that alder. The goldcrest! Isn't it lovely?"

She watched the bird, no bigger than her palm, perched on a branch. Something stirred in the underbrush, disturbing the goldcrest, and it took flight.

If only she could escape so easily.

A traitor lived within the walls of Lochaber Castle. Ranald knew this and didn't know what to do about it. He scanned yet another time the cryptic message on the shred of paper he had found in the stable. The paper smelled of dung. The letters were scrawled—written by someone in a hurry?

Ranald and his Reivers ride to Glenfinnan within the fortnight.

Only someone sitting in on the council meetings could know have information . . . or an eavesdropper.

For instance, the Lady Enya?

Crumbling the paper in his hand, he started toward the castle keep, then sighted the maiden Mary Laurie. Her shoulder resting on the doorjamb, she was talking to Cyril, whose job it was to salt the carcasses of the weaker beasts unlikely to survive the winter months.

By the signs he had been noticing—heavier moss on the north side of trees, early-morning redheaded woodpeckers, increased activity by the squirrels, and the thickness of the spiderwebs—this winter was going to be a nasty one.

A heavy winter would be a blessing this year. The mountain roads would be impassable, giving his reivers respite from the English, giving the weary Scots time to regroup, rest, repair.

"G'day to you," he said, bracing a hand just above her head. Inside the salt house, the husky young salter knelt in front of a slain cow. Its long, rust-colored coat was matted with blood.

Mary Laurie looked up at him with eyes the color of a tranquil loch: not quite blue, nor gray. Her soft mouth widened in a timid smile. "G'day to ye, sire."

From beneath her mobcap, brown curls peaked with caution. Something her mistress assuredly did not practice. What was the Lady Enya doing in the woods with Jamie? He trusted Jamie. More than he could say for the Lowland woman. "Tell me, lass, can your mistress write?"

The thickly lashed eyes grew wary. "Of course."

"Does she do so these days?"

"You would have to ask her, though I doubt it. She is kept busy performing menial chores."

So, the maidservant was loyal. And courageous enough to brave his wrath. "Ach, but ye do menial chores." He caught one chapped and roughened hand.

She withdrew it. "And I am rewarded for it with bed and board."

"So is your mistress."

"Aye, but she does not work here of her own choice. I read and write, but it is by choice I work for me mistress. She pays far better than I would receive elsewhere."

"Ye read and write?"

"Some."

Mayhaps he was a fool. What if this seemingly reticent maid either wrote the note or hoped to find someone to smuggle it out? His eye fell on Cyril the Salter, a trusted lad from the hamlet.

But Mary Laurie no longer had the note, if she ever had it, to pass to Cyril, which meant she was talking to him purely out of interest. He ruled her out.

Perhaps it was time to change bases. He had found Lochaber Castle an excellent stronghold for sallies and a good defense position, since large armies could not advance on its mountaintop location. It had the added advantage of being unreachable until spring, once snowfall blocked the passes.

Mary Laurie slid him a nervous glance. "Is that all, sire?"

"Aye." Watching her go, he wondered why he did not simply confine her mistress to the castle rather than let her stroll about at her whim.

He wondered, too, why he should give the Lowland Amazon any thought at all. The woman was obstinate and arrogant. The defiant tilt of her cleft chin symbolized these abrasive qualities. Nevertheless, she had proven capable of surprising fortitude and resiliency.

Admittedly, she was no beauty. Not compared to the slender, petite, and passionate Lady Hayward. Mayhaps another expedition to Oban and Lady Hayward was required before winter's snow locked in Lochaber.

* * *

"The man, this Ranald, is not one of the superstitious Scots' Auld Folk." Simon Murdock's flint-colored eyes stared over his pyramided fingertips at the nervous, scarlet-coated staff officer standing at attention. "Anyone who can slide a dirk between Captain Fenwick's ribs so deftly has to be human. I want him found and brought to me. Alive."

The lieutenant, his plumed hat tucked beneath his arm, saluted smartly. "Aye, sir!"

After the officer left Simon adjusted his scarlet coat's turned-back cuffs and the small coil of gold braid on one epaulet before having his aid usher in the waiting couple.

His gaze traveled past his desk to the scribe, Archibald Alistair. He stood behind the woman's chair. Why was he here at Fort William with Lady Kathryn Afton?

Snowflakes still flecked those tendrils of pepper-and-salt hair that curled beyond the range of her mantle's hood. Were she younger, he might seduce her. A pleasant *menage au trois,* her daughter, her, and himself.

However, before that delightful scenario could be played out, he had to find her daughter, his wife.

"I apologize for the chill of my office, madam. The Jacobites blew up portions of the fort, and Parliament did not see fit to include an office fireplace as part of the restoration."

Good King George, fat King George, could not afford to build forts and pay the troops to garrison them. It cost the king £80,000 a year to fortify newly won lands, and he received but a fifth of that sum in taxes from the Scottish people.

Lady Afton waved a hand of dismissal. "I am impatient with your progress. Two months is long enough to, at least, locate the renegade."

He didn't understand it himself. The man had not yet asked for a ransom.

He withdrew the wrinkled leather pouch from his waistcoat pocket. "We've set a reward on the reiver's head, madam. 'Tis only a matter of time until someone betrays him for the proverbial thirty pieces of silver."

And only a matter of time until he acquired another pouch made of a fool's testicle.

Chapter Eight

Enya's mouth compressed. The Highland "mist" filled her wooden clogs like bathtubs as she squished across the bailey toward the bakehouse. The mist was more like sleet.

Now she understood more fully how the Gaelic word *dreich* encompassed so many descriptions—dreary, dismal, drizzly, misty, gray.

The Reiver was back. From her window this morning she had watched him, astride his shaggy, big war horse, and his men canter from beneath the twin gatehouses through the morning dark toward the stables. The booty this time was a wagon-load of English muskets with powder and ball. Enough to keep the raiders supplied through the winter.

She hoped anyone searching for her would not undertake the trek to the mountain village of Lochaber any later than the end of October. After that, it could well be spring before Buachaille Etive's retreating snows yielded their bodies.

October's end. All Hallow's Eve. The height of supernatural activity. What demonic activity did the Reiver plan for her?

The long, covered wooden trencher she carried was crowded with loaves of bread dough. She spared her red and roughened hands a sympathetic look. At least her hands, and an occasional backache, were the worst she had yet suffered.

But the Reiver would be riding out less and less as the winter deepened. By All Saints' Day his attention would be directed at her, if not before.

"M'lady?"

She turned at the sound of Annie's voice. The young Highland woman, hurrying to catch her, slackened her pace. Once Enya had reassured her she had no romantic interest in *any* of the Cameron men, especially Jamie, the young woman had accepted her and accorded her the courtesy due a noble lady.

A hoary mist frosted Annie's reddish brown hair. At Enya's suggestion she had ceased using henna and allowed Enya to take a pair of scissors to the dead ends. A definite improvement. Regular baths in cold weather, no matter how heated the water, were not yet a consideration. "Aye, Annie?"

"Ranald's sister . . . uhh . . . requests your presence."

She watched the young girl's breath steam the air while thinking rapidly. Unlike Annie, Mhorag would have nothing to do with her. Why summon her now? Unless she had seen Duncan talking to her in the greensward of the inner courtyard yesterday and believed Duncan and she were plotting to escape?

"Let me slide the bread into the oven first."

The brown eyes admonished her. "'Oo'd best 'urry, me lady."

"I shall."

The bakehouse's communal brick oven was used by the villagers also, but was not in service at the moment. Its flaring red coals scorched her cheeks. As scorched as the rye bread would be if she were not careful.

While she waited her backside froze and her face and hands blistered. At last, the loaves were an acorn brown, and probably as hard. A harping Flora despaired of her culinary abilities. "God help the puir chief when he eats yer meals."

Enya hurried back through the mist, dumped the loaves in a kitchen basket, and sped up a turret stairwell to the fourth landing and Mhorag's private chambers. Except for being more spacious with a few more odds and ends of furniture, the room was almost as bare as her own. Elspeth had reclaimed some war- or weather-damaged tapestries from the castle's ruined wing for Enya's chambers. A threadbare tartan carpet warmed the cold stone floor.

Mhorag paced its perimeter like a hungry cat awaiting kitchen scraps. She wore knee pants, green lisle stockings, and a long-sleeve woolen shirt covered by a jerkin. Obviously, the young woman scorned feminine clothing. And scorned Enya herself.

At the sight of her, Mhorag whirled, fists planted on her hips. Her eyes were more full of arrows than a thistle of nettles. "Well? Did I give ye permission to dally, mistress?"

"The bread, I—"

Mhorag's palm smacked Enya's cheek. "I don't want excuses. I want obedience. Is that understood?"

Astonished, she put her fingertips to her smarting cheek. Never had she been struck. She turned a sulfurous gaze on Mhorag, so much smaller that Enya could have pummeled her to bread dough had she so chosen. "Touch me again, and I'll—"

Mhorag's mouth curled in a tight smile. One finely delineated brow rose. "Ye'll what?"

Sudden comprehension enlightened her. "This isn't about my quality of service, is it? 'Tis about my quality as a woman."

"Ye are daft."

She struck at the young woman's most vulnerable spot. "You are afraid to be feminine. I make you uneasy, don't I? Each time you see me you are reminded of your cowardice as a woman."

The blue eyes were agates. "Aye, 'tis about your quality. Ye have chosen for a husband a man who widowed me, then caused me to lose the bairn I was carrying. Once Simon Murdock filled me with his seed, his officers took their turn."

Treacherous sympathy filled her, but she retorted, "Then strike out at *him!*"

Her smile was chillingly sunny. "I do. Through ye. Now fetch a basin of water and a scrub brush. Ye may clean the privies. A task the castle's former occupants overlooked."

"What?"

"Surely ye understand the King's English?"

Enya's fingers curled. "I pledged my service to your brother, not you."

"Did ye now? Then let me tell ye that my brother's plans for ye are far more unpleasant than the task I have set for ye."

She clasped her hands in repose. "I'll deal with that when the time comes."

Mhorag's head canted, and a *cafe-au-lait* lock tumbled over her shoulder. Her eyes glinted. "Besides, with the smell of the privy about ye,

I doubt my brother will visit his attentions upon ye more than is absolutely necessary. So, in me fashion, I am helping ye, am I not?"

"Are you afraid I'll find favor with your brother? Take your place, since he's all you have left?"

"Clean the privy, mistress. Now."

The medieval fortress that aspired to be a temporary manor was decidedly unprogressive in terms of its privies. Each private chamber included a privy set into an outer wall, built over a shaft fed also by latrines on other floors. Dirty water and other deposits were discharged through the gargoyles on the outside of the building.

Cleaning out privies was a most odoriferous experience for Enya.

At the end of the day she forwent dinner and retreated to the privacy of her own small chamber and a bath drawn by a reluctant Elspeth. "By me troth, bairn, but ye smell like a pigsty."

"Pigs have it better than I." She sighed and closed her eyes. She slid down into the copper tub until the steaming water topped her shoulders. "The master and mistress I serve are worse than pigs. They behave like villeins of the vilest—"

"Is that so?" asked a male voice.

She recognized its smooth, trilling timbre. Her lids snapped open; her head jerked around. Arms folded, Ranald stood in the doorway. A swath of cream-and-whisky hair fell across his wide forehead. Over a linsey-woolsey shirt, a leather tunic stretched the breadth of his chest. His knee-high boots of soft Spanish leather were splotched with mud.

Her mouth crimped with annoyance. "What is the source of your ire now?"

He crossed to the tub. Tall, his strapping body roped with muscle, he loomed over her. His eyes, this time the green of lichen, bore into her. "Ye, mistress. There was not enough bread to go around today. Ye forsook your duties."

She sat upright, then, seeing her breasts almost exposed, slid back into the steamy water. "Your sister dragged me from my duties. Had me clean—"

He wrinkled his nose. "Don't tell me. The stench in here is explanation enough."

She sprang to her feet. She was strong of limb and well formed and would not be shamed by this man. Physically, she was his complement, though the idea repelled her.

Elspeth gasped. "Enya!"

His eyes followed the water trickling between her porcelain white breasts, dripping from the peaks of her suddenly cold-taut nipples and the reddish cluster of curls at the apex of her legs.

"Aye, dunce," she taunted. "Stare."

She glimpsed the knotting of his large hands; then it appeared he checked himself. He motioned with his head at Elspeth. "Bring me razor and strop, woman. I wish to shave."

Elspeth darted a glance at Enya, who nodded. There was no reason for Elspeth to take the brunt of the man's anger. And angry he clearly was.

After the door closed behind a reluctant Elspeth, he reached for a threadbare linen towel the old woman had laid out and tossed it to her. "Dry yourself. I don't wish ye to die of pneumonia before ye bring sufficient Highland bairns into the world."

"I'll jump from the battlements before I bear your seed."

His massive shoulders shifted with a shrug. "It won't be my seed, madam. Your red hair offends me."

A curious statement. She searched his face for the intent behind his words, but his expression was, as usual, stolid. Apparently emotion only overtook him when he played the pipes.

He began removing his tunic, then his shirt. Hair, darker than that of his head, whorled across his chest. He tossed the white shirt over the open lid of a sailor's chest that served as her armoire. "No, don't get out of the tub," he told her.

She hesitated, puzzled. "Surely you don't intend to get in here with me."

At that moment, a sharp rap on the door diverted his attention. Elspeth stuck her long nose inside. He took the razor and strop she passed him. Enya saw the querulous look the old woman fired at him, followed by the more concerned one she spared for her charge.

Then he shut the door on Elspeth's huffy countenance and turned back to her. He held out his other hand. "The towel."

With an inquiring look, she passed it to him reluctantly. Her earlier anger had overridden her embarrassment. Now, mortified, she crossed her arms before her nudity and her less-than-svelte body.

He flung the towel, along with the strop, on the chest. Dipping the razor in the water, he said, "Hold still, mistress. Or else I shall cut ye."

Aghast, she watched as he knelt before her and laid the razor's edge against that triangular patch of rust-colored curls. Her breath was a sibilant inhalation. "You can't mean to shave me . . . there!"

"Like maple leaves in autumn," he murmured, anchoring a shovel-size palm against the lower portion of her flat belly. Wherever he touched her, a spasm rippled inside her. His other hand deftly wielded a path through the soft, short curls.

Her fingers arced, aching to dig into the ridge of muscles banding his shoulders, but the slightest move could jar the razor. Tears of humiliation sprang to her eyes. "I hope you do your own barbering."

"Aye. Each morning I sacrifice meself to the ritual of bloodletting over the shaving basin."

"How comforting."

At her tart tone, he grinned up at her. The smile took her completely by surprise. That defenseless instant made her weak also. "Careful," he warned, "me hand may slip on a stroke."

Still reeling from that singular smile, she braced a hand on his shoulder. The touch of his warm skin could have sizzled her fingers.

"Spread your legs."

"Please, no," she whispered.

"Would you rather another do it at me command? Nob, perhaps?"

The suggestion was enough to prompt her to move her legs apart, though only the breadth of the razor and no more. "Why?" she demanded. "Whipping me would have been punishment enough."

He cocked a broad brow at her. "Do ye wish to be whipped?"

"Of course not."

"This is not punishment. I told ye. Red hair is unlucky."

She nodded at the hand holding the razor. "Left-handed people bring bad luck."

He shrugged. "Red hair offends me."

Her stare was arrow-tipped. "You mean to shave my head, also?"

He shook his head, and his queue brushed against her fingers. "Nay. That you may cover beneath one of those big caps."

"A mobcap," she supplied with a saccharine smile.

"Aye." He finished with the last stroke. His fingertips explored her now smooth pad of flesh, as if examining his expertise with the blade.

When those probing fingers lingered at the convergence of her soft folds of flesh, she trembled.

His voice took on a husky pitch. "Keep yourself shaven here, mistress. Or else I'll have it done for ye. Do ye understand?"

"I understand that I shall never forgive you for this, Ranald."

At her use of his given name, he flinched. Her fingers felt the flinch in his back muscles. He rose and strode to the door, where he paused and turned. The look he speared her with was merciless. "Do ye think I care?"

Enya removed the tortoiseshell comb from her tresses and shook them out as she climbed the stairs to her room. Only a few minutes until she had to be back in the kitchen. The play she had been reading to Annie—*The Conscious Lovers* by Sir Richard Steele—had so absorbed her that she had forgotten the time. The play had dealt more with the plight of family than lovers.

She hadn't realized how much she would miss her mother and father and her homeland. Mayhaps, if she had been ensconced in the loving arms of a husband, the longing would not be so acute.

As it was, she was ensconced in servitude. And not a loving servitude. There was nothing loving about her situation. At least at home she had been unique, the lone daughter, the daughter of a baron. Even her features had been unique, if not beautiful. Now she was simply a serving maid, and a less than comely one, with what her mother kindly described as a generous figure.

Enya's mood was less than convivial when she opened the door to her chambers and saw Mhorag. The young woman was in the act of spinning around. Against her body she held one of Enya's formal gowns, a pink silk damask with a white satin quilted petticoat and cuffs and a low neckline of pink ribbon and silver lace. The ball gown's lace hem swirled around her boots.

"You look much better as a woman," Enya said, entering the room.

Mhorag's guilty look instantly changed to one full of more arrows than a thistle of nettles. "I was just . . . just . . ."

"Trying *my* clothes." The gown's hem now

draped over the floor a good six inches.

The Highland woman's eyes were stones of blue fire. "You were late starting dinner, and I came to find you—and I found—"

"—found that it might be pleasant to dress as a woman, after all."

She had struck at the young woman's most vulnerable spot—her denied femininity—and had made an implacable enemy. Mhorag tossed the gown on the bed. "A tart's gown!"

"What's going on here?" Ranald stood in the doorway, an oilskin draped over his large frame as protection against the rain and snow.

"Tell the tart to get out! To go start dinner!"

"I might point out that this is her chamber." His look was inscrutable.

"There ye go for a damned cowardly Italian, Ranald!"

She would have stomped past Enya, but Enya detained her with a hand on her arm. "Here." She passed her the tortoiseshell comb. "That snarled mat of hair will look better pulled away from your face."

Mhorag's glare was a holly stake in Enya's heart. Then she grabbed the comb and stalked from the room.

"Get to the kitchen," Ranald said and followed his sister out.

Enya stared after him in real amazement. A real monster the man was.

* * *

The snowflakes pelted her face and clung to Mhorag's lashes. Her spurred heels dug into the dappled mare's steamy flanks. The cold wind, tearing at her furred hood and hair, almost revived her flagging spirits.

Behind her, Duncan strove to keep astride the shaggy Shetland. The Lowlander's lanky legs barely cleared the bracken and Queen Anne's lace. She hauled on her mount's reins, and the horse swerved around. "Well, what keeps ye, knave?"

The shetland trotted up alongside of her. "I told ye, mistress, I am not a horseman." His labored breath frosted the air. "'Tis sea legs I have."

"Ye bore me with your excuses. Come along." She applied her whip to her mount's rump, and the horse spurted forward again. Beyond the next knoll was Lochaber. The villagers, as bored as she, were preparing festivities for All Saints' Day, tomorrow.

Already, a score or so men, mostly ploughmen and harvesters, were curling. Playing on the small frozen loch at the base of the mill, they vied with each other to slide a granite stone over the ice as close as possible to the tee, the center of a marked target.

Before the village pub, she bounded from her horse. Tossing her reins to a startled lad of no more than fifteen, she said, "Watch my mount and there's a pint of bitter awaiting ye inside afterward."

The dour interior of the public house suited her mood perfectly. The pub was empty at this hour. There was the pungent burnt smell of very raw whiskey. She sauntered over to one of the barrel tables. In its center was a red candle in a brown whiskey bottle.

The host hurried to set a plate of crusty maslin bread, slabs of tangy hard cheese, and knobs of pickled onions. "A mug of cider," she told the portly man.

Behind him, Duncan came straggling in. His ruddy cheeks, sea-blue eyes, and shock of wheat-hued hair were the only bright colors in the murky pub, if she discounted the tiny flames of fire licking the smoke-blackened fireplace across the room.

He pulled out one of the wooden chairs at her table. Before he could take a seat, she kicked the chair over. "I didn't give ye permission to sit, lout."

His mouth lost its usual merriment. "I'm a servant, not a serf."

Her lids half masked her eyes. "Ye are a captive. A captive granted a certain measure of freedom because ye took the Bond of Manrent. There is no recanting. There is only punishment for disobedience."

The host returned with her cider. Duncan's lips hardened in self-imposed silence. She opened her man's small purse and doled out six black pennies.

The host bobbed his thanks and left her and Duncan alone once more. Shivering, wet, and weary, Duncan eyed her steadily. "Ye annoy me, mistress."

She laughed and began stripping off her riding gloves. "Do I now? Good!"

He stepped aside for the host to set the brimming mug of steaming cider before her. "Why 'good'? Have I harmed ye?"

"Ye are a man, aren't ye? Right the chair. And remove your cap in me presence."

A vein ticked in his temple, but he did as she commanded. "Ye would punish me merely for being a man? When half the earth is filled with men?"

She wrapped her hands around the hot mug, warming them. "Ye are also slow of wit. Or else ye would know better than to question me."

He leaned forward, bracing his weather-reddened hands on the cask-top table. As much for support, she suspected, as for a show of power. "Me thinks ye are afraid, mistress."

She dipped her fingers in her trencher's mushy pool of lard and spread it atop her bread. "I think you talk too much, Duncan of Ayrshire."

"Me thinks you are afraid of caring too much

about a man, afraid ye will lose him."

"Ye are impertinent, too." One by one, she licked her sticky fingers.

"Right now, ye look like a satisfied cat. Except I don't think ye are. Satisfied, that is."

She was beginning to regret taking the Bond of Maintenance in behalf of this annoying man. She had done so in retaliation against the Lowland woman. If Duncan was a part of her retinue, then let her lose something she valued!

"You test me patience, Duncan. Go to the kitchen and beg a morsel. But be quick about it."

She didn't want to miss the opening ceremonies for the eve of All Saints' Day. The fire feasts and dancing. Or, perhaps, it was merely that she didn't wish to be out after dark.

It was said that Samhain, the Celtic lord of death, allowed the souls of the dead to return to their homes for this evening. This was a time when witches and warlocks roamed. And houses were shuttered.

On holy days, ghosts were freed. The holy, or hallowed, eve before All Saints' Day marked the beginning of the season of cold, darkness, and decay. On the Hallow'een, the auld Druids had burned animals, crops, and even humans as sacrifices.

Mhorag swigged a draught of the hot cider. Because her brother was laird of a clan, he was the traditional symbol of Samhain. As Lord of

Death, would Ranald order a human sacrifice tonight? Like Murdock's wife?

Mayhaps there was such a thing as the biblical "measure for measure."

Chapter Nine

Cold air whispered through the castle chinks. The rustling draughts disturbed the tattered bed hangings, tapestries, and Enya.

The hour was late, shortly before dusk. All day she, Margaret, and Annie had cooked and baked for the coming pagan celebration.

Which was just as well. The taxing labor had taken her mind off the approaching encounter with Ranald. For weeks now, she had been mentally and emotionally preparing herself for the possibility that Ranald would indeed make good his threat.

She was trying to convince herself that for one of his men to get her with child was but a physical act; that the act would have had the same aftermath should Simon have bedded her first.

Only much, much more unpleasant.

When she entered her chambers Elspeth and Mary Laurie were busy with her bath—Elspeth adding rose and chrysanthemum petals, and Mary Laurie shaking the wrinkles from a mint-green court gown.

Silently, Enya blessed the two women. She knew they were there to make the coming evening easier for her, if that were possible. Prayers and miracles were more in order.

"The eve doesn't bode well," Elspeth grumbled as a salutation to Enya.

So much for moral support, she thought. She peeled off her blood-and-grease-splattered apron, kicked off her patents, and flopped into the deerhide-covered armchair. "Why is that?"

"'Tis the Highlanders." Mary Laurie nodded toward the window slit. "Wild ones, they are."

Obviously the farm girl wasn't going to elaborate. Enya pushed herself from the chair and crossed to the window.

In the courtyard below, oak branches, which the Highlanders' pagan ancestors had considered sacred, were mounded in blazing bonfires. Shadowy figures moved in the flames' shifting light. Some added more wood to the conflagration. Others appeared to be dancing.

"The bonfires are to drive away witches and other evil spirits," Mary Laurie said in a hushed voice. "Cyril the Salter told me so."

Enya affected a shrug. "What can you expect from heathens?"

"Ye're not looking, bairn," Elspeth said. Her hooked nose twitched with disdain. "Look again. At those heathens. And listen."

Now Enya understood the apprehension of the two women. The revelers wore masks, stag's heads, and wolf and bear skins. The Highlanders' shouts and laughter sounded more like howling.

"So, 'tis come to this at last," she muttered. She could only hope Duncan's idea worked. By the end of the evening, she would know.

"I fear for yer life," Mary Laurie said, coming up behind her.

Enya squeezed her hand, now no more reddened and chapped than her own. "If the chieftain had wanted to kill me, he would have already. Dead, I am worthless to him. Alive, I am bait for his prey, my husband."

The hot, scented water beckoned her body. But she had kept Ranald's depilation of its red triangular thatch a secret from her maidservants. At the memory, mortification flushed her cheeks. "Now I want to be alone to ready myself."

The two exchanged looks, but her adamant expression nudged them toward the doorway. "I'll summon you when I need you," she said.

The steam-clouded water did not completely conceal the expanse of newly revealed flesh where her thighs conjoined. Already downy red tufts were growing back. If she didn't shave herself, she knew Ranald would. And this time he would probably do so in the presence of the entire population of Lochaber.

Furious, she held the razor he had left her up to the last light of the day. The time would come, she vowed, when she would use it on his throat.

The eerie wailing of the bagpipe transfixed Enya and the rest of the inhabitants of the great hall. Tonight it was darkened, with only the candlelight glittering eerily from lanterns that had been made from scooping out large turnips, or neeps.

Frenetic shadows danced across the castle's weapon-adorned stone walls. The heat of the fireplace did not drive the chill of fear from her as she listened to the piper.

He wore a domino of black velvet and a white robe, as befit the Samhain, the Lord of Death. At the moment, he played for the hereditary laird of the Clan Cameron, Ian. His son Jamie stood at his side, ready to pass him his crutch.

Jamie had donned the furred mask of a lynx head in concession to the pagan activities. The lame man wore no mask, and his white robe was bisected by the Cameron tartan.

Enya would have sworn her head had never hurt so much. When would this horrendous night be over?

First, there had been the interminable procession of Lochaber families with their torches. In keeping with tradition, they had put out their hearth fires and had come to relight them from the Hallow'een's bonfire in the outer bailey.

The last strains of the bagpipe died away. Ranald Kincairn put aside the instrument and returned to his Justice Chair.

The moment had come for a'souling, or begging.

The villagers, many of them costumed, formed a line before their appointed laird, who listened to their requests. The requests were simple, things like apples or nuts or pastries, called soulcakes.

Simple until Enya, who had slipped into the line, came to the forefront.

In addition to her half mask of green silk, she wore a mobcap with side lappets that completely concealed her hair—and her identity.

She dipped a curtsy. When she looked up into Ranald's face the mouth below the domino was set in hard lines. Did he recognize her?

"My laird, my request is a modest one."

"Aye?"

"To select a husband for myself."

In the mask's slits, the turquoise eyes glittered. "And if he is unwilling?"

"Oh, he is willing enough. I merely seek your permission on this night a'souling."

He braced his chin on one fist. "And who is it ye wish to take for a husband?"

"Duncan of the Clan Afton."

From behind the chair, Mhorag stepped forward. She, also, wore a white robe. "I forbid it. The man belongs to me."

Enya resorted to Duncan's suggestion, made days earlier, in the event just such a thing should happen. "Then you gain two servants by the marriage, do you not?"

"I find your request unusual," Ranald said, his brogue rolling and soft. Deceptively soft. "Seeing as how ye are already married."

So he did recognize her. She peeled off her half mask. She had half expected him to know her if by nothing other than her extraordinary height. Then, too, there was her carriage and her speech.

Duncan might have anticipated Mhorag's objection, but Enya had anticipated Ranald's. "A technical point," she said. "You see, I went through a formal ceremony with a proxy. Simon Murdock was not present and no ring was given. The exchanging of vows with my intended was never completed."

"Then, as your laird, I will select your husband for ye."

She was losing ground. "But 'tis the eve of All

Souls'. The night to go a'souling. I beg the right to choose my own husband."

"Your begging goes unheeded. But not your marital status." Crevices creased at either side of his mouth. "You are herewith betrothed to Nob of Glenorchy of the Clan Cameron."

She gasped in real amazement. This she had not anticipated. She had not truly believed he would give her to Nob. Any of the men—stuttering Patric, wild-bearded Colin, paunchy Macdonald, one-eared Robert of Macintosh, even Jamie—but not Nob. A neat trap Ranald had sprung on her.

A murmur of surprise rustled among the onlookers. "Why, thank ye, me laird!" Nob cried out from somewhere amid the crowd.

Ranald nodded, then turned his attention back to her. "As your laird, I claim the right to bed ye first. Your betrothed will escort ye to my chambers."

So, she had lost. Despair sagged her shoulders. Then she was overtaken by the hysterical urge to bolt, to run and hide somewhere no one would ever find her.

A hand at her elbow jarred her. Nob's broad face beamed at her. "'Tis a caring husband I'll be, Mistress Enya. After our marriage there'll be na more heavy work for ye."

She tried not to shrink from his touch. Nodding, she managed a "Thank you, Nob."

Beneath the low forehead, his little eyes twinkled. "With a bairn in ye, ye'll need to take it easy," he said, leading her toward the staircase. "Na more hefting firewood and buckets of water."

"What if 'tis the laird's child within me?" she demanded, anger replacing her momentary apathy. "What then, pray tell?"

Nob's grin displayed uneven, yellow teeth, reminding her of the ghostly neep lanterns lighting the great hall. "Why 'tis even better, mistress."

"Oh, God!"

With much pomp, he ushered her into Ranald's chamber. She stood just inside the doorway and surveyed her oak-paneled prison cell for the night with apathy.

Embers smoldered on the hearth, where lay the faithful Thane. A furred spread covered the curtained four-poster. Her gaze darted away. She was unwilling to face its implications. Not just yet.

"Thank you, Nob." After all, the troll could not fathom that she would not feel the same pride as he at being selected for the laird's attention.

The gruff-looking little man didn't move. His thick lower lip hung loosely, as if he were unsure what to do next. He couldn't be thinking about watching what was about to happen—or was that a Highland custom, the right of the betrothed?

"I will await him, our laird, alone," she said firmly, her smile frozen.

Nob's head bobbed. "I'll return on the morrow to escort ye back to your chambers."

"You do that."

When he had gone she leaned back against the closed door and shut her lids, shut out all that awaited her.

If Ranald Kincairn were taking advantage of that barbaric Highland tradition of the *droit du seigneur* merely to satisfy his carnal lust, she might be able to accept the man with a blank mind. Many a bride with husband selected for her, either by parents or by a sovereign, had done just so.

But Ranald was using her body for revenge on another. And tonight wouldn't be the last of his imposed punishment upon her; she was certain of that.

If only she could go back to Afton House and the security it had represented. Now all was about to be changed—irrevocably.

Her head came up. Hadn't her mother suffered a similar fate?

Then her mother's daughter could behave no less courageously. She would meet Ranald Kincairn with courage and dignity.

Chin tilted, she left the comfort of escape the door afforded and strolled around the man's chamber, as if merely inspecting a guest room.

Thane's ears perked up, those soulful eyes followed her. The collie's furry neck was ruffled. As if he, too, sensed this was no ordinary evening.

She stooped to scratch behind the collie's ears. "So, you, too, are awaiting our laird."

Studiously, she ignored the feather bed to wander over to a simple commode of planked pine, where reposed a ewer and basin of water—and a formidable claymore with its blood-rusted blade.

Common sense told her, she couldn't even begin to lift the claymore. But, oh, what a marvelous way to split hairs with her captor.

A bureau bookcase with a drop leaf and small glass panes, most of them cracked or missing, attracted her attention. Empty of books, as she had suspected. If the oaf's formal schooling went no further than a year at Winchester, she doubted his literary efforts went beyond the rudimentary.

She bypassed a sturdy chair built in the pattern of an *X* and fully covered with fringed material of a Turkish design to reach a desk, where a wax candle sputtered. It smelled of honeysuckle. The mahogany writing table with fretted detail on the pediments was of quality workmanship; doubtlessly booty from a raid.

Then she noticed the open book. A Bible. Wonderingly, she ran her fingers over the thumb-worn parchment pages. The Highland warrior read this? She peered closer at the text.

> He delivers me from my enemies; Surely Thou dost lift me above those who rise up against me; Thou dost rescue me from the violent man. Therefore I will give thanks to Thee among the nations, O Lord.

Her eye skipped farther down the page to another passage.

> . . . in them He has placed a tent for the sun, which is as a bridegroom coming out of his chamber.

"I see that ye can read."

She whirled. Guiltily, she stared at the masked Cameron laird. "Ye knew that I could! Ye knew almost everything about me before ye abducted me, ye did!"

"Your speech is betraying your nervousness."

Thane padded joyfully over to him, and he bent to pat the collie's head. Then he straightened, and Thane, content now, trotted back to his guard post before the fire.

Ranald removed the domino that masked his eyes, tossed it atop the bookcase's drop leaf, and crossed the room. Reluctantly, she conceded that the big man moved with grace akin to a lithe sailor who scaled a ship's mast.

She held her ground. Would he take her now, without preliminaries? No, his form of cruelty was more subtle, more insidious. He would delay the act to prolong her torment.

She miscalculated. It wasn't she he desired, but a pipe.

He removed a long-stemmed clay pipe from a desk drawer cluttered with more pipes and writing utensils. With a modicum of motion, he tapped tobacco from a pewter box into its clay bowl. As he lit the pipe, he watched her, as if gauging the effect on her of what he would next say.

"But you are right about me knowing *almost* everything about you. For instance, I know ye enjoy the pipe yourself. Smoke it when ye think ye are alone."

Those three sentences did more to rattle her than anything she had yet experienced. "How long did your men spy upon me?"

He studied her through the haze of smoke. "Do ye think I would allow someone else to watch your most intimate of activities?"

Her jaw dropped. "You? You spied upon me?"

"Gaining entrée to your mother's salons was but a wee thing." He crossed to the Turkish chair. Sitting, he puffed on the pipe stem, all the while measuring her reaction.

She hoped her panic was not revealed in her expression; hoped he couldn't hear her heart's frantic beating. "This is madness!"

Staring up at her, he held out the pipe. "Care to try?"

She slapped it from his hand. The clay bowl shattered on the floor. Aghast, she looked from the scattered fragments back to him. When he made no move to strike her she regained a portion of her courage. "You will not get away with this."

"And ye will learn to control your temper. Teaching ye will be most rewarding, I think."

She put her hands on her hips. "You think! Your thoughts are geared for warfare. And that will be your downfall!"

"Oh?"

"It will be unexpected, because I shall make you fall in love with me."

Those angled brows flared in astonishment.

Her statement surprised her also, but she maintained her equanimity.

A slow smile stretched his long mouth. "That will prove interesting."

"You don't think I could?"

"'Tis highly unlikely. First, as I told ye, I find red hair uncomely. I am not attracted to ye in the least."

She wanted to screech at him, scratch out his eyes. She smiled superiorly.

"Second, ye are to be Nob's wife, not mine. I don't think ye can accomplish your intention in the space of one night. For that matter, not ever. Now, pick up the pipe shards."

Her hand jerked, and he warned, "Don't. Should ye strike me, I would have no alternative but to return in kind."

She sought an unguarded place, hopefully his Achilles heel. "Does not the Bible say turn the other cheek?" she asked, stooping to collect the pieces of clay.

"It also says an eye for an eye. It is full of such paradoxes."

He was a paradox. She would have to unravel this man's skein of complexities if she hoped to best him. For the moment, she ceded him the battle.

" 'Never seek a fight,' " he told her. " 'If it comes, step back. It is far better to step back than overstep yourself.' "

"From the Bible?" she muttered.

"No. 'Tis a Chinese admonition. Ye are shaven, mistress?"

Her hand clenched. Crimson seeped between her fingers. She opened them and stared at her palm. Tiny welling cuts crisscrossed it. Oblivious to the pain, she looked up at him. "Aye, I am shaven."

He grasped her wrist. His brows met above the bridge of his decidedly Roman nose. "A bloody mess, ye are."

He rose, tugging her along behind him to the

commode, where he poured the ewer's water into the chipped basin and dipped her hand. Scarlet swirled the water. Removing her hand, he gingerly probed the cuts.

"Oh!" she gasped as his big fingers found a tender place.

He peered at her through his dense lashes. "Tonight, it will be not only your hand that bleeds, I trust."

Grasping his meaning, she yanked his hand from hers. "You are merciless!" With a swipe of her hand, she toppled the basin of bloodied water onto his robe. Blood red was stark against the robe's white.

His eyes narrowed. "On this night, this robe will also be smeared with virgin's blood."

He yanked her by her wrist toward the curtained bed. Released, she fell atop it. Dispassionately, he gazed down at her. "Disrobe. Or shall I call the village women to assist ye?"

Her lips formed a taunting smile. "Do you need someone else to accomplish your purpose, my laird Kincairn? Tell me, how many betrothed lasses have lost their maidenhood to you?"

"Dozens."

She tried not to wince. Keeping her eyes on his brooding countenance, she sat upright and began unlacing her stays. "You must be proud." Off came her garters and yellow ribbed stockings. "A grand stud horse, you are. How many brats have you sired?"

"I may recant giving ye to Nob. Better Simon Murdock endure your waspish tongue." He blew out the candle. Only the fire's embers lit the room. "Alas, Murdock's life span is due to be shortened drastically."

With only her ivory satin shift to hide her nakedness, she tugged off the mobcap. Like a red flag, she let her flaming hair tumble out and cascade over her white shoulders and breasts, thrusting against the shift's thin material. Her heart was pounding, but she squared her shoulders and said in a tone of indifference, "Have done with it then. I am tired and desire to sleep."

He stared at her. "The shift, mistress."

True, he had seen her naked. Still, peeling off the shift's straps and letting it fall around her ankles was probably the most difficult thing she had ever done.

The first time he had beheld her nudity had been an accident. This time, what he was requiring of her was a violation of herself that was almost as painful emotionally as a physical violation would be.

His eyes traveled from her wild red curls to that smoothly bare mound at the apex of her thighs. After a moment he said, "I told you. Your red hair leaves me indifferent. Go on to sleep."

Her expression betrayed utter surprise.

He laughed. "Ye had prepared yourself for martyrdom, hadn't you?" He drew the curtain about the bed, then flopped down beside her and closed his eyes. "I, too, desire sleep."

She felt like smacking him. Because of him, her energy was running high, her thoughts were scrambled, her nerves were stressed.

Lips compressed, she fell back onto the bed next to him and turned on her side, away from him. Without clothes she was chilled, but because of his weight she could not tug the fur coverlet over her.

She rolled back over and nudged his shoulder. "You are no better than a beggar, Kincairn, sleeping with your clothes on."

Without opening his eyes, he ordered, "Go to sleep."

"I'm cold."

He sighed, grabbed one end of the coverlet and wrapped the two of them in it. His heavier weight created a valley in the feather mattress, and she rolled down and against him.

Breathing shallowly, silent and unyielding, she lay trapped along his length. Maybe half an hour passed. At one point he slung a heavily muscled arm across the indentation between her hip and her rib cage. His warm breath fanned her ear. Gradually the coverlet and his own body heat drove the chill from her.

When, in his sleep, he cupped her breast with

one hand, she stiffened. Nothing happened. Then, without her volition, her nipple began to harden. She shifted so that her breast was not thrusting into his palm.

"Quiet," he murmured, his hand slipping down to palm her belly, as if a most natural act between him and her.

"I can't."

He stirred, nestled his head in the pool of her hair. "Why not?"

"You are touching me."

He didn't say anything, but she knew he was fully awake now. His palm stayed where it was.

She squirmed. "I canna sleep like this."

"Then leave me bed."

"No."

He raised on one elbow and glared at her. The firelight glinted green in his eyes. "God's blood, but ye are an argumentative wench."

She pushed herself upright, holding the covers over her bare breasts. Why she did so made no sense to her, since he by this time doubtlessly knew every freckle on her body. "If I leave now, the people below will know you did not find favor with me. It will make my position just that more untenable in the castle."

Then, too, Nob was waiting below. At the moment, he seemed the worse of the two men.

"God," he groaned and rolled over to his other side. "Stay then."

She had only to figure out how to stay here—and stay safe until rescue came. Besides, she had a promise yet to keep: to make Ranald Kincairn fall in love with her.

The south end of Loch Siel was shallow and reedy and, from Kathryn's vantage point, she could see the garish flats of cluttered fish cages. An old cattle-drive trail passed within sight of the coaching inn. Its view was depressing, with a steady afternoon drizzle and lowering gray skies. Herons stood muffled and miserable on the shoreline.

Kathryn deserted the single window in her room to pace the red-and-green-plaid carpet. All the while she rubbed her chilblained hands. Since Arch had trod off into the mist earlier that morning the mantle clock had ticked off more than four hours.

The mantle clock was one of the few amenities offered by the half-timbered coaching inn of Acharacle. The village had little to recommend it beyond the nearby Castle Tioram. The ruins were once the home of the chief of the Clan Ranald, who burned it in order to keep it from falling into the hands of his enemies, the Camerons, during the 1715 Jacobite rebellion.

Her concern must have summoned Arch, because at that moment the door swung open. "I may have a lead!" he said, shedding his drenched cloak on the plank floor.

"Oh, Arch, I've been worried. You were gone so long!"

He slapped his floppy, black felt hat against his knee. Rain droplets splattered everywhere, reminding her of a wet dog shaking the water from its coat. "By accident I found a clue to Kincairn, Kathryn." He crossed to the fire to warm his hands.

She poured the fragrant green tea she had induced the innkeeper's wife to bring up. "So many leads, so many tales, with none having any substantial results."

"This one may prove out. An old man, mayhap all of seventy-five years, lay dying along the roadside. I half-carried him, half-dragged him, to a close-by tithe barn. I tell you, the thatched roof was leaking like a sieve. Anyway—"

"You're shivering, Arch. Here, let me get you my blanket."

He crossed to the wheel-back chair and eased his frame into it. "As I was saying, I laid the old man on a bed of straw and covered him with my cloak. I was trying to ease his last moments. Without thinking—I hope to God I don't burn in hell for this—I began murmuring, administering the Last Rites."

She laid the blanket over Arch's long legs. It was the least she could do to comfort him. One of the few things he allowed her to do. He had become so self-sufficient. Maybe he always had been. She really knew so little about him after he left Ayrshire to study at the Benedictine monastery across the channel in Normandy.

"At that," Arch continued, "the old farmer opened one eye and said, 'Ye be a priest.' "

"Oh, God, Arch. You take too many chances!"

"I thought this might have been my last chance at anything. In a country that has become staunchly Protestant, my head would fit nicely on a pike."

She knelt at his feet. Her black taffeta dress pooled around her. "What happened?"

"I was half off the mark before his next words stopped me. He said he wanted to die with the chief of the Ranald clan. I thought the old man had gone daft, and told him the last chief had died in '15."

He paused to sip the tea, which had bits of leaf swirling through the liquid. She thought he would never swallow. "Well?"

"The old man insisted that a descendant of the Ranald chief is head of the Camerons."

"How can that be?"

"According to him, a warrior of the Clan Cameron, with a family name of Kincairn, carried off a Ranald lass. One of their eight offspring was endowed with his mother's maiden name as his own given name. It seems we're looking for a Ranald Kincairn."

"So this Ranald Kincairn is the man we're seeking? Of Ranald's Reivers?"

"Aye, so it would appear."

"Were you able to find out anything else about him?"

"His men, it seems, are cat-footed Highlanders, swift in movement, apt in concealment, artful in stalking, silent in execution.

"The hallmark of his attacks, Kathryn, are forest ambushes, sudden raids, night attacks, and the total destruction of anything of possible use to the enemy."

"Including the enemy's wife," she whispered.

He put the cup down and took her hand. "Apparently, Ranald Kincairn is laird of the Camerons into the bargain."

Her shoulders sagged. "Now we have the Cameron rebels to track down as well."

"Maybe not." He leaned forward and almost pushed a wayward curl from her cheek before quickly removing his hand, as if her skin scorched him. "The measure of Kincairn's genius is his strategy in shifting headquarters. Winter is soon upon the land. The Reivers will surely have to go into hiding. They would choose a most inaccessible place, would they not?"

She rolled her eyes. "All of the Highlands are almost inaccessible."

"An inaccessible place, Kathryn, that is loyal to the Camerons. The type of warfare Ranald's Reivers wage is dependent on support of the local populace. Think about it."

Her eyes narrowed in concentration. "The most inaccessible place in Cameron territory?" She remembered staring from Fort William's ramparts at the forbidding, snow-capped mountains. She almost genuflected. "Holy Mother, Arch. Are we too late?"

Even she didn't know which she was asking—too late to scale their heights or too late to reclaim Enya.

Chapter Ten

Enya threw open the shutters. Gray-pink rays tinged the predawn heavens. The scent of crystal-tipped grass stirred thoughts of happier times, childhood times in Ayrshire, when the worst she had to worry about was her brothers' teasing. Both Gordon and Andrew had plagued her with frogs until Elspeth would chase the two boys with a rug beater. Later on, Enya chased them herself through dew-wet grass.

Now Gordon and Andrew were dead—and she felt like the walking dead. She had to remind herself that she was human and not a wild beast, caged. Even Thane, still asleep by the fire, fared better than she with their master.

Behind her, Ranald stirred. "What—you—?" He leaned on one elbow, barechested. Sometime during the night, he had stripped off his clothing. She couldn't remember seeing a chest so broad, naked or clothed. The coverlet lay dangerously low around his hips. "You're still here."

"Aye." With only the faint light of dying embers, she had dressed. She crossed now to the Turkish chair, and, bare feet tucked up under her, drew on a briarpipe. Mutinously, she exhaled a wreath of smoke. The eddying circle expanded, grew more indistinct.

"Where did ye get that? Me pipe?"

"From the drawer of your writing desk."

He propped his back against the wall and, head canted and arms crossed, watched her. "Me grandmother smoked a pipe."

"Did your grandfather know?"

One side of his mouth cocked a grin, completely obliterating the pleat on that side of his face. "She taught him. She was from the Clan Ranald. He was the Cameron's official piper and was charged with playing the call to battle."

She smiled through the haze of smoke. "So the bagpipe was the closest your grandfather ever came to a pipe—until your grandmother."

"Smoke is mysterious," he mused. "Like a woman."

"Let me stay."

"What?"

"'Tis not my shame you want, is it? Or else you would have made it much more unpleasant for me. Like last night, for instance."

His brows lowered. His pleats deepened to menacing grooves. "Don't underestimate me."

"I think 'tis my husband you—"

"I explicitly recall your announcing to all that you weren't married."

"—Simon Murdock you want. I'm merely the bait, aren't I."

He shrugged. "So?"

"Do you expect me to entice him up here?"

"No. I expect to meet him on the battlefield. You are not me bait. You are me trump card."

She uncurled her legs and leaned forward. "Then you have nothing to lose by giving me your protection as long as I am under your roof."

Now the pleats curved ever so slightly. "Why should I?"

"Because you need someone you can trust. You see, I know someone in the castle wants to betray you."

He uncoiled from the trappings of the coverlet and strode toward her. His blatant nudity—and his indifference to it—shocked her. She yanked her gaze from his swaying genitals and fastened on his face. His expression was more brooding than Buachaille Etive. "What makes you say that?"

She maintained her indolent position. "A letter."

Arms akimbo, he asked, "What did it say?"

She found it very, very difficult ignoring his

masculinity when it was so boldly displayed less than an arm's length from her face. A rapidly heating face. "I don't have it."

His lids lowered to half masts. "Ye try me patience, mistress."

The way that large cylindrical member dangled so blatantly from its nest of brown curls was extremely distracting. "'Tis the truth. I don't have it."

Realization showed on his face. He swung around and strode to his desk.

"The letter is still there," she said, laying aside the pipe. "I would recognize the handwriting of my own companions. Neither Mary Laurie nor Elspeth penned it. And Duncan canna write."

"Why should I believe you?" He tunneled his fingers through his rumpled hair, bypassed her, and strode toward the open window. Watching the shift of his muscled buttocks, she drew deeply on the pipe. Never had she more needed its soothing effects.

"Even you could have written it," he said, without turning from the window.

"Aye," she said. "I could have written it, but I dinna."

She rose and went to stand behind him. Gently, she touch his shoulder. The feel of his warm flesh beneath her fingertips made her pause. The man was flesh and blood. Very much human. "Canna you trust?"

"Nae. I am responsible for too many people to risk that."

"Because I am a Lowlander, Murdock's wife, and," she added with a touch of humor, "a red-head?"

He caught her hand and pulled her around between him and the window embrasure. Their faces were bathed in early-morning light, as they gazed into each other's eyes. "No, because ye have the power of the Auld Folk. Of fairies and monsters of the deep."

He looked perfectly serious. "And that is dangerous to you?" she asked.

"It could be."

What would it be like to be kissed by this man? A man so much taller and larger and stronger than she. A man who had the effect of making her feel extraordinarily feminine at the moment. And very vulnerable. "How can I convince you I willna harm you?" The briskness of her voice was her armor against him.

"Ye will have to prove it to me. By actions, not words."

She removed her hand and stepped around the fire, putting distance between her and this man she suddenly desired. "I will attempt to prove I can be trusted. Will you do the same? Do I have your word that I will remain a maiden as long as I am your captive?"

He half turned, one brow raised. "Ye do not ask for your release. Why not?"

She picked up the briar pipe once more. "I doubt you'd go that far."

"Ye are discerning."

"I want your guarantee of Duncan's safety also."

He faced her now, muscled legs spread like the Colossus of Rhodes, fists planted on his narrow hips. His look was inscrutable. "Duncan? Your care for your servants is admirable."

"You will see that Duncan is treated well?" She drew idly on the stem of his briar pipe, as if nothing vital were at stake here.

"No. First, Duncan is not mine to guarantee his safety. He belongs to me sister. Second, he was not part of our bargain. As for ye . . ."

Her breath locked in her lungs. Had she pushed her luck too far?

" . . . your maidenhood will not be taken from ye without your consent. I guarantee this. I will see that Nob is recompensed."

Relief whisked the pent-up smoke from her mouth in a burst of dragon fire. She started coughing, and Ranald pounded on her back.

"Stop!" she gasped. "Stop! Ye . . . are taking advantage of me."

His smile was, at best, polite. "Something I have no desire to do, believe me."

His total lack of interest affronted her. Was she that homely?

He returned to the window. The rising sun

highlighted his craggy features. With a dismissive wave of his hand, he said, "Hie thee to the kitchens, mistress."

She spared one backward glance for that magnificent body. Lamentable that it should suffer the executioner's ax.

At least, before she had the opportunity to make him fall in love with her.

A bowed psaltry's spirited music enlivened the castle's occupants that evening, which meant that Mhorag's uncle must not be suffering one of his debilitating headaches.

Mhorag had her own. She wearied of the women's diversions—working on their embroidery, gossiping, telling riddles. Chess or *chemin de fer* required more thought than she was willing to give tonight.

The dice game in progress at the end of the guard room beckoned her. "Doug, Patric, Scott . . ." she acknowledged the half-dozen clansmen who hunkered over the dice by name or nod.

In return, they accorded her the deference of "M'lady." Other than hasty glances darted in her direction, they kept their attention focused on the game. They knew their places. That was it, she thought. Duncan of Ayrshire did not.

Going down on one knee, she tugged the pouch strings from her girdle and tossed it near the mound of shillings and other English and Scottish coins. “My wager. Twenty-three pounds sterling.”

Looks flickered among the men. She knew what they were thinking. Dared they best her, the laird’s sister?

“Cast the dice,” a voice said behind her.

She looked up. Duncan stood over her. His silly grin, with one front tooth overlapping another, irritated her beyond all forbearance. “Ye have finished stocking my hearth with wood?”

“Even at this moment, m’lady, a fire licks your bricks.”

The smirk of the other dicers made her want to pummel the lout. She wouldn’t lose her composure. She retrieved the dice and tossed them. One landed atop the other.

“A cock,” he said behind her. “Cast again.”

Exasperation issued from her lips in a grunt, but she kept her own counsel. This time the dice came up eleven. She grinned. A point for her.

Duncan knelt between her and the man to her left. He dropped a gold chain before him. “This says ye throw seven.”

“Where did ye get that?”

His grin faded to a dolorous droop. “’T’was me dear mother’s.”

“Now why is it I doubt ye? Ye probably raided me own jewelry box.”

He looked shocked.

She collected the dice. "I accept your wager, Duncan of Dunce."

He had the temerity to grip her wrist. "One moment. Your wager—" He nodded toward the bag. "I'm not interested in the twenty-three pounds sterling. English or Scottish. I beg something else."

She had to admit, the oaf wasn't boring. "And that is?"

"A night in your bed."

Her eye sockets felt seared with her hate. The memory of being pierced with the putrid-flesh swords of Murdock and his soldiers burned through her brain like molten, red-hot lead.

The smothered chortle of the gap-toothed man called Doug, the amused expressions of the others, snapped her control. Her hand lashed out in a slap that surely echoed against the other end of the hall. "You seek above your station, knave."

As if caressing the red imprint of her palm, he fingered the spot on his cheek. "Ach, 'twas worth the try, m'lady."

Doubtlessly he was also bedding the Lady Murdock and every castle wench, as well. "Would a night in me bed be worth the flogging of twenty-three lashes, ye insolent villein?"

His gaze held hers in a tenuous tryst. "Aye."

"Your words are bold." She glanced at the other men. "Should I summon the stable master? Wallace is handy with a whip."

No one said anything. That infuriated her even more. "Get Wallace," she told Patric.

With a reluctant, "Aye, me—m'lady," the fair-haired youth backed away quickly. Tension strained taut every expression.

Next, she rounded on Duncan. "Where is my brother's whore?"

He affected a confused look. "I know not of whom ye speak, m'lady."

"The tart, Enya."

His fingers curled into fists.

She didn't know whether to be pleased she had succeeded in goading him or envious of a woman who commanded such devotion.

"I believe the Lady Enya is with your uncle, playing backgammon." He spoke evenly, and his eyes told her nothing.

Contrition mixed with chagrin. "Why hasn't Patric returned with the stable master?" she demanded of Colin, the hapless man standing nearest.

His lids blinked rapidly. In the midst of his scraggly beard, his tongue licked his lips. "I'll go find them, m'lady."

"Stay. They come now." She waited for the shuffling stable master and Patric. Why hadn't Ranald returned from the grouse hunt? His intervention could end this tragic farce.

As if sensing something was afoot, most of the occupants in the great hall followed Wallace and Colin, a river of white, puzzled faces on either side. Why had Duncan insisted on calling her bluff?

Wallace tugged at his forelock. Greasy hair as long as the thong of his whip strung down his shoulders. Her nostrils quivered. He smelled of the stables as well. His gaze studied the hard clay floor. "M'lady?"

She nodded her head in Duncan's direction. "Flog him. Ten lashes."

In dumb, blind obedience, Wallace uncurled his whip. "With the barb?"

"No. The man doesn't want death, ye dolt." *Just my body beneath his.* Without turning, she said, "Duncan, come here. Shed your shirt."

He lumbered forward into the semicircle of curious, excited, and fearful on-watchers. He peeled off his coarse woolen shirt to reveal a wiry body. His rib cage and shoulder blades stood out prominently. He had none of her brother's bulk to recommend him.

She searched his eyes for a sign of rebelliousness. In that unguarded moment she saw calculation, cold reasoning, a measure of insecurity, and a lust for the fullness of life.

Did he think she was part of that fullness? "Do ye recant your wager?"

He shook his head in the negative. His flaxen hair fell forward over his forehead.

"Then kneel."

He dropped to his knees, his back still poker-straight. His gaze challenged her.

She nodded at Wallace. "Begin."

As the whip lashed upward, a collective intake of breath could be heard. Then the leather thong sliced through the air, sliced through the pale skin fleshing Duncan's back. He jerked; almost pitched forward but caught his balance. Incredibly, he grinned.

An impudent grin, by God. She stilled the flutter in her heart and ordered, "Another!"

The whipped flashed up, slashed down. A thin crimson welt appeared. His jaws clenched. Still, his country-boy gaze held hers.

She would not weaken. "Again."

Duncan tensed. The lash whistled another time. Its tip curled under Duncan's jaw. He buckled. Blood trickled off his neck, under his armpits, and splattered onto the floor.

Ten times more she ordered the application of the lash. Ten times more she heard its shrill keening. Ten times more she winced inwardly. Still, he watched her. His eyes reminded her of a scarecrow's. The coppery tang of blood filled her nostrils.

The big blacksmith was finding his rhythm. Duncan's body jerked spasmodically with each bite of the whip. His head drooped like a horse recently broken to the bit.

A reasonless, empty ache clawed at her insides. "Halt!" she cried. "That is more than half. With the full measure of twenty-three, the simple fool would never make it to my bed, anyway. Take him to his quarters."

His head still hanging, his bloodied body quivering, he made a croaking sound that carried authority nonetheless. "Nae."

She felt the accusing stares of the others. Was there no way out of this to save face, yet save him? Another part of her mind questioned this: Why save him? "You heard me, Colin. Patric, Doug—take him to his quarters. I will send salves for his cuts."

Duncan raised his head. His hair dripped with sweat. His eyes had a glazed focus. His mouth managed a merry quirk. "Come yeself, m'lady."

"God Almighty!" she swore. "Begone from here. All of ye." She lifted her skirts off the pink-splashed floor and swept past the tottering Duncan.

Alone in the turret stairwell, she put a steadying hand on its walls. Its cold stones revived her. Why *had* she saved his worthless hide?

Because he had undergone a measure of pain in order to lie with her when her own husband had cowardly abandoned her to Murdock and his soldiers?

Kathryn was sun-starved. Where she was going, sunlight was but a memory.

The old military road was a partially cobbled wynd twisting around the face of Buachaille Etive. This stretch of road straggled up through a glen white with aspen and birch. All that sparkled here came from the large amount of rain, or snow, as the case was now.

Clouds billowed ominously around the Grampian peaks. A bitter, driving wind had sprung up. She sensed an infinitude of rock far beyond the snow's white wall. Occasionally her mount's big hooves slid on ice patches glazing the road. Below, far below, a cold mist shrouded a burn that fed into Loch Linnhe, guarded by Fort William.

Many hours ahead was the tiny hamlet of Lochaber and its castle. She and Arch might have discovered this latest clue to Enya's whereabouts too late. They were taking a calculated risk. They both knew and accepted the obvious: that once they reached Lochaber, they were locked in for the winter.

If Enya were not at Lochaber . . . Kathryn would not let herself finish the thought.

The alternating whinnying and neighing of the small, shaggy horses Arch had procured from a Fort William blacksmith brought her back to the present. She cast a whimsical glance at Arch, riding at her side. "You remind me of a wolf. Lean and lined and famished."

He flicked her a wry grin. Snow melted on his

burning-red brows. "A mangy wolf, I'd wager."

"Never that. Only a hungry wolf." The source of her young lust had always hungered for lost causes. God willing, Enya was not a lost cause.

"How much farther?"

He shook his head. "Too far. Another six or seven hours in this weather."

The snow was turning to sleet that stung her cheeks. "The horses need rest."

"I am afraid to stop. We may freeze in our tracks. 'Tis getting colder by the hour."

Indeed, the breath descended from the Shetlands' nostrils in icy white columns. The winter wind was biting cruelly. She pulled her bright plaid clan tartan up over her nose. The strong, sour smell of wet wool made her want to gag. She felt hot even though she shivered. She tried to keep from swaying in the saddle.

"Kathryn!"

The sharp word refocused her. She looked across at Arch. He was scowling blackly. "I am all right." But her voice was hoarse in her ears. And distant. "'Tis just the tartan is so bloody hot."

In her ears, she heard ringing. 'Twas the *pibrochs* calling to her, those sad songs of the bagpipes. Calling like omens.

Suddenly, she was falling. Snow swirled inside her fiery brain. Warm breath burned her cheeks. "Kathryn, don't give way now!"

Where was her breath? "Rest . . . just for a wee while."

"We'll rest soon. I promise you. Only a few miles farther."

She heard the lie in his voice, but his dark eyes would not release her. She could get lost in them, forget who she was. Lady Kathryn, wife of Malcolm Afton of Ayrshire. "Your smile has the charm of sunrise, Arch. You should have been a Druid priest. You weave spells and incantations so expertly."

"I would charm you if I could," he said, his voice sounding like the distant crackling of autumn leaves underfoot.

She felt his arms around her. Lifting, soaring. Then she realized she was merely being transferred to his horse. He cradled her against him. His body heat and his cloak were stifling. "Un-uhh," she moaned.

He would not release her. "Only a wee bit longer, my love."

His love. At one time she had been just that. His love had almost hidden her path from her. But she had left the tempestuous girl in the illusions of the past. She was old now. As lined as he and graying rapidly. And too wise to betray all that was good and holy.

Her eyes drifted close. "I am as dead as mutton," she said with a rattling laugh. Why did she feel so hot when it was wintertime?

"No!" His lips touched her forehead. "Do you know that I still love you?"

"Do not say these . . . things. I have been . . . content with my life as it is."

"You lie. But I ask not your love, my dearest one. Only that you stay here on earth that I may end my own days in peace."

She found the strength for a dry laugh. "Peace, you say? Peace would . . . be your death knell. You thrive on challenges."

"You were a challenge. I remember the first time I saw you."

She knew he talked to keep her from drifting off into that peaceful place between sleep and awakening. Still, she feared the moment. Never before had either of them made specific reference to the past.

"I was at the loch, helping my brother haul in a net of haddock. I glanced up and saw you riding toward us as if chased by the wind. At first I thought you were a boy. You were clad in breeches and a short tunic, and your feet were bare."

"Please, say no . . . more."

"You leaped neatly from the bay's back. I was impressed. More impressed when I saw your hair, braided in loose plaits."

"Three loose plaits."

"A bonny lass, no less!"

"Aye, though I rebelled . . . against it at the

time." It was her beauty as a girl that had cost her her freedom and made her an adult too soon.

"Sunlight glinted in your eyes, Kathryn, and you shielded them with a little grimy hand. I looked down, and your toes were dusty. I was enchanted. Have been ever since."

"And I," she added with a longing sigh, "I was newly married."

"Aye. I couldn't believe this was Malcolm Afton's bride. This young slip of a lass with her braids—all three—" he said with humor in his voice, "bouncing on her back. Somewhere along the way, you became a grand lady."

"And the fisherman became a priest." In between, she thought dreamily, was one glorious moment I shall never repent.

"You don't remember that afternoon at all, do you?" he prompted.

"I weary of talking." She curled close into his body warmth. "I am tired, Arch."

"You cursed me as a scoundrel, taking the fish without tithing to the laird."

A half smile tugged at her feverish lips. "You were astonished."

"Aye. The mere fact that your husband was a baron had nothing to do with tenant tithing in the Lowlands. We Lowlanders come from a long line of scoundrels and smugglers and—"

"—and spies!" she challenged, teeth clattering

with the cold. She gazed up at him through the mist of snowflakes. "Are you one, Arch? Are you a spy for the English?"

Beneath the tasseled cap his face was set in lines as granite hard as the mountains surrounding them. "You ask questions whose answers might endanger you."

"I am not afraid of danger."

"I am."

"What?" The single word was but a whisper. She felt lightheaded but forced herself to speak aloud. "What are you talking about?"

"Aye. Each time I risk . . . take chances . . . my stomach churns. Have I endangered others needlessly? I bite my nails. I feel alone against enemies who have all the advantages. Is my indignation merely self-righteousness? Do I have the intelligence and ability to do the things I believe are needed? Or am I being pompous to a fatal degree? There are nights when I can't sleep, I am so afraid. 'Tis then I remind myself I am not alone."

"Your faith . . . supports you?"

He glanced down at her, his grin cocky. "That's why they call me Arch. I always need support."

"You were never serious with me!"

His grin faded. "For once I shall be. Each of us needs someone to support us when the high road is rocky. You embody that faith, Kathryn."

"But there have . . . been years go by . . . when you were—"

"You were there for me whenever I returned—needing a handout, a change of clothes and a bath, or simply a listener. You've always been wrapped around my heart. Your memory is a living shield."

"I don't want . . . to hear this." The arctic wind turned the perspiration on her forehead to crystals.

"Make up your mind. Do you want me to be serious or not? If so, I—"

He broke off as horsemen clattered from the density of trees on the left. She stirred, tried to sit erect. The riders brandished swords and dirks that could cut down herself and Arch with the ease of a scythe in a field of wheat. Fear slithered down her back. Beneath her cloak, against her belly, she felt the prick of a blade.

"Use it if you need to," he whispered against her cheek.

The warning glance he gave her told her more than his words. The knife was for her to use on herself.

Chapter Eleven

Duncan, flat on his stomach, turned his head to one side. That wide, slow smile boiled Mhorag's blood. "Say nothing, Duncan of Ayrshire, or I shall rub your wounds with salt."

Terrible wounds they were. Pulps of gored flesh fringed the welts that were like scarlet satin ribbons. He did not wince when she rubbed in the moldy-smelling salve, but his spindly hands gripped the rough pine frame of his cot.

She should have left him to the Lowland wench who demanded to tend his wounds, but she herself was responsible for what had happened. Damnation, but the dolt had forced her hand!

"Is Mhorag a Celtic name?"

She knew he talked to keep his mind off his pain. She fancied she glimpsed bone. She shuddered. "Aye. Mhorag is an ethereal mermaid. Daughter of the dragon of Loch Ness. She lives in Loch Morar, not far from here."

"I should have known," he muttered.

"What?" She dabbed rapidly at the blood that trickled lazily toward the straw mattress. It was already soaked in one spot with the thick red fluid: Duncan's life sustenance.

"That ye would take me by surprise. This was unexpected."

Her hand paused. "Ye make no sense. Your body has no fever, so ye canna be hallucinating."

"Nae. I am rhapsodizing." He lifted his cheek, pillowed on the back of his hand, and looked over his shoulder at her. "Ye took me by surprise. This love was unexpected."

"I dinna love ye, idiot!"

"Nay, but ye will."

"A plodding fisherman? Do ye not realize I have been tutored in Latin and French, astronomy and literature? I doubt ye can even do your sums."

He shrugged. "Ye can do them for me."

He amused her. "And what will ye do for me?"

"Temper yer bitterness. Gentle yer wildness. Slow yer headlong rush. Ease yer pain. As ye are doing mine at this moment."

Her hand slowed, then halted. Tears blinded her. She wiped angrily at them.

"Easy, lass," he cautioned with a wry grin.

"Yer tears are salt to my wounds."

She swallowed her tears and snapped, "I should put you under the whip another ten times."

"But ye will na."

"Ye are not even a virile man. Look at ye. No muscle. All bones and flesh."

He grimaced. "Mangled flesh."

The door of his quarters opened with a bang. Enya stood framed in the doorway. Her sun-burnished red hair straggled from its crown of braids to curl wildly about her square jawline. In that half light, the cleft in her chin looked even more pronounced. "What have you done to my Duncan?"

Mhorag sprang to her feet. "Your Duncan? I dinna see your name signed on his Bond of Maintenance. 'Tis my name. Duncan belongs to me."

Enya stormed forward, her loose hair flying. "Ye swore to defend Duncan and his rights." She stopped within a cloth's yard of her and stared past her at Duncan. "God's blood, but you are inhuman, woman!"

"She's a mermaid," Duncan put in.

Enya glanced down at him. Her eyes widened. "Dear Lord, look what she has done to you, Duncan!"

A droll smile exhibited those two overlapping teeth. "I did it to myself, Enya."

Enya's gaze swung back to her. "He's delirious! You self-indulging, unfeeling bitch!"

The urge to smack the impertinent woman flitted across Mhorag's mind. She rejected the desire in favor of a more striking taunt. "He suggested the flogging in exchange for my bed. More than my brother wants from you, 'tis said by the chambermaids."

She watched with delight as a pink flush rose up Enya's neck and over her cheeks, to clash with the burnt red of her hair.

Immediately, the flair of rage was shuttered in those dark eyes. The Lowland woman smiled with condescension. "The lack of bloodied sheets tells nothing. I never claimed to be a maiden, did I now?"

Duncan groaned. "Do ye two mind? Me back is killing me."

"My poor darling." Enya went to bend over him.

"Touch him, and I'll have you flogged." She ached for a reason to flog the Lowland woman herself. To strike at the symbol of her own agony.

After Simon Murdock's violation of her before a dozen ogling soldiers, her mind had imprinted his face forever on the backs of her lids: his saliva-dripping mouth, his eyes drowning in devouring malice, his teeth bloodstained by her own teeth ripping at his tongue. For weeks afterwards she had not been able to sleep, but had sat crooning gibberish to herself. Or so she had been told. Those weeks didn't exist in her memory. Only Murdock's evil raven's face.

And now the Lowland woman had stolen away the security of her brother's comforting affection.

"Milady!" From the doorway the old hag Elspeth beckoned her wayward charge with the curl of a gnarled finger.

Duncan moaned. " 'Tis a sewing circle me quarters have become."

"The laird has returned," Elspeth hissed.

Enya directed a guestioning glance at her maidservant. "Aye? So?"

Elspeth flung a cautious look at Mhorag. "Go on with it, old woman," she said.

"He has returned from the hunt with more captives. Your mother and Brother Archibald."

"Mother!" Enya grabbed up her skirts and rushed from the room with Elspeth in her wake.

Mhorag stared after the young woman. "Your savior has abandoned ye to your fate," she drily told Duncan.

With a visible shudder of pain, he rolled onto one side. "Ach, but what a fabulous fate."

She slapped away the fingers that sought hers. "Ye did not earn your night in bed with me."

His face contorted into a mask of mock misery. "Surely, m'lady, thirteen lashes earns me at least a kiss from thy lips."

She stared at his mouth. Flecked with blood, as had been Simon Murdock's. She cringed at the thought of kissing the Lowlander. Even had his lips been spotless.

But then, she was no longer spotless, was she?

She brought herself to do the deed. Leaning down, prepared to withdraw should he make a lunge for her, she dropped those softly mocking lips a hasty kiss. Just as hastily, she withdrew. At least he had not tried to hold her against her will. Not that he could.

"Ye are stingy with yer lips, m'lady. Was the kiss that unbearable?"

"I felt nothing. Absolutely nothing."

"I'm told 'tis quite pleasant. Why don't ye try again?"

She shrugged. "Why should I?"

"Why shouldn't ye . . . unless, mayhaps, ye are but a lass? Skittering away from feeling like a real woman?"

Her eyes flared. Her lips bared in a snarl. "A real woman, ye say? Does sex with a man make a woman real? How about hollow? How about burnt-out inside?! How about hurting and used and—"

"How about soft and surrendering and loving?"

Never again would she have those qualities of innocence. That gossamer thread of sanity snapped. Her hand, aching to swat something, found a target.

His head snapped to one side. Again, that silly grin. "Does that count toward the twenty-three lashes?"

So hot was her anger, she couldn't even manage a single word of scolding. What she did do was stalk from the room with scalding tears blinding her eyes.

Some might have termed her exit an escape.

Enya's world seemed to be falling apart around her. First her own capture. Then Duncan's flogging. And now her mother and Brother Archibald were captives.

Rage overrode all caution. She had forgotten lessons in watching her father cope with his disease: that rage was really fear. That there were only two feelings in all the world: fear and love.

She sallied into the great hall like a Celtic warrior queen into battle. Her gaze fell on Brother Archibald first. Hands tied behind him, he was dressed in rough garb. A bloody furrow bisected one cheek.

Her mother was dressed no better, in common attire that might have clothed a Glasgow harlot. Her hands, too, were tied. The two captives trailed behind Ranald, who swept through the halls calling out orders.

Enya pushed through the scurrying servants to reach the two. "Mother!"

The woman halted, turned. A suspicious tint reddened her cheeks. French rouge? Her mother never used cosmetics. Enya enveloped the older woman in a tearful hug. "Oh, Mother!" Intense heat emanated from her mother. Dismayed, Enya drew back. "You're feverish!"

"I'm all right, Enya." Kathryn swayed unsteadily. "Now that I know you are indeed safe."

"You are . . . unharmed, Enya?" Brother Archibald demanded. His eyes searched hers with such anguish that she realized what he feared.

"Aye. I am unharmed. Truly, Brother Archibald. But you—what happened to you?"

He raised his fettered hands to finger the still-bleeding wound. A rueful grin tugged at his mouth. "An enemy picked me to pieces."

She whirled away. Her gaze scanned the heads, finding the one that towered above the others. "Kincairn!"

He half turned and looked over his shoulder. His brows drew together over warning eyes.

She stalked toward him. The others in the great hall parted a path for her. He wore an oilskin against the wet weather, a brace of grouse slung over his shoulder. He looked weary.

Only when she could see his eyes, the color of a frosty blue moon, did she halt. "Is there nothing you won't stoop to? Is your thirst for revenge so great that you must harm innocent people? My mother and Brother Archibald had nothing—"

"*Brother* Archibald?"

"Ye—you heard me! How many must suffer at your bloody hands?"

"If you wish to protest, appear in the Justice Hall on the morrow."

"My mother can't wait until the morrow. She is ill! Can't you see, you simpleton!"

The sharp intake of breaths warned her she had overstepped her boundaries. Still, she would not back down. She would not show weakness. "For all your education," she said, enunciating each word distinctly, "you are little more than an ignorant heathen. You represent well the idea that Highlanders are barbarians!"

Veins stood out in his temples like pulley chains on the portcullis. Both apprehension and anticipation strained the silence of the room. "Jamie. Take her to the donjon."

Jamie stepped forward. Regret mingled with reproof in his countenance. She jerked her arm from his clasp. "I won't go without my mother."

"Milady," Jamie murmured, "do as—"

"Jamie." The single word rent the air. Ranald merely raised one brow, but the glowering gaze was not misspent. Like a steel-tipped arrow, it pierced her. "Mistress Enya has obviously lost all reasoning and caution. I do not wish her running amok in the dark of night. She might hurt herself. See that she is clapped in chains."

She would have flown at him, screeching, and scratched his eyes from their sockets had not Jamie's grip manacled her. "Ye forget your Bond of Maintenance!" she cried out over her shoulder.

Jamie dragged her with him. "Hush, milady. Dinna you see that you are only making things worse? Ranald is in a foul mood."

"Willna make a difference. If you kicked the man in his heart, you'd break a toe."

"He lost Nob today."

"What? The princely troll?" She almost tripped over the first step of the stairwell. It twisted downward into a dark hell. A cold hell.

"Aye." Jamie's handsome face wore a haunted expression. "Took an arrow through the back."

The rickety staircase spiraling down to the buttery was lit only by intermittent sconces whose candles sputtered. "One of the other hunters?"

He shook his head. "None of the arrows in their quivers matched the one that killed Nob. Nob was riding with Ranald at the time. He thinks the arrows may have been meant for him."

Cobwebs brushed her face. "He canna believe my mother or Brother Archibald had anything to do with it! My mother doesn't have the strength to bend a bow, and Brother Archibald's never hefted one in his life."

Jamie's expression was skeptical; however, he said, "Your mother and the priest—if that is what he is—have been in the confidence of Simon Murdock."

Hope quickened in her. "He's nearby?"

"Not near enough. Another few days and even Hannibal and his elephants willna make it up that pass."

He led her past a twisted heap of barrel staves and cooper's bands, past the buttery, and let her into a room littered with trunks, cast-off furniture, water casks, dilapidated saddles, and rusting firearms. The room smelled dank.

"Here we are. Watch your step. Sorry to have to do this, my lady."

Before she could react, he clamped handcuffs on her. Her anger, dissipated by the story of Nob, was resurrected instantly. "Ye canna do this, Jamie. I am not a slave! I am not a dog or bear to be chained!"

He looped the cuff's chain through a link waist-high on a wall that had not seen a scouring brush since the glaciers scoured the glens. "You are lucky to be getting off with confinement, Enya. Ranald could have made it much worse for you."

She shivered so badly her chain rattled. "How am I to undress? To feed myself?"

"If ye remember, I've fed ye before," Ranald said from the doorway. "I imagine I can do so again."

Her head snapped around. "I spit on you and your Highlanders!"

"Now who is the barbarian? Jamie, arrange for Nob's burial."

Jamie eyed him inquiringly as he brushed past the larger man on his way out.

Ranald strode in and, stepping over a rust-eaten washtub, seated himself on an upside-down churning bucket. She half expected his weight to splinter it. He stretched out his long legs and crossed them at the ankles. "Your mother is indeed ill."

"If she dies here beneath your hands, I swear I'll see you join her and Nob if it's—"

Anger wrought in him a choking laugh. "Do not threaten me."

She stared at him stonily.

"Your mother is being treated by that old hag of yours, Elspeth. With any luck, she should improve."

Still, she said nothing.

"I canna give you what you want from me!" he said suddenly.

Her teeth ground. "I want nothing from you."

His sloping brows climbed. "Not even your freedom, Enya?"

Something in her prodded her to taunt him.

She wanted to make him feel her pain. "You poor deluded savage. The times have changed, and you have been left behind. The days of the laird and his clan are past."

His frustration erupted. "Damn it to bloody hell, woman! Do you want me to admit that I am mean and heartless and relentless? Aye, all those things I am. And more. But I canna save my people by being any other way."

He braced his forearms on his knees and leaned forward. "Don't ye think I tried? We peacefully surrendered. We gave up our language and our customs, our weapons and our words.

"Docilely as cows, we let them lead our lairds to the slaughterhouse, until we realized it wasn't just our leaders they meant to exterminate. It was a whole way of life. They meant to vanquish an indomitable people who would not bow their head. The Romans annihilated the Celts here seventeen hundred years ago. I do not mean to let the English do it to the Scots."

Her dimpled chin came up. "I am a Scot."

His lips curled in a sneer. "Not anymore. You have been diluted by English ways."

"Dinna you see," she asked softly, "you have become the very thing you hate?"

The brackets at either side of his mouth deepened. "I canna let them go. Your mother and Archibald."

"Not ever?"

"Not until I have buried Simon Murdock."

She couldn't keep the pity from her voice. "There will always be another Simon Murdock. This isn't the way, Ranald."

Her tone caught his attention. His gaze was unyielding. "You swore to make me love you. I swear to make you hate me."

She didn't believe him. Wouldn't let herself. "Shall we see who wins?"

He peered at her through lowered lids. "What happens if we both succeed?"

She cast him a sorrowful look. " 'Twill be tragic for you."

He shoved back the bucket with a booted heel and stood. "I don't give up. I won't lose as long as I draw a breath. Come along and amuse me."

She watched him release the chain from the link. "What do you mean?"

He tugged her along after him. "I am tired. You are safe enough. I told you, Enya. I find redheads unattractive."

"Really?

He took the donjon steps two at a time, his spurs clinking against rickety wooden steps. She had to hurry to keep pace with him. "Aye," he said, "thy skin is bloodless. Too pale and freckled. Not for me the calm, cold kiss of a virgin. Give me the wild, sweet and warm love of a brunette."

His words both wounded her pride and fired her indignation. She would have tackled his muddy boot had she the use of her hands. "Ranald Kindairn, you do not know how to love."

"Oh?" he asked over his shoulder. "And, pray tell, ye do?"

At the landing, she caught up with him. The single sconce pooled them in an intimate light. "You are afraid of me, you are!"

"I, afraid of a Lowland traitress, who in the bargain, I might remind you, is my captive and in chains? You jest, mistress!"

"Then kiss me."

The grooves at either side of his mouth quivered. "Who would have thought? A captive begging to be taken?"

She could have gnashed her teeth. "I only said kiss me."

He rolled his eyes, then lowered his head, as if humoring her. Suddenly she was afraid. How, with one kiss, could she bestir him to look at her in a different light?

She closed her eyes and puckered.

He laughed.

Her eyes snapped open. "You mock me!"

"Nae." He stood, gazing down at her, his dark eyes musing. "Should I teach ye the rudiments of lovemaking, do ye still think ye could turn the tables on me and make me love ye?"

She searched his face for a ruse. She saw only intent. Intent on making her suffer. "I will yet do it."

"Me laird," he prompted.

"Ranald." She smiled.

He jerked on the handcuff's chain. "Come along. This has been postponed long enough."

She yanked on her end. "A moment. My mother?"

He emitted an exasperated grunt. "What about her?"

"She must recover her health first."

He cocked his head and gave her a quizzical stare. "Do ye understand that you are my captive?"

"Of course!"

"Do ye understand all that that implies?"

"Do ye understand that I will make you love me?" She stood on tiptoe and kissed that hard mouth.

He did not respond, only waited for her to withdraw her lips.

Her ego bruised, she moved back a step, as far as the chain would allow. She stared at him with an unnamed fear. Had she, indeed, been trapped in a dungeon, a sun-flooded dungeon of love? " 'Tis your blood that runs cold."

"Then heat it. Tonight. I tire of empty promises."

Chapter Twelve

Enya dropped the mob cap atop his desk. Her hair pins she scattered across the open Bible with its marked verse: *Praise the Lord from the earth, sea monsters and all deep.*

She furrowed her fingers through her hair, and its fiery waves plunged over her fair shoulders to swish against the small of her back. If submit she must, then let it be on her own terms.

Ranald's eyes darkened. Lust, disgust—or delight in the opportunity to degrade her—might have been the emotion playing across his chiseled countenance. But not love. Not yet.

Without taking his eyes from her, he propped his musket against the fireplace and slid the leather thong holding his powder horn over his head. He dropped the powder horn on the hearth. "Take off your apron."

She reached behind her back and pulled on the bow's strings. It fell to her feet.

He unbuckled his dirk's scabbard and dropped it beside the powder horn. "Now your jacket."

Button by button she loosed the short serge jacket. Her cambric shift barely contained her full breasts. She watched to see if passion flared in his eyes. They were shuttered.

"Now your skirt, mistress." His heavy leather tunic was tossed on a chair, so that only his tight knee breeches clad his lower torso. That, and his white woolen stockings. He settled himself in the Turkish chair and, unbuckling his knee bands, rolled down the stockings.

With his attention diverted from her, it was easy enough to divest herself of her bodice and skirts. It was not so easy to tear her gaze from that wide expanse of bared chest. The same dark hair that was sprinkled across his lower arms matted his chest and converged in an arrow tip traveling down the plated muscles of his stomach.

Entranced, she watched him rise, unbutton the knee breeches, and drop them. The arrow shaft aimed past his navel to that other shaft, much thicker. Even as she stared, it seemed to take on a life of its own . . . arousing from its present dormancy to harden. It lifted, thrust outward and upward.

She swallowed. Her gaze locked with his amused one. "Your shift, mistress."

Her cleft chin tilted upward. "No. I am your bondwoman, not your slave."

His smile was most pleasant. "Ye heard me. Your shift."

All those years of trying to be compliant and cooperative, to behave as a lady, as dictated by polite society, rather than as a female, resisted further pressure. "And you heard me. No."

With three purposeful steps he bridged the plaid carpet to halt within a hand's span of her. His gaze was hotter than any forge. "As I expected, a Lowlander canna keep his word."

"*Her* word." Her fingers fumbled at drawing off her shift. "And I keep it." Nervous, she couldn't make her fingers function. Strands of her hair looped over a small pearl button. At the sharp tug on her scalp, she gasped. "Drat!"

In one fluid move, he grasped the front of her shift and ripped downward, loosing her snarled hair. Nevertheless, the renting of the garment and the crackling of the fire were the sounds of a battlefield.

His reckless gaze journeyed over her exposed breasts, belly, and hairless mound. "Good. I see that ye have kept yourself shaven."

A wild woman in her emerged. Not a woman out of control, but one who had reintegrated with her natural life. In that single instant she shed the burden of domestication and rediscovered that track of her wildness. She sprang at her captor. Claws bared, she knocked him to the floor. Straddled him.

Shock widened his eyes. "Ye witch!" It was more an exclamation of admiration than condemnation.

Then he grasped her upper arms in an effort to restrain her swiping hands. They rolled together, limbs entwined, as each strove for supremacy. Her ancient female instincts boldly reclaimed their wildest nature. From her subconscious boiled a ghostly memory of Celtic kinship with the wild woman outlawed by a controlling male society. A wild woman living a life natural to her, one now bound and constrained and imprisoned. A captured witch.

Ranald's stronger body gained the top, his powerful legs anchoring hers motionless. His hands pinned her wrists to the carpet. "You weigh more than a draft horse!" she ground out.

He laughed lowly.

She arched and snarled. He ducked her thrashing head and nibbled her earlobe. She stiffened. Her fingers curled, her feet arched.

"On nights like this, witches come to the clearings in the moonlight to prance and howl," he growled at her ear. His beard-shadowed jaw rasped her delicate skin.

She howled her anger. Howled and moaned, grumbled or purred according to where and how Ranald touched her naked body.

His battle-scarred fingers rolled her hard nipples between them. "Ye are the Greek goddess Artemis," he whispered against her parted lips, "the soul of the wild who roams through the forests and guides the moon across the sky."

She bit his lip, drawing blood. "And when the wild woman finds her wild man?"

His big fingers dipped into the wet, warm folds between her legs. "When that at last happens the wild woman wants to be touched, cajoled, ravished," he murmured, his lips journeying the valley between her breasts. "Night is her time. My wild woman craves the moon and the stars and wood fires."

"And her wild man craves *her,*" she said. Her fingers did not quite encircle the rigid, enormous organ pressed atop her groin. She guided it between her thighs, already moist with her need. "Create a place for it," she told him, her voice thick with wanting.

He paused, lifted his head, scanned her face. She felt at once young with innocence and ancient with wisdom, both wild and magical. She raised her own head; her tongue stole out to lick his bottom lip as an encouragement.

In acknowledgment, he thrust his tongue inside her mouth at the same moment his shaft thrust inside her. She bucked at the unexpected pain and cried out her anger. Her teeth nipped at his muscle-striated neck.

He drove into her again. She screamed out. His mouth silenced her. His persistently pumping hips desensitized the pain in her cradling flesh. His arrow shaft became a wand that healed. No, more than that: It imparted a throbbing pleasure that demanded assuagement.

Suddenly he groaned out and collapsed like a wounded beast atop her. For a moment she lay paralyzed, listening to his grasping breath, feeling the burning heat of his body and its incredible weight. Then she realized what had happened.

Furious, she pushed him from her and rolled to her knees to crouch over him. "You'll not take your pleasure without giving me mine!"

He stared up at her in real astonishment. "What? What did ye say?"

She really wasn't sure just what she meant. But recollections from a mist of time assured her she had drawn near a feeling that was akin to a spiritual ecstasy. A bliss that was hers if she but risked the courage to claim it. "I want you to make me feel what you felt!"

A slow smile added to the grooves at either side of his mouth. He nodded at the wilted wand. "The laddy there will have to be persuaded."

Comprehension dawned on her. She grasped the limp organ. With awe, her fingers investigated its length, the network of pulsating veins, the mushroom caplike tip; the change of color from light pink at the root to dark purple at the head; how velvet-smooth the skin was, yet steely hard beneath.

With fascination he watched her exploration. Lightly, she stroked him as she would the soft, velvety nose of a skittish stallion. She peered up at him through the thicket of her lashes. "You are wondrously made."

His low moan elicited her own slow smile. She watched him grow in length and thickness. Then she guided him into that part of her that she deemed her wilderness. Astride him, she began to move her hips in rhythmic oscillation, like that of a grandfather clock. Time's pendulum swung her faster. Her hair lashed back and forth with her thrashing head.

Gone was all thought of her determination to seduce her captor. She was consumed with the desire to be the woman she now knew she was meant to be. The wild woman for which her body was meant, the wilderness vessel for the wild man watching her. She was experiencing a dissolution into the joy of the present moment.

Every muscle, every ounce of flesh cried out for release from the tension building in her.

Suddenly something inexplicable happened. Her body trembled throughout in violent spasms. She laughed, she wept, she exulted.

Gradually she became aware that Ranald had sat up with her, that her legs were wrapped around his hips. They rocked together to some unheard melody, as if this were the last moment, the last dance, and there were just the two of them to make it last forever.

He was stroking her hair and crooning to her in Scots Braid mixed with Gaelic, "*Mo Coinneach,* me fair one." All the while he dropped soft, warm kisses on her bare neck and shoulders. "*Mo kinruadh,* me redhead. *Mo Cinaed,* aye, ye are indeed firesprung."

So this was what it was about. How glorious!

She pulled away and sprang to her feet to stare down at his surprised expression. "I have yet to make you love me, but you canna make me hate you. Not after what happened between us."

His dismay gave way to a knowing smile. "Dinna be so sure of that, Enya. Ye are inexperienced at what has just happened between us. Should I put my mind to it, I can have ye begging for me touch and hating me for your weakness—all at the same time."

For once she was totally sure of her feminine powers. She returned his smile, her own supremely female. "You will want me again."

"Aye. I mean for ye to be ripe with child come the winter thaws and me meeting with Simon Murdock."

Her blood ran cold. She had been overconfident. She collected herself and said with a simulated yawn, "I weary of this game of yours." She began to dress. "Daylight is near, and the kitchen fires need to be tended."

When she was dressed and at the door, her hand on its latch, he said, "Enya."

She looked over her shoulder, steeling herself for his next diabolical move.

"Cover your hair next time. And be sure to keep yourself shaven. Understand?"

Her eyes flashed their contempt. She said nothing, but closed the door behind her with a thud that rattled its latch.

From Duncan Enya found that her mother and Brother Archibald had been quartered in rooms just off the gallery in the south wing. "Yer mother is weak but holding fast to life, Enya. Elspeth has been tending to her."

"What about you, Duncan?" She reached out and touched the red stripe that plowed the skin beneath his left ear. She ached for her childhood friend. They stood beneath an arched window embrasure, talking rapidly, as both had chores awaiting them.

He grinned. "As well as can be expected. And ye?" These days his usually merry eyes were serious. They searched her face intently. "He did not . . . harm ye, did Ranald?"

The memory of the night before was vivid. She could still smell the scent of heather and fresh rain and wet leather on his skin. And the after-scent of their lovemaking. "No, he dinna harm me, Duncan."

A few minutes later, from a narrow bed, her mother asked nearly the same question of her. "The reiver did not hurt you, did he, my darling? You are looking wan."

She sat on the edge of the straw-stuff mattress. She tugged the cover up over her mother's shoulders. The room was cold with drafts, and her's mother's face was unnaturally pale. "As I told you and Brother Archibald last night, I am unharmed."

But not unhurt. Her thighs and delicate inner flesh ached. An ache well worth the pleasure she had experienced.

"This was dangerous, Mother. Traveling to the—"

"The wolf's lair?" Her mother's smile was weak.

"Aye, the wolf's lair, in weather like this."

Her mother's hand crept out to take hers. Gone was the fever of the night before. Elspeth's remedies had worked cures before. Hopefully, this time, also. "We were hoping to arrange for . . . your ransom."

She sighed. "Mother, he'll not release me until the day Simon Murdock is dead. I don't think all the coffers of the Lowlands would set me free."

Her mother's grip tightened. "There must be a way to escape."

"Not now. Not until the thaw is over." *And by then she might be large with child!* Gently, encouragingly, she squeezed her mother's hand. "I think that before then we will have a better knowledge of both the castle and its inhabitants. Escape will be much easier."

Her mother managed a feeble smile. "Arch—Brother Archibald is already seeing to that. You know him, how easily he makes friends. He has gone below to mingle."

Her mother's sudden flush pleased her.

"He will succeed, Enya. These stubborn Highlanders are staunchly behind a priest."

"Mother, I am needed in the kitchen, but I will return at the end of the day."

She did not go directly to the kitchen, but went in search of Brother Archibald. She felt an affinity for the irascible priest. When she saw his red hair some of the tension ebbed from her shoulders, which always hurt these days, what with carrying the cast-iron kettles of water and the heavy armloads of firewood.

Brother Archibald stood before the enormous fireplace. Warming his hands, he was holding forth with several early risers in a lively discussion of the triumphant biblical King Ahasuerus. "So, the warrior king, after going on a wild party spree, went looking for a queen. His search brought him in close contact with the most beautiful virgins in the land."

"What makes that so unusual?" asked the bearded Robert, who had lost his eye in battle. His good eye fell on her. "The Highlands had the most beautiful virgins in all of Scotland 'til Murdock and his Lobsterbacks arrived."

She knew Ranald's men were all wondering if she, a Lowlander, also was still a virgin.

Seeing she was the focus of disgruntled attention, her mother's old friend said smoothly, "What makes that so unusual is that a Persian king would even consider marriage to a woman of unknown lineage." He held out a welcoming hand to her. "Ah, Enya, I am glad to see you looking so winsome this morning." His words were spoken with the ease of a guest, rather than a captive, who was merely visiting the abode of a hospitable host.

In keeping with his light tone, she said, " 'Tis the crisp mountain air, Brother Archibald."

"I looked in on your mother this morning. She seemed to be resting well."

She wanted to evade the prying eyes of the men. "Mother is asking for you now."

Excusing himself, he joined her. She waited until they were well away from the others. "We may have an ally in the castle, Brother Archibald."

He flashed her a rewarding grin. "You have always been resourceful, Enya."

She spoke in a whisper. "I found a scribbled message in Ranald's desk giving the destination and date of a raid Ranald was going to make. The handwriting wasn't Ranald's. Only the council members could have known."

"Or someone within earshot." Voice low, he climbed the stairs with her. "Mayhaps one of them let slip the message to a wife or companion-in-arms."

"True enough."

"Does Ranald know you know?"

"Aye. I tried to use the message to buy the safety of Duncan and myself and the others, but Ranald would have none of it."

"You realize whoever wants Ranald out of the way may care less about our fate?"

"I thought if you were aware of this note, you could keep a watchful eye."

"Do you have any idea who may have written the note, lass?"

She considered. "Ranald has usurped Jamie's rightful claim as the chief's heir. But Jamie doesn't want the position."

"Or so the young man says."

"And the old chief, his father, canna ride." She reflected on the game of backgammon she had played with Ian. "The man is sharp, though. He plays aggressively. Nearly beat me." He was also taciturn and said little that was of a revealing nature, however much she tried to engage him in conversation.

"From what I've learned, Ian was a brave and fearless leader of his clan. Harsh in victory and unyielding even in defeat."

"Ranald is the natural choice."

Brother Archibald gave her an inquisitive glance. "The way you say his name—this Ranald—is it feelings you have for this man?"

"Aye," she said with a grimace. "Mixed feelings. Fury for being treated like a—a piece of barter. And hurt. But I give him credit, Brother Archibald. He is a natural-born leader—unyielding, ruthless, heartless."

"And a brilliant tactician," the priest mused. "At least, that is the talk among the English troops and their leaders. Tell me, can you get a sample of handwriting from the council members?"

"I could try. Of the eight, only four could write. Nob may have been able to, but he was killed the—"

"Aye, I know. Ranald suspects me."

"He suspects everyone. One of the council

members, Robert—the one-eared man below—has a handwriting that is barely legible. Ranald is, naturally, ruled out. That leaves Jamie and his father. I haven't had an opportunity to search their belongings. You have to remember that this castle is a layover, a base for the winter only. They keep very little to haul around with them."

"Talk to this Jamie. See what you can learn. Don't discount anything."

As the priest let himself into her mother's room, she eyed him thoughtfully. There were times when she thought he had missed his calling. His bearing, his thought processes, his commanding presence all bespoke a man well capable of leading other men, not leading Latin masses.

Flora and Annie were full of questions about the latest arrivals to the castle. "Ye mean they braved the trowies to come here?" Annie asked, eyes wide.

"The trowies?"

"The trolls," Flora explained. She fixed a beady eye on Annie. "Ye talk too much."

"Trolls?" Enya asked. Were they talking about Nob?

"Aye," Flora said, her thin lips quivering with imaginary fears. "After dark the trolls guard the glens of Buachaille Etive against outsiders. Many a traveler has been found at the bottom of a glen, the body all twisted and broken."

The kitchen was hot. Enya wiped the sweat from her receding forehead and picked up another leek to dice. "Annie—Flora, don't you think that, in the dark, a traveler unaccustomed to the mountain might miss a turn in the road?"

"Our Shetland ponies don't miss turns," fat Annie scoffed.

God, she could use a smoke right now. After breakfast Ranald would be presiding over the Justice Room. A puff from one of his pipes would ease the stress of the last few days. Surely she could find an excuse to take her out of the kitchen for an hour or so. Then, too, there was Jamie's room to search.

Escaping Flora's carping presence was not that difficult, after all. An argument arose in the Justice Hall over a trained bear that had bitten off the hand of a spectator. The bear's bellowing roar summoned the castle servants and other curious eyes into the Justice Hall. Ranald sat in the Justice Chair with a half-amused smile playing at his lips.

"Cruickshank had been tormenting the bear!" a droopy-nosed man said. He pointed a finger shaking with anger at a balding man whose right arm was heavily bandaged with dark, dried blood discoloring the white, gauze-wrapped stump.

Cruickshank, the owner of Lochaber's jute mill, brandished his stump. "The bear should be killed—before it kills some wee innocent!"

The bear prowled in agitation back and forth between his owner and the Justice Chair. Murmurs for both sides ran through the hall. Enya did not wait for Ranald to make a decision. She would know the outcome soon enough. She backed away from the fringe of the crowd. Lifting her skirts, she ran up the staircase, heading for Ranald's room—and one of his pipes.

Would he miss one of maybe half a dozen pipes? Not likely. She took tobacco from the leather pouch and tapped into the bowl of a porcelain pipe. She lit a reed from the hearth's fire and held it to her pipe.

With the first intake of the heavenly smoke, she closed her eyes. This was as near ecstasy as a body could come . . . unless she discounted that too quickly fleeting moment locked with Ranald in passion's embrace.

Only in reviewing those moments did she recall his reference to Artemis, goddess of the hunt and the moon. He had had an education of sorts, though too often the heathen in him permitted his knowledge to be colored by his superstition.

Lips pursed, she blew away the haze of smoke to better see the open Bible. This morning Ranald had marked another verse. Reading it, she felt her scalp tighten and the hair rise on her arms.

Where has your beloved gone,
O most beautiful among women?
Where has your beloved turned,
That we may seek him with you?

The metallic clink of spurs echoing in the hall alerted her. Quickly, she shoved the pipe back into the drawer. The door opened. Ranald stood glowering in the doorway. He closed the door behind him. "Any reason why ye are in my quarters?"

She collected her wits. "Do you not remember granting me protection under your roof?"

He sauntered toward her. "Under my roof. Not in my private chamber."

Her smile was derisive. "You wanted me here last night."

He stopped only a handsbreadth away. "Oh? You have returned to beg for a repeat of last night?"

"Beg I'll never do."

He took her chin, gently brushing its cleft with his thumb. Then he angled her head and brushed his lips across hers. More than once. "Soft." His mouth lingered against hers, unmoving. "Yet firm."

A queer feeling swirled deep in her belly, just

below her navel. A sweet weakness swept over her. She almost swayed against him, collecting herself at the last instant.

He must have sensed her sudden restraint. "I'll beg, Enya. Kiss me. Now ye are no longer a cold virgin. Kiss me with the fires of your uncovered passion."

She moved back as far as the desk allowed and tugged off her mob cap. Her thick red braid tumbled free to swing over her shoulder. She stood on tiptoe, feathered her lips across his, and whispered, "My uncovered passion is symbolized in my uncovered hair, Ranald. Fiery red. Are you afraid?"

He grasped her shoulders and drew her against him. "Aye, I am afraid, *mo cinead.* Of feys and witches and trowies."

Nervous, she laughed lightly and tugged from his embrace. "Ah, so 'tis a trowie I am now?"

He caught her wrist and towed her over to the bed, where he pulled her down alongside him. Head propped on one hand, he stared down at her. "Trowies are whimsical creatures." His free hand toyed with her braid. "To be under the spell of the Highlands' little people, its elves, is to lose one's soul."

His fingers were working free her plaits. "These little people . . . do they behave like ordinary people?"

"Ach, no. They live cheerfully below ground,

in chambers carpeted and richly hung with arras and abundant tables set with the best china and silver. But their doorways are but modest entrances, looking for all the world like gopher holes."

This playful side, almost innocent in its heathenish backwardness, could be endearing. "Being a trowie has its good points."

"Aye. They say that trowies are lovers of good music, and many Shetland fiddle tunes have been learned by listening at a trowie doorway."

He spread loose her hair, fanning it across the bed. "The wee folk have always been here, ye know. They are disdainful toward humans."

"Why?" She barely got the word out of breathless lungs.

He began unlacing her stomacher. "Because we mortals only just got here—at least in the slow-ticking watch of the trolls. A man stolen by a troll for what seems like just a few hours may be surprised to learn he has been away for days or weeks or even years."

Free of her stays, her breasts spilled into his palms. She strove to contain her gasp of pleasure as he dipped his head and licked one nipple. "Are . . . are there both male and female trowies?"

His hand slipped beneath the layers of her skirts. "Aye, but sometimes they go masqueraded as human men and women."

Her thighs spread for his invading fingers. Her voice was little more than the rusking of dead leaves against the windowpane. "I fear 'tis I who have been witched by a trowie."

"Enya?"

"Hmmm." She barely found the energy to answer as his fingers worked their magic on her.

He rolled from her, rose, and grinned down at her. "Next time, damp the pipe before ye put it away."

She bolted upright. "Where are you going?"

He tugged her skirts down over her exposed thighs. His lips curled merrily. "I'm off to free a bear. G'day to ye, mistress."

"The wisdom of Solomon," she murmured with a wry twist of her lips.

Once she was dressed she did not return to the kitchens, but instead went to Jamie's chambers, farther along the hall. She knocked, and when there was no response, she slipped inside. Her heart was beating rapidly. She scanned the room. Much like the others, it contained a rough-hewn bed, an armoire, and a rustic pine table that apparently served as a desk.

It was that to which she crossed. A few books, befitting a man of learning and letters, were stacked at one end: Defoe's *Robinson Crusoe,* Pope's *Essay on Man,* Swift's *Gulliver's Travels,* and Voltaire's *History of Charles XII.*

A brass pot for sealing wax, a sander for drying an inked signature, an inkwell of sandalwood, and a broken quill were scattered across the desk, but there was no evidence of any penmanship itself. Neither were there paper or parchment or even scribbled notes inside the pages of the books through which she flipped.

A queer chill in her neck made her glance over her shoulder. The door was still shut. Feeling nervous now, she went through the armoire: shirts, tunics, knee pants and trousers, jerkins, and a frock coat, buckled shoes and boots of fine Spanish leather.

She abandoned her search and fled the room. With no one in the cavernous hallway, she felt lucky to escape undetected. Or, at least, she thought so.

After she finished her kitchen duties she had no more returned to her chamber than she heard an imperative knock at her door. Her hands halted at unlacing her bodice. "Aye?"

Without waiting for permission, Ranald entered, with Thane close on his heels. Saying nothing, he crossed to the fireplace, sank down on his haunches, and began rearranging the smoldering embers with the poker. "The flue is so primitive that more smoke swirls in the room than goes up the chimney."

"True enough," she said carefully. Smoke had discolored the walls' wainscoting and painted paneling. She watched his profile for any revelation as to the purpose behind this visit.

"What were you doing in Jamie's chambers today?"

"How did you know?" she blurted.

His smile was enigmatic. "I'm the seventh son of a seventh son."

"What?"

He settled down before the fireplace and crossed his ankles. Thane dropped down alongside him.

She remained standing, arms folded, and studied him as he talked. "Every Highland glen and braeside has its resident wise man or woman. Traditionally, 'tis the seventh child of a seventh child who, through the power of fairies, inherits the gift of *taibh-searachd.*"

His rich accent didn't make any clearer the Gaelic word. "The gift of what?"

"*Taibh-searachd.* Prophecy. Or seers."

"Oh, spare me the nonsense."

" 'Tis true. For instance, a century ago a Highlander, Kenneth Odhar, was given a magic white stone with a hole in it by the fairies and was able to see the future in it. It seems that Kenneth paid dearly for his gift. He was *cam*—blinded in one eye."

She squinted at him. "You don't really believe this, do you?"

He shrugged those massive shoulders. "Kenneth predicted the Battle of Culloden over a century before it happened."

"Coincidence." Yet despite his everyday tone, he sounded profoundly arcane. "I wager not everything he predicted happened," she challenged.

"Weel, he did speak of a string of black carriages, horseless and bridleless and led by a fiery chariot, that would pass through the Highlands. I admit that sounds farfetched." That grin again. "But then, how do I know ye were in Jamie's room?"

Her eyes narrowed. "You spied on me."

"And were you spying, mayhaps?"

So, he had neatly boxed her into a corner. "I had gone to get a book for Annie to practice her reading."

"And where is that book?"

"There wasn't one easy enough for her to read."

He brushed off his hands and rose to his feet. Thane rose, also, and looked to his master for a signal to leave. "Me thinks, Enya, ye are practicing your own kind of predicting."

"What?" she asked again, taken aback.

He crossed to the door and paused with his hand on the latch. "Aye. Your confinement to the donjon, after all, should ye continue to make it difficult for me to treat ye as a guest rather than a prisoner."

"Does the host make love to every female guest?" she retorted.

"Don't mistake that, mistress, for lovemaking," he said, and shut the door on her.

Chapter Thirteen

So the redheaded one had been a virgin after all.

Ranald tried to keep his mind on his surroundings. On the noises that belonged—clink of metal bits of harnesses, creak of saddles, occasional snorting of horses, the baying of a hound. On aspects of the landscape that belonged—untrammeled snow; the glide of a golden eagle in a clear, cold sky; a single plume of smoke from a trapper's cabin.

When one failed to notice small things that didn't belong was when large things occurred. Like ambush. The long night march, followed by an early-morning raid on a small patrol party of the enemy, had left his weary men dozing in their saddles.

For over a year now it had been a matter

of stalking and attacking whenever he could, sometimes moving his headquarters from day to day so no one knew where he would strike next. In this he was helped by people of the countryside who gave him the most recent news of the English movements.

On the northern horizon, blue clouds lay in a smooth line, a foreteller of heavy snow. Within another week the pass would be blocked. For the winter, Lochaber would be a snowbound island.

Why was he seeing dragon ships in wind-swept clouds? Why was he infatuated with a redheaded wench who seemed to wield over him the power of a pagan priestess? It was merely that she was so bloody unbiddable, distracting, and unpredictable.

At his side, Jamie said, "Hopefully, this was the last battle before winter. But after that, Ranald? Do we do battle for the rest of our lives?"

He glanced across at Jamie—his cousin, his friend, his confidant. A Redcoat's bayonet had opened a small gash along his left sleeve. Jamie had not the eye-hand coordination of a warrior born. Seeing the bloodstained wool, Ranald was sorely tempted to reply that the fighting was ended forever.

Mayhap Enya was right when she had told him yester morn, "Don't you see, Ranald? Surrender doesn't bring the inability to survive but always the birth of something new."

He had just committed that small surrender, that giving of himself, of his seed. That moment when man is at his most vulnerable. And yet, she had held him to her, caressed him and crooned softly to him in her lyrical Scots Braid. And he had been renewed. In a sense, resurrected. If not spiritually, then, at least, physically. The sight and feel of her heavy breast in his palm was enough to accomplish that feat.

"Your thoughts are not of battle," Jamie said, bringing him out of his reverie.

His answering laughter felt liberating. "Nae. They were of a battle of sorts. With the Lady Enya."

In his thoughts was the image of her yester eve, sitting by the fireplace and teaching the village maid Annie to read. From his own Bible, no less.

Had the Lowland lass no limits?

She was not sweet-tempered as Ruthven had been. Tall, taut, and trying instead of small and soft and submissive, like his intended. But he was not afraid of crushing either the breath or the spirit out of Enya. Her body fit his well, and she challenged his perspective.

Fragile Ruthven. Redheaded Ruthven.

"Let her go, Ranald," Jamie urged.

"There ye go for a damned cowardly Italian," he joked, mimicking his sister.

" 'Tis not Simon Murdock I'm concerned about. 'Tis the Lady Enya."

His lighthearted mood vanished. "Has the vixen witched ye, also?"

He recalled too easily Jamie's earlier declaration of what an entrancing conversationalist she was: "Spirited, she is, Ranald, with a mix of wit and wisdom." And he knew how big and awkward he was. Awkward both of body and words, especially when it came to women.

"You know better than that," Jamie said. "You must put the past behind you and trust again."

Ranald pretended to scan the fields, where oats for the cattle were rotated with potatoes, turnips, and rye. Privately, he wondered if this redhead who presently occupied his bed could be trusted, as she claimed. There were mornings when he half expected her to try to bury his dirk in his heart while he slept.

Or, at least, she thought he slept. Experience had made a light sleeper of him.

Remarkably, most mornings she had been content to sit quietly and puff on one of his pipes. He knew she waited for an avenue of escape to present itself for her and her retinue.

Truly, he was going to be sorry to make the Lowland lass hate him.

Kathryn was sitting up, more than she could do a fortnight ago. December's wan light filtered through her room's high, narrow window and yellowed her skin.

"I feel old," she told Enya. "When someone has to spoon-feed you you might as well be buried."

Enya held another spoonful of the watery gruel for her to swallow. "Ridiculous, Mother. Bairns are spoon fed, also."

"But the we'ans have a lifetime to look forward to. Mine is over."

"I hardly think so," said Arch from her doorway. He stood so tall, the lintel concealed the top of his head.

Neither Enya nor she had heard him open the door. He was the same age as she. How did he manage to look so full of energy and strength? "Come in and talk to us. Enya is regaling me with castle gossip while she feeds me."

"I'll take over," he said, "though I doubt the village gossip I have been sorting through is more entertaining."

Enya passed the wooden bowl and spoon to him, and he took her chair beside the bed. "Anything about any accomplice we might find here in the castle?" Enya inquired.

He shook his head, and his thick red hair fell across his brow. "Not a thing. If anyone is disloyal to *Cean Mòr*—"

"To whom?" Kathryn said.

"*Cean Mòr*. That's Celtic for what the villagers

call Ranald—Great Chief. And none of them are about to betray him. At least, not to me."

"I wonder why the fierce loyalty when he isna from Lochaber?" Enya mused.

He shrugged those yard-wide shoulders. "Have you learned anything?"

Enya shook her head. "I haven't been able to find even a scrap of paper with writing on it. I went through some books in Jamie's room. I couldn't even find his name on a flyleaf."

"If you could get him to write something for you," Arch suggested.

"Which might prove nothing," Kathryn said. "The person who wrote that missive might have deliberately disguised his handwriting."

"Open your mouth," Arch told her.

Obediently, she did as he commanded and swallowed the gruel. "Tell Elspeth even her potions taste better than this," she said to Enya.

After her daughter departed she asked, "How do you keep your passion for life, Arch? I tire so easily."

"You are my passion."

Her heart fluttered. "Don't talk that way."

"Why not?" He set the bowl and spoon on the floor and leaned over her. "If you are determined to languish away, then I shall speak my mind."

"You already did," she said, and held up a forestalling hand. "We'll speak no more about this!"

"Aye, my love. The time for words is past." He gathered her in his arms. She was too weak to push him away. He cradled her to him, his smoothly shorn jaw resting against her temple. "You are me one true love. As I am yours."

"No," she protested. "Do not say these things."

"If not in this lifetime, then in the next you will be mine." He lowered his head even farther. "If I can do no more than kiss you now, then in the next lifetime I will make you mine and give myself to you in return."

His breath warmed her, fanned inside her the embers of life she thought had died. Her heart took flame as his lips kissed hers. Her body, aglow, responded as it had all those many years ago. If only for this one wondrous moment, she was young again.

"Mother!"

With a gasp, she yanked away from Arch to behold her daughter in the doorway. Enya's expression was aghast. "Enya, you don't understand—"

Arch drew her back within his encircling arm. "Come in, Enya. 'Tis time you knew the truth."

Her daughter's gaze of astonishment darted from him to her. Slowly, Enya closed the door and rested her back against it. Her expression was one of incomprehension.

"I love your mother, Enya."

"Obviously," she said dryly. "What about your priesthood vows?"

"I have yet to take them. I am only a brother."

Surprise stunned Enya momentarily. Then she looked at her. "What about my father?"

She was grateful for Arch's strong supporting arm. She drew a deep, steadying breath. "Arch is your father, Enya."

Their daughter's eyes widened. "You betrayed *your* vows then, Mother. Your vows of marriage."

At the anger in her voice, Arch said harshly, "Do not judge, Enya. That is the worst of sins. The only sin, mayhaps."

Her words were a mere whisper. "How could this happen?"

A measure of strength restored, she drew away from Arch. "Does it matter? We were young. Unwise. Inexperienced. The important thing is that we dinna want to hurt anyone, least of all Malcolm. We still don't. What you saw was a moment of weakness on my part."

"No," Arch declared, "it was a moment of love on my part! It will not happen again, but I will not let even you make something ugly or evil of what was—"

"Did you know this?" Enya asked. "That I was your daughter?"

"I suspected the truth a long time ago."

Enya sank into a hidebound chair.

"I never told him—or Malcolm," Kathryn said, "that he was your father."

"I think I always knew," he said, releasing her. "But I thought it best for everyone to leave the matter be." He rose to his feet. "As far as I am concerned, Enya, things don't have to change. Malcolm need never know. 'Tis up to you."

Enya bit her lip, glanced down at her knotted hands, raised her eyes, and smiled. "I'd like to know you better. As more than an old friend."

Arch grinned. "Clearly, we've nothing better to do for the winter."

"Look! See there, off above that peak. The golden eagle." His breath frosted the air. " 'Tis the biggest bird in the Highlands."

Enya pulled up on her pony. Her gaze followed the direction in which Jamie pointed. Above the snow-capped summit the bird's wings were stretched wide, seeking a warm current of air in which to glide.

Warm air would be difficult to find today. Even so, she was willing to brave this newest onslaught of cold weather. With her work in the kitchen finished early and Ranald absent, she had pestered Jamie to take her riding to escape the stale air of the castle.

Where was Ranald? Was his heart's devotion given over to some maiden in the village? A

Highland lass whose hair color did not offend him?

Sometimes he called her to his chambers; a few times he came to hers; often he ignored her. He had not summoned her in weeks now.

When teaching Annie to read she had asked her subtle questions in regard to her laird, but Annie never mentioned any dalliance to her. That he occasionally called her to his chambers was a duly accepted fact—the right of the laird.

Come morning, she was still a kitchen maid, was she not?

Still, she often wondered if all of his time was truly spent in deer stalking, visiting local crofters and burghers, hawking, hunting, presiding at justice halls, and counseling with his reivers.

The one person she found herself turning to more often for solace was Jamie. He was well read, educated, and of a pleasant nature. And, it went without saying, a very handsome and charming man.

Sometimes she plied him with questions about Paris. Other times she listened wistfully as he told her anecdotes about luminaries he had discoursed with, men of influence like Voltaire and Franklin and Rousseau.

"The golden eagle is monogamous," he was saying now. "He mates for life."

"How perfectly fascinating. Can the same be said of the Highland laird?"

Jamie shot her a penetrating glance. "Are you inquiring about my cousin? If so, aye. Ranald mated for life."

Anguish struck like lightning. "Ranald is married?"

"No. The marriage never took place."

"What happened?"

His eyes shuddered over. "You had best ask Ranald about Ruthven."

Her enthusiasm in the ride went out of her. She rode on in silence for another league.

"Speak your mind with me," Jamie said at last. "I beseech you."

Ranald was ever on her mind. She admitted as much. "I know that Ranald has suffered under Simon Murdock's administration. And I can understand Ranald's bitterness, but sometimes I feel that he . . ."

She could not finish the thought. It would have been a betrayal of him. For all his fiendishness, he had never treated her brutally, as her intended had treated him and his family.

Jamie paused. They had dismounted and stood on the perimeter of a fallow field. Jamie put his hand on her shoulder. "I canna agree with what he is doing to you, Enya."

Rustling in the shrubbery behind them spun them around, is if by complicity. Ranald stood there, the merlin riding his gloved arm. The lacings of his leggings were filled with shreds of leaves and bits of bark. His face was smudged with a two-day growth of beard. Wrinkles of weariness fanned his eyes and mouth. His unnatural calm clad his presence with a kind of total menace.

How much had he heard? Nothing about his expression foretold the possible scope of his intentions. "My captive. Ye find her entertaining, Jamie?"

"Well, of course. She is a lady, for God's sake, Ranald."

"She is not to go out alone with you."

"You are afraid I shall seduce your cousin into eloping with me?" she asked, her tone scathing.

"Neither is she to be left alone with Duncan," he persisted calmly.

Jamie's mouth flattened with a mixture of both disgust and disappointment. "You should know me better than that, Ranald."

"I ken that flattered men can behave like fools."

He looked at her. It was an impersonal appraisal that seemed to take no heed of her disheveled red hair or her becomingly flushed cheeks or the flame of resentment in her green eyes. "I want ye to keep in mind that I am no fool." With that he strode on past the two.

Jamie glanced at her, shook his head warningly, then turned to follow Ranald.

* * *

When the weather wasn't inclement, which wasn't often, Enya would sit on the castle ramparts after her chores in the kitchen were finished.

Often her thoughts turned to Brother Archibald—or Arch, as she now called him. It was difficult to address him as Father just yet. She didn't know if she would ever be able to do so. At least she had come to the point where the thought of him as her father was no longer so utterly strange.

This afternoon was cold, but the usually blustery wind was lying low. Sunlight had melted the most recent snow, and she pulled back the hood of her cloak.

Soaking up the crisp, fresh air, Thane lay stretched out at her side. The collie heard the noise first. His ears pricked up, then he leaped to all four paws. She turned to see Ranald approaching. Tail wagging, Thane trotted over to his master, clad in a deerskin coat and leather trousers against the elements.

She also rose. "Thane was keeping me company." She hoped her words sounded casual. Whenever around Ranald these days, she found herself getting absurdly shy. Like a nervous maiden, she was.

One of those rare smiles eased the hard line of his mouth. "I wanted him to keep *me* company."

"Another raid?" Surely she could think of something better to say.

"Only on the trout."

"You're going fishing?" The thought of escaping the castle confines tantalized her. Of all the castle's inhabitants, she, alone, was forbidden to leave. Even old Elspeth and Mary Laurie were permitted to visit the village. "Please, may I also accompany you?"

He looked askance. "Ye fish?"

She smiled demurely. "A wee bit."

His eyes took on a boyish gleam, his face alight. "Ever fished for trout?"

She shook her head.

"Then come along. The best bait is the mayfly, but until the insects hatch again we'll have to make do with minnows."

She couldn't believe this wild, unsophisticated chieftain, the leader of a formidable band of reivers, could be so congenial.

Sunlight glinted in his tawny hair as he led her along a snowbanked road, then cut across crystal-frosted rye grass, and picked up a path leading to the burn. Thane trotted at their side, his tail wagging happily. Ever so often he would leave them to explore a hazel thicket or prickly gorse, then come romping back.

The burn's water rushed so rapidly that ice had no chance to form. Ranald halted beside a denuded, pale gray mountain ash. Here the river narrowed, slowed, and deepened. "There should be something in the riffle between the gravel bars and yon bed of watercress."

She watched him impale a minnow on the hook of his fishing pole, doubtlessly booty from a recent raid. He cast the line in a dark area that marked deeper water and twitched it a few times. Within seconds, a juvenile trout took the bait. Ranald hauled in his catch, unhooked it, and held it under the belly until it swam off. "Not bad for a brown trout, but not large enough to be a gift fish."

"Cast in the farthest riffle," she suggested, "the one closest to the sheep pasture across the river."

He flicked her a challenging look. "Ye do it."

Before she could reply he passed her the pole. She searched his face, ruddy with the cold day. His expression held a look of patient good humor. "This outing had been planned," she accused.

"Planned? More like ordered. The good hag Elspeth trapped me in a draughty passage and wouldna let me by until she had lectured me on your virtues. I ended up giving me promise to provide ye with the opportunity to stretch your legs—limbs," he finished lamely.

His magnanimous gesture, then, had been at Elspeth's prompting. In a dour mood, Enya accepted the fishing pole. Her cloak hampered her cast, but when she could control the line she dragged it crosswise, remembering how mayflies flutter upstream just before their wings are dry and are unable to lift off the surface.

The trout came up out of a dark area in the farthest riffle and took the bait with an almost angry motion. She said a quick prayer to whoever was in charge of brown trout. Her excitement was contagious, and Thane began to yip.

"That's it!" Ranald encouraged. "Keep jiggling the line."

The trout stopped once to try and bury itself in a patch of watercress before she tugged it ashore. Bright and clean-finned, it stared up at her with a dour eye.

"It shall make a marvelous meal," Ranald said, unhooking it.

"Let it go for another time," she suggested.

He spared it, and it slipped away to the center of the river. Then he turned on her an accusatory glance. "Ye've fished a lot."

She laughed with pure delight.

He grinned up at her. "I didn't realize you, also, have a dimple in one cheek."

At the soft gleam in his eye, she sobered. What if she fell in love with him instead? On the way back to the castle, both she and he were silent. Did he ever think about the woman he had been going to marry? "Tell me about Ruthven," she blurted.

A muscle in his jaw flickered. "Ye ha' been talking to Jamie."

She said nothing. By now they had reached the portcullis. He nodded to the posted guards and continued on. "What do ye want to know?"

In the bailey, she circumvented a squawking hen. "Why didn't you marry her?"

His long strides lengthened even more. "She died."

"Oh." She swallowed. "I'm sorry. Murdock's doing, also?"

Ahead of her, he climbed the stairs two at a time. "No."

She hurried to catch up with him and followed him into his chambers. "Do you think you could manage to be less monosyllabic?"

He peeled off his deerskin coat and went to stand before the slow-burning fire. His voice was low. "Ruthven and I grew up in the village of Achnacarry, the Cameron ancestral home near Fort William. When I went off to the university we were pledged.

"Later, Bonnie Prince Charles returned, and I joined the ranks. Not out of Jacobite zeal, but because of anti-Hanoverian feelings. With his defeat I became one of the holdouts. Me younger brother Robby and I joined Ian and other rebels. Always on the run, striking here or there at a lone patrol, and off again.

"Whenever I thought it was safe I would slip

into Achnacarry with Davy to see Ruthven and Mhorag, who was living with Ruthven's parents. One night, as I lay in Ruthven's arms, I found a Sassenach bayonet pointed at my throat. She had betrayed me."

She swallowed. "You killed her?"

He rounded on her and grabbed her arms. "Do ye think so ill of me?" He shook her once, then released her. "Nae, Enya, I didn't kill her. I wanted to, God knows. But the Redcoats bound me and Davy and shipped us to Tolbooth prison in Edinburgh."

She gasped. The prison was known to be a hell-hole, a museum of torture devices. She wrapped her arms around him and laid her cheek against his broad chest. "Oh, God, Ranald!"

His voice, above her head, was harsh. "I learned later that her father and brother had been arrested. To save them, she had sold me out. I canna blame her. Fear will drive people to betray their verra selves."

"How did she die?" she whispered against the soft chest hair curling above the lacings of his shirt.

He wrapped his arms around her and pressed her against him. "Mhorag said that the villagers gave Ruthven two sacks of silver: the proverbial thirty pieces. Weighted them to her waist, they did, and threw her in the burn. She sank out of sight."

She shuddered. Knowing Mhorag, the young woman probably prodded on the villagers.

Apparently, Ranald didn't realize he was swaying back and forth with her in his arms. With an almost maternal instinct, she drew him down with her onto the braided rug, where she cradled and rocked and crooned to him. "Oh, my dearest, my darling, my love."

She was using her hands to heal, but what might have begun from maternal feelings gradually altered to something equally as powerful. That primal drive to procreate. In a frenetic drive, she disrobed him, tearing at the lacings of his shirt.

He caught her fire. Wildfire. His hands ripped away her own clothing, so that she, too, was naked. Gone was her worry about being too large. His eyes told her she found favor with him.

Without conscious effort, as if in altered states, they turned to touching each other. Massaging, fondling, embracing into a perfect pulsation. Moving as one, female and male in synchronization. Seeking that oneness with each other and gathering their life forces. They rolled, entwined, before the fire.

They were performing that dance of creation, that act of love that Ranald sought to deny as such.

Wherever he touched her, that part of her felt

aglow with brilliant light. "Open your heart to me, Ranald," she whispered feverishly between his wild kisses.

"I canna."

" 'Tis easy." She kissed him in return. "Now. Tell me you love me."

"Words. They are unreliable, *mo cinaed.*" He moved up over her, into her, filling her. His hands wound through her hair with strokes that bespoke wonder.

Intermeshed with him, she felt as though she lost her own separate identity. Her emotions rapidly vibrated with ecstasy, then rapture and lastly an unsustainable bliss. She felt that burst of exquisite sensations that overflowed her.

Breath rasping, heart pounding, she lay silent, locked as one with Ranald. Gradually she became aware that something in her was irrevocably changed.

Ranald's weight grew pressing, but she didn't stir beneath him, only continued to hold him. What an unusual man he was. Brave and bold, educated more than most, yet a visionary, and charmingly superstitious with his belief in clans of wee folk and fairy legends.

She would have sworn she felt on her cheek the dampness of tears not her own. " 'Tis over now," she gentled. "Those nightmare years are over."

He lifted his head to stare down at her. His

eyes, dark with another form of passion, glistened. "Nae. 'Tis never over." He took her hand. Forced it between his legs. "Feel me."

Confused, she let him guide her fingers down the length of his hot, hard flesh to those still-swollen twin sacs. "Touch me, there," he urged.

She did as she was told and felt the line of puckered flesh.

"In prison the gaolers were going to castrate me. At Murdock's orders. Ye see, *mo coinneach*, your congenial husband's prizes of war are a collection of human testicles for such conversational pieces as coin purses and snuff pouches."

Chapter Fourteen

The depth of winter embraced the hamlet of Lochaber in its dark, swirling shroud, obscuring the distinction between minutes, hours, and days. Enya moved through this precarious interlude like a tightrope walker, balancing these days between Mhorag's viper tongue and Ranald's beguiling arms.

There were times when she doubted she would escape with her sanity. She couldn't go to Duncan. He was determined to turn the shrewish Mhorag docile.

Confusion prevented her from going to her mother and Arch just yet. And Elspeth, who had never been in love, would not understand this tug-o'-war feeling she was experiencing.

Surprisingly, or mayhaps not so surprisingly, it was Annie who provided perspective.

They sat before the guardroom fire, absorbing both its warmth and light. These days, noon was as dim as twilight. The fireplace was big enough to roast a stag. The walls, at one time adorned with weapons, were bare if one didn't count a halberd and spear, which were of little use in grouse hunting. Which was what occupied Ranald's Reivers today. The castle was empty of all but staff.

Her eyes narrowed with concentration in deciphering the unrecognizable words, Annie read, " 'And it came to pass in an—an—' "

"Eveningtide," Enya supplied, scratching Thane's head. Disliking this latest blanket of deep snow, he had chosen to keep her and Annie company.

" '—eveningtide, that David arose from his bed and walked upon the roof of the king's house: and from the roof he saw a woman washing herself and the woman was very beautiful to look upon.' "

She read slowly, letting her forefinger point out each word. " 'And David sent and inquired after the woman. And one said, Is not this Bathsheba, the daughter of Eliam, the wife of Uriah, the Hittite?'

" 'And David sent messengers and took her; and she came in unto him, and he lay with her.'

"Oh, mistress!" Annie said. "I dinna ken that the Book held such stories! Bathsheba was married, and still she slept with King David? Did she have no choice?"

Enya shrugged. "Mayhaps she wanted to." How did you explain that you lust after the very man who is holding you captive? "Read on, Annie."

The young woman's words came more quickly now. " 'And the woman conceived and sent and told David, and said, "I am with child." ' Oh my. Now what?"

Enya watched with satisfaction as the maid, without prompting, read on. " 'And it came to pass in the morning, that David wrote a letter to Joab and sent it by the hand of Uriah.' "

Annie paused to scan back through the previous passages she had read. "Uriah was Bathsheba's husband?"

Enya nodded.

Annie's words came faster now than her finger. " 'And he wrote in the letter, saying, set ye Uriah in the forefront of the hottest battle, and retire ye from him, that he may be smitten and die.' "

She glanced up at Enya. "David kills Uriah to have Bathsheba? Why, mistress, that is what Ranald is doing. Killing the Lord Lieutenant to have ye!"

Christmas, regarded as a pagan festival by the kirk, came and went with but little notice in

Lochaber and its castle. However, the festival of Hogmanay brought celebration.

On December 31, Enya was kept busy in the kitchens from dawn to dusk in preparation for the great quantities of food that would be consumed the next day, the first of the year.

Flora basted and roasted the traditional haggis: minced lamb's offal with oatmeal, onions, and spices packed into a sheep's stomach.

In addition, large roasted boar, replete with an apple in its mouth, was served, as well as flambéed peacock; marinated duck with orange and ginger; and grilled venison with lemon and rosemary. The array of meats was an indication of the successful hunt of Ranald and his men.

Enya helped cook the flummery and bake the apple tarts. Hogmanay's traditional shortbread and black bun were added to the holiday fare. By the day's end there was still the evening meal to be served. She could have cared less about the beginning of Hogmanay.

Clearly, not everyone felt as she. Laughter, singing, and music could be heard coming from the great hall. Fiddles, a bowed psaltery, and a lute—but no bagpipe. Where was Ranald?

"Oh, mistress," Annie said, "let me serve the men at the head table."

"With pleasure," she said, dropping down on the three-legged stool. With Flora downstairs in the buttery, she would enjoy a respite.

Annie, excited about waiting personally upon Jamie, hurried out with a tray ladened with goat cheese, hard bread, and ale. The handsome young man had yet to notice her, for all that she was now bathing regularly and taking to brushing her teeth with pressed rice.

At last Flora dismissed Enya. As she climbed the turret stairs to her room, revelers were already spilling over into the offshooting halls and chambers. Hogmanay promised to be a long, drawn-out affair, lasting at least another twenty-four hours after the clocks chimed out the old year.

Every bone and muscle in Enya's body protested the event. Her head ached. She was too exhausted even to heat water for a bath, much less rouse Elspeth. The old woman had to be as tired as she. With the approaching holiday, the villagers had besieged the spinning house, buying out its bolts of newly woven cloth for their costumes of finery. Elspeth spent a goodly amount of time at the spinning house and, through singing the work songs, was becoming proficient in Gaelic.

Enya placed a warming pan filled with hot coals beneath her bed's covers to heat its coarse linen sheets while she undressed. No sooner had she snuffed her lamp and, with a blissful sigh, slid into bed than the door burst open. "I should have known," she muttered, staring up at Ranald, candle in hand. "Don't you ever knock?"

"Ye are not yet with child?"

"What?" She sat up, pulling the bedcover up over her bare breasts.

He crossed to her. His expression was brooding. He bent over her and cupped her face in his free hand. The light he held aloft to study her face. "No, the signs aren't there."

"What signs? You've been drinking!"

"Aye. *Uisge beatha.* The water of life—the best of Scotch whiskey. Come along." He released her face to tug on one of her hands. " 'Tis Hogmanay. A new year."

Obviously there was no gainsaying him. "Turn around while I dress!"

His eyes narrowed. His hand dropped to her stomach. She realized what he was doing, feeling to see if her belly was "rounding." She grabbed her pillow and pummeled his chest. "You wretch! I am not a cow to be bred!"

"I want ye showing by spring—when I meet your Simon Murdock and cut out a hole where his heart should be." He grabbed up her smock and tossed it at her. "Dress, mistress."

Without moving from her citadel of sheets and covers, she slid the smock over her head, yanked it down about her waist, and began jerking the strings through their eyelets. "You would look delicious served on a platter with an apple stuffed in your mouth!"

His lip curled. His lids lowered in a speculative fashion. "You will look tempting with witches' milk dripping from your nipples."

She threw off the covers, smoothed down her skirts, and slid her feet into her clogs. "There are ways to avoid being—impregnated." She was disgusted with her embarrassed flush and turned away to replait her hair before the chipped mirror.

He came up behind her. His fingers wrapped around her braid. He tugged ever so slightly, but just enough to tilt her chin upward. "Ye better go down on your knees and pray for conception. Your welfare and that of your companions depends upon it."

She stared at his face reflected in the mirror. "What happens if I don't . . . conceive?"

He released his hold on her. "Then ye no longer serve me purpose."

"And?" she asked, forcing her breath past the cork of fear in her throat.

"I withdraw my protection. Do ye think there is a door that would open to you—Murderous Murdock's wife? Widows in the village would just as well stone ye; families who have suffered beneath Murdock's bludgeon would as leave watch ye starve or freeze than turn a hand to give ye bread or shelter.

"Which reminds me," he added, in his irritating, offhanded manner, "ye'll need your cloak.

We go down to the village tonight. And make certain your hair is tucked beneath your hood."

Despair churned her stomach sour. She squared her shoulders. Always that tightrope nightmare: to survive until spring when Ranald planned to clash with Simon—and to do so without bearing Ranald's brat!

A steady stream of merrymakers poured between the castle and the village just below. More celebrants crowded the lantern-lit town square, so many that it had been stamped dry of old snow. Their shouts of *auld lang syne* frosted the nippy air. Lively music from pipers and fiddlers rounded out the gaiety.

Obviously this was a time when the Highlanders' reserve broke down, with kisses and embraces shared equally among relatives, friends, and strangers. Lochaber's burghers were parading banners bearing Ranald's black dagger insignia.

As Ranald, with her in tow, wended his way through Lochaber's carousers, a daring young woman seized the opportunity to grab him and tug his head lower to plant a robust kiss on his lips.

He laughed, wrapped an arm around the blond maiden's waist, and returned the kiss, to the rousing cheers from bystanders.

"Ye're a stag, ye are!" the blonde said loud enough for those nearest to hear, including Enya.

"Ye're a randy laird!" shouted an inebriated old man wielding a ribbon-wrapped cane.

"Aye," Enya muttered, "that he is."

Piqued, she followed him into the pub. Revelers occupied every table and stood shoulder to shoulder. Even the bar was flanked by imbiders, lifting their mugs with ale-slurred toasts and sloshed whiskey.

Stopped here and there by greeters and well-wishers, Ranald finally hauled her before a cheery fire that smoked the planked ceiling. The harried host hastily cleared a table for his laird.

"Malt whiskey for my bondwoman and meself," Ranald ordered.

She sat stiffly. "A wee dram will be enough," she said in a tart tone.

"'Tis the night for beginnings, eh, my laird?" asked a grinning, peach-fuzzed young man, deep in his cups.

Ranald took one of the mugs the host handed him and passed it to her. "Drink up, mistress. We won't enjoy the fire's warmth for long."

Sullenly, she eyed him over the mug's rim. "What else now?"

He swallowed a deep draught. "After midnight, 'tis the time for first-footing."

She rolled her eyes.

His grin was amiable. "We select a house to visit, with the aim of being the first foot over the door in the new year." He took another drink, then said, "I might add, tradition demands the first-footer should be carrying a lump of coal— and should be tall, dark, and handsome. Red-heads are—"

"I know." She scowled. "Unlucky."

Just the thought of summoning energy to rise from the table made her tired. The whiskey had made her sleepy. She yawned and stretched.

She caught Ranald's gaze following the emphasized curve of her breasts. He tossed down the last of his whiskey. "Time for first-footing."

She plunked down her half-full mug on the dented copper table and rose to her feet. "Let's get this over with. Where to?"

He stared at her with an odd look. As if he were already regretting something. "A hunting lodge. Not far from here."

She followed him outside through the press of merrymakers. Where the crowd thinned and its din lessened, she said, "Please, Ranald, I am tired." She could only hope the party-goers were more congenial than he.

"We're almost there."

Ranald forsook the cobbled street for a snow-bordered lane. Away from the warmth of the throng and the shield of stone buildings, she could hear the wind soughing in the pines and hidden crags surrounding the village. Far overhead, the phosphorescent curtain of the aurora borealis lit their way.

Her cloak was not thick enough to ward off the cold. She shivered. Ranald seemed unaffected by it. She had to quicken her pace to keep up with his long stride. At least his immense frame blocked the cutting wind.

The wend gave way to a narrow, tree-bordered road. Hard-packed snow and dead leaves crunched beneath her clogs and his heavy boots. The scalp-tightening thought occurred to her that he might be taking her out into the woods to kill her. Maybe the Highlanders celebrated Hogmanay with human sacrifice.

She really was crazy! And tired. "How much—"

"There," he said. "Through the trees."

Situated on a rocky bluff was a small two-story building with a thatched roof and darkened windows. No one greeted them at the barred door. Ranald let them in to a darkened room.

"This is first-footing?" she asked, an uneasy feeling gnawing at the pit of her stomach.

"Wait," he said, and then deserted her.

She stood in the darkness and wondered if she shouldn't flee now and take the chance of perishing in the trackless wastes of his country.

Soon a candle's light spread its inviting rays across a bark-paneled room, bisected by a rough-timbered staircase. Rustic chairs braced a smoke-blackened fireplace. He crossed to it and knelt to hold a taper to the chips clumped beneath stacked wood.

She stared stupidly before realization dawned on her. "Ye—you—planned this!"

With a flare, the chips caught fire. "I leave nothing to chance."

With growing trepidation, she eyed his broad back. "What do you plan to do?"

"'Tis the time for welcoming in a new year. 'Tis the time for begetting in you a new life. Here, we won't be dist—"

Rage beat furious wings against her rib cage. "You savage! Do you think I'll spread my legs for you so docilely?"

She turned to leave. She got the heavy door open by only the breadth of a belt before he slammed it shut with an echoing bang. He whirled her to face him. His hands dug into her shoulders. He shook his head, as if trying to clear it of whiskey fumes. "What is it between us?" he growled. "When I touch you—when you lie with me—'tis not enough."

"You fool! 'Tis my love you want, and that you canna have without giving me your own!"

"Your love?" he scoffed. "I want only my seed in you."

With that he swept her up into his arms and strode toward the staircase. She would have struggled but did not relish taking a tumble down the stairs. Instead, hands balled, she lay unresisting in the cradle of his arms. She could smell the wood smoke in his shirt. Against her cheek she could feel the powerful and preternatural beat of his heart.

He kicked open the door of one of the rooms and dropped her on the bed. Staring down at her, he loosed the buttons of his trouser band.

As always, when made aware of his physical nearness, like awakening beside him in the middle of the night or coming upon him unexpectedly, there stirred in her a thrill of excitement as powerful as the sudden clash with an adversary.

He did not tarry to undress further. He lowered himself atop her and, taking her arms, stretched them out at either side of her. His hands pinioned her wrists to the bed. His knee spread wide her thighs. She waited, breathless with throbbing anger and something else. Without preliminary, he drove into her, sheathing himself to the root.

She arched and cried out his name. He silenced her not with a kiss but with his mouth over hers, his tongue penetrating, invading. She bit his lip and tasted salty blood.

Incredibly, he held her to him tenderly and began to move more slowly. Entering and withdrawing with velvety precision. Entering and withdrawing with a relentless will. Her body responded treacherously, harmonizing with his movement.

"You are mine, Enya. Should you run away, I

would come after you. Again and again. The first time I saw ye at Afton House, I knew—"

She froze. She had forgotten that fact. "I know you came to one of my mother's salons, but when was the first time you saw me? You could only have entered by invitation. Were you disguised?"

"As a servant. I waited upon ye, m'lady." His mouth curled sardonically. "When I learned ye were to be Murdock's wife I knew I would have ye first."

"Why?" she whispered. "If you had ridden that far into enemy territory, why not ride on to London? Steal his horse, burn his house, butcher his dogs? Why me?"

His breath was hot and rapid. "I saw ye," he said simply.

Recalling the biblical story of David and Bathsheba, she needed no explanation. Her body yielded and molded itself against him.

He released her wrists to began his rapacious stroke again. Her body signaled its acceptance in its creamy release. She trembled, groaned, clutched him to her. Still he went on with a determination to make her yield completely.

"Say ye belong to me," he said, his breath harsh.

Her thighs felt battered, yet she wrapped them around him and rode that tumultuous crest. Her nails raked his back. Her passion answered his.

The need to be one with him consumed her.

It was as if he was consumed by the same savage need. His teeth nipped the hollow of her neck. "Say it, Enya. I want to hear it!"

From somewhere, she dimly heard her voice, like a distant cry. "Aye! Oh, God, Ranald, aye!"

As if that night was an admission of Enya's surrender to Ranald, he began inviting her to ride with him on the days the weather permitted. Like the day he took her fishing, she supposed this was another way he was acknowledging her need to escape the confines of the castle occasionally.

Or was it his way of curtailing her sylvan outings with Jamie?

One gray, cold morning, Ranald took her with him. She rode her Shetland, he a great shaggy horse, bred for the rugged Highland landscape. He was visiting a crofter's widow who wished to wed.

"Do you ever think about a normal life?" Enya asked him as their mounts picked their way across a bed of shale bridging the river. "Marriage, children, that sort of thing?"

She expected him to scoff, but his reply was thoughtful. "Aye, occasionally. But the Sassenachs wouldna let me live in peace."

"If you could . . . if the British came to terms—"

"They never will," he said, his full mouth stretched flat with grim finality.

She flashed him a gentle smile. "But if your trowies worked magic, if the British did capitulate, what would you do? Buy a commission in the military?"

His laugh was short and harsh, his expression as gloomy as the mist. "Nae, soldiering is not what I want from life." He shook his head, and his queue brushed away a dead leaf clinging to the back of his doeskin jacket. "I love the land. But the Highlands is nae such a place for crofting."

She rode on in silence. Come spring, come the confrontation between Ranald and Simon, what would happen to her and the others? If Simon should triumph, she didn't think she could bear to remain his wife. Better that he cast her off.

And if Ranald triumphed? What would happen to her then? Conversely, she didn't think she could bear it if he should cast her off.

Dame Whitaker's cottage was a thatch-roofed hut walled with timber and cob just beyond a sheep *fank* along a burn. An iron plowshare and rusty-bladed scythe and sickle that had harvested autumn's crops lay unattended next to the doorway. Smoke eddied from the stone chimney.

Before Enya could dismount Ranald put his hands around her waist and lifted her from the saddle. For just a moment her hands lingered on his muscled shoulders. She found herself wanting him though they had lain together scarcely less than twenty hours earlier.

Her gaze met his. For once she saw in his eyes an absence of bitterness. Then he released her.

The widow met them at the door. She had ruddy cheeks and graying brown hair. Two children, a boy and a girl each under five years of age, clung to her heaven woolen skirts. "My laird," she said, her eyes shining with the honor of his visit.

He picked up the boy and sat him on his broad shoulder. "You are taking good care of your sister, son?"

Eyes wide, the boy nodded solemnly.

"I expect you to help your new father care for your mother. Understand?"

Again, the boy nodded.

"Come in, my laird," the woman said. She dipped a curtsy as Enya passed inside. "M'lady," she said with a more reserved tone.

The floor was bare, trampled earth. Two flock mattresses girded one wall. Smoke from a peat fire stung the eyes before fleeing up the chimney.

Ranald put the boy down and rumpled the girl's matted brown curls before addressing Dame Whitaker. "A kinsman tells me ye wish to marry outside the Clan Cameron."

"Aye, me laird." Her pale lashes fluttered,

and she looked five years younger. "Morven Finlaggan. Of the Clan MacDonald."

Ranald nodded. "Staunch Stuarts. I would welcome the man. Bring him to the great hall when ye are wed."

The little girl had been eyeing Enya. Enya dropped down and smoothed the straggling hair from the girl's oval face. "What is your name?"

The girl fastened her gaze on her wooden clogs. "Bonnie."

"Well, Bonnie, you have the bonniest eyes."

The girl smiled. Two teeth were missing.

Then Enya spotted the still-smoking pipe on the chimney mantle. The bowl was a carved dragon's head. "How clever! May I?" she asked the widow.

The woman darted a nervous glance at Ranald. "I only smoke when the bones git to hurtin'."

"I see," he said, keeping his countenance sober. "May the lady examine your pipe?"

Dame Whitaker's head bobbed in permission, and Enya picked up the pipe. The workmanship was crude, fitting even better the concept of a fire-breathing dragon.

Ranald's usually impassive eyes glinted with amusement. One of the few times she had seen him let down his guard. She thanked the woman and followed him out.

When they were once more mounted she

asked slyly, "Do you think pipe-smoking could become a feminine habit at Lochaber Castle?"

"I think you are more trouble than I bargained for," he grumbled, but the glint still sparkled in those unusually colored eyes.

Ranald treated Enya with a hint of gentleness she would not have credited in his character. His gentleness lasted until three mornings after the visit to Dame Whitaker, when he strode into the still-darkened kitchen and found Jamie helping her rekindle the embers in the fireplace.

"I never had to do this at home," she was telling Jamie. "And with Margaret ill with the ague, I—"

"Mayhaps ye dinna understand me?"

Both she and Jamie glanced over their shoulders. Jamie sprang to his feet. She rose hastily, the soot-crusted poker still in hand.

Ranald's brows were drawn down over flashing blue eyes. "Go to your room, Enya."

Jamie's hands balled. "Enough is enough, Ranald. This high-handed treatment of her dinna serve to strike back at Murdock. She is not your concubine."

"You are protective of the Lowland lass. Do ye seek to bed her, my cousin? Or perhaps ye already have."

"Nothing has happened between us. But she deserves better than—"

"Dinna answer him, Jamie," she warned. "He only wants to make you submit to prove something to me."

She whirled back to Ranald. "I'd rather be bedded by any of your men than you. Even Nob, as ugly as he was, had compassion and caring. Ye are an—unfeeling—" she was so choked with anger she could not breathe "—insensitive toad! Your touch repulses me! Do ye understand!"

Without thinking, she lifted the poker to strike him. He grabbed it, snapping it from her hands to fling it across the tiled floor, where it clattered against a copper cauldron.

Deliberately, he raised his hand and slapped her with his palm. The slap was not a hard one, but she yelled with fury. Jamie started forward, and Ranald set her aside. He stared at Jamie. "Is she worth it?"

Jamie drew a long breath, then his shoulders sagged. "You have proved you are stronger, Ranald. But you may have lost more than you kept."

Chapter Fifteen

The long winter months affected everyone in the castle, especially Kathryn, who had still not wholly recovered from that near-death ride up to Lochaber. Stale and smoke-laden air, bitter cold drafts, repetitious fare, and, of course, close quarters made for short tempers, but today, Kathryn's short temper had nothing to do with the castle confinement. She paced the parapet. The night's prevailing westerly wind whipped her cloak around her tall, slender frame and tore at her braided coif.

Arch stood, arms folded, and watched her. "Deny it, then."

"I won't deny I have . . . tender . . . feelings for you," she said, nearly shouting as she strode past him in the opposite direction. She whirled around. "How could you do this, Arch? I trusted you!"

"You still can," he said calmly.

"I trusted you as a holy man!"

"Trust me as I am."

"Trust a spy!"

As she made her next pass, he caught her arm and turned her to face him. "'Tis not the trusting that bothers you, is it?"

She put her hands on his chest and pushed, trying to put space between him and her. "A spy for the Colony of North Carolina!"

"For Governor Johnston," he corrected, "and you are evading my question."

She still couldn't believe it. She had been suspicious for some months now that something was awry, but the mask with its hourglass cutout that she had found in his satchel was indisputable proof. She had seen one like it brought by an Edinburgh parliament member to one of her salons. A quaint device placed over a seemingly innocent letter to reveal a communique.

Arch pulled her against him and stared deep into her eyes. "'Tis the fact that your feelings for me were safe as long as I was committed to becoming a priest someday. That is it, isn't it, Kathryn?"

"I'm married, Arch!"

His mouth flattened in a grim line. "Then your feelings for me are still safe."

Her forehead dropped against his chest. She couldn't control the long shudder that rippled through her. For so long she had been the strong one. Making all the decisions. Decisions that affected not only a household but an entire clan, a way of life that had to move into the future and yet preserve the integrity of its past.

Now, here was the love of her youth. This strong, loving, and compassionate man. Holding her. Supporting her both physically and emotionally. If she would but let him. Who would have thought that at her age she would be feeling like this?

He took her chin and raised it, forcing her to meet his impassioned gaze. "Trust me, my love. All this time, all these years, I have come to you when you called. Trust me, even in this."

Her eyes closed. She could feel his warm breath, almost caressing her lips. His mobile mouth, so alive . . . so different from Malcolm's anguished, pain-contorted lips . . . she could not . . . surrender.

Slowly, reluctant to give up the dream, her eyes opened. "I call upon you now to help me be strong. To help me remember the man who has loved me faithfully all these years and who awaits my return."

He smoothed her unbound hair down over her back. "My attention is focused exactly on that—getting us back to Ayrshire safely."

She moved a little away and immediately missed the comfort and warmth of his embrace.

"You've found the person who would betray this Kincairn?"

He shook his head, and his shaggy red hair was caught by the wind. "No. I've talked with everyone in the castle from lackeys to council members. No one professes even the least criticism of Kincairn. Including both Ian and his son. Ian claims the Cameron clan would have been decimated without a man like Kincairn to ride at its head."

"Enya says she is keeping an eye out for scribbled notes. Short of asking for samples, she hasn't turned up any proof of handwriting as yet."

Kathryn frowned, and Arch read her thoughts. "You are worried she is coming to love the man who could most hurt her."

She managed to smile. "The way you put it . . . isn't that true of anyone we come to love? That they are thus given the power to hurt us most?"

Ranald tossed onto the table the message brought by the merlin. "From me contact at Islay." He glanced from face to face. Which of the men assembled for the council was his betrayer?

Ian picked up the folded scrap of paper and scanned it. "So, Murdock knows we are holed up here at Lochaber. Well, ye expected him to learn sooner or later."

"He'll be at the pass come spring thaw," one-eyed Robert said.

"Does Murdock know you have his bride, Ranald?" Jamie asked.

Ranald studied his cousin's bland expression. Could this man whom he had known all his life, who had fished and fought and fared with him, betray him?

No, Ranald decided, Jamie might be in love with Enya, but he would not betray the Camerons. It was not in the man.

Colin, who had picked up the message, fingered his wild beard. "God help our laird."

"What—what does it sa-say?" stuttered Patric.

Colin passed him the message. He peered at it. A blush suffused his peach-fuzzed face.

Ranald enlightened the other men at the table who had not seen the message. "It seems that Murdock threatens to not only take from me his wife but to also take me nutmeg, something he failed to do the last time his men had me beneath the knife."

At the knock on the door everyone at the table tensed, then relaxed when Annie entered with a tray bearing a cheap tin teapot and cups.

If Ranald hadn't been staring at the girl's face, wondering what was different about it, he would have missed the look that passed between her and Jamie.

Dia's Muire! It wasn't Enya, but Annie, whom Jamie was courting!

Whatever affinity and trust that might have developed between himself and Enya had been obliterated by that awful morning in the kitchen when he found her talking with Jamie.

Regardless of the estrangement between them, it had not affected the volatile passion that took place between them in his bed or, for that matter, in the stables, a corn crib, or the forest.

Ranald felt like a fool. But how to remedy his error?

After the council meeting was over he asked Jamie to wait. His cousin eyed him warily. When Jamie and he were alone in the doorway he said, "I've been *glaikit.* I ask your forgiveness, Jamie."

Jamie eyed him dourly. "Stupid isn't half of it. How about blind, as well?"

Ranald grinned. "Did Annie do something to her hair?" He fluttered his hand about his own head. "Like comb it or something?"

Jamie slapped him on his back. "Enya's work, my cousin. It would appear she has been working on you, as well."

That was exactly what he feared. Mayhaps what he feared most.

* * *

Memories danced to a Scottish ballad as Ranald played the pipes. But the fiery-haired young woman who tapped her foot to his music was not Ruthven. Enya had yet to betray him. At some point both he and Enya had to start believing in each other. If there was no trust between two people, there was nothing.

He finished the tune, one of magic rowan trees and monster sea hags, and put down the pipes.

"*Port na bpucai,*" Ian said, clapping his contorted hands. "Fairy music. By the best of the pipers. Me headache is all but gone."

Ranald still had his own headache to vanquish: his pride.

Now was as good a time as ever to do it. He signaled Patric to take up the fiddle. The young man's bow played a haunting strain that was like the soft sighing of night wind.

Feeling like a lumbering draft horse, Ranald crossed the great hall. Enya sat on a bench with Elspeth. Both women eyed him balefully. Plucking up his courage, he ensconced himself on the bench beside Enya. Hands clasped between his spread knees, he said, "Legend says the tune is the funeral song of fairy spirits gone to bury one of their own."

She said nothing.

Mentally sweating, he tried again. "Ye see,

fairies are not immortal, but weep and mourn and die as we humans do."

Without taking her gaze off Patric, Enya said, "I believe and trust in what I can see."

Her expression was so unyielding, he doubted his apology would be accepted. It was just as well he didn't apologize. He should never have sought her out in the first place. Not with all eyes upon them.

He started to rise and thought better of it. He wouldn't run like some befuddled boy. "Teach me to dance, mistress," he blurted.

Real dismay showed in the expression she turned on him. "You've never learned to dance?"

He shook his head. He fastened his gaze on his clasped hands. "Nae. Me feet are like boats."

The ends of her mouth curved upward. A delightful mouth. "My own feet are nae wee things, but 'tis not a difficult thing to learn, this dancing."

"Weel, will ye? Teach me?"

She rose and held out her hands. "Come along, my laird." A sly smile dimpled one cheek. "You've put yourself in good hands."

With everyone in the great hall watching, he sincerely hoped so.

In the middle of the room, cleared of tables and benches, she positioned his arm around her waist, his hand at the center of her back. "Hold me firmly."

"I'm beginning to like this already."

"Pay attention!" she rapped.

He tried. He felt like a clumsy oaf. He glanced up from his disobedient feet to see that Annie had selected Jamie as a partner. His cousin was dancing with the grace of a born courtier. And Cyril the Salter had summoned his courage to select Enya's maidservant, the Lowland girl Mary Laurie.

So Highlander and Lowlander *could* mingle!

Soon his own feet seemed to gain a musical inclination. His body followed next. A slow smile eased his strained expression.

"Before you know it," she said, "you will be performing the Highland fling with the grace of a gamboling deer."

He drew her closer. "Me thinks that dancing was difficult because I had wee women for partners. All the while, what I was needing was a woman to match me size. An Amazon of a woman."

She eyed him quizzically. "You are more educated than you would allow."

"Ye are more of a woman than I had allowed."

At once he could see that his intended gallantry had hurt her feelings, but it was too late to make reparation. The tune had ended, and she left him standing alone in the cleared floor.

By God, had she gone and done it? Had she made him fall in love with her?

Nae. She was a mere Lowlander. She had not

the power of the Auld Folk.

Did she?

The man was lazy. Unreliable. Without ambition. Undependable.

Mhorag lifted her skirts and picked her way across the bailey's muddy yard. At least the snow had given way to drizzle. Spring couldn't be too far away, not with March only a fortnight off. Another two months and the sun would have melted away the snow.

Another two months and Ranald would be moving the reivers down from the winter camp of Lochaber. The idyllic months of peace would be past.

The peace in the castle bailey was presently disrupted by a steady thudding. So, the oaf was just now getting around to taking the cabinet hinge to be repaired. The double doors to the ironforger's shop were open. Heated air beckoned her enter. The smell of bare earth and rusty iron tickled her nostrils.

Battle axes and claymores and swords and steel-tipped arrows, all awaiting repair, lay in random piles, as well as domestic items like waffle irons and tea caddies and bed warmers. A pitchfork with a broken tine waited its turn for repair.

The heavyset ironmonger was not in sight. Instead, at the anvil Duncan, naked to the waist, wielded a hammer. A leather apron was tied over his faded breeches. The reflection of the forge's blaze danced across his torso. The flames' red light mingled with the red lash stripes that snaked around his rib cage.

Bemused, she stood in the doorway's shadows as he repaired the hinge. A swath of sweat-dampened, butter-yellow hair fell across his forehead. Sweat sheened his skin and ran down the channels where his tendons and ligaments and muscles came together, then separated with each lithe movement of his chest and arms. Until he had need to strain, to apply power and pressure, his slender build cunningly concealed its sinewy muscle.

The blast of heat sapped her energy. She pushed back her woolen jacket's lapels. Still, the heat entered her body. Ran through her veins like molten lead. Her heart seemed to pound in tempo with the thud of the hammer against the red-hot metal hinge. Inside, deep inside her belly, another throbbing began.

He lifted his forearm to swipe it across his sweaty forehead and stopped midway. His warm brown eyes locked with hers. Embarrassment flooded her. Surely he could not help but notice her awestruck countenance. He laid aside the hammer and hinge and wiped his soot-smudged hands on the leather apron. During this time, his gaze never wavered from hers.

When, at last, he ambled toward her, she was

able to collect her scattered wits. Too many more dangerous male adversaries she had faced to let this country bumpkin beguile her. "Ye tarry overly long. When I give an order I want it carried out at once."

"The ironmonger has taken ill. I—"

"I dinna want excuses."

Deliberately, he let his gaze move insolently from her frosty-blue eyes down past her sullenly set lips to her man's shirt. The sweat-dampened linen clung to one pouting nipple peaking around the fold of her jacket. "What do ye want, Mhorag? What do ye really want?"

Her hand crept up to the shirt's topmost button. Her tongue stole out to lick her heat-dry lips. "Nothing." Realizing the word had come out a barely audible whisper, she said it again, this time louder. "Nothing. Nothing from a man."

That easy smile displayed his crooked teeth. "Now while I was working, I was thinking all the while how I would like to fashion a girdle of mailed gold for ye. It would be of this thickness." He took her hand from where it lay between her breasts and measured off the first joint of her small finger.

"Half an inch?" she murmured.

"Aye. And this long." He slipped his hands beneath her jacket and spanned her tiny waist with his long, slender fingers.

She didn't move. Her breath had stalled in her

throat. Perspiration trickled between her breasts. Soaked her inner thighs. Her lips parted. Her breasts heaved. Had the forge's blaze consumed all the shop's air?

"I would set stones in the girdle," he went on. "Stones the color of your eyes. Aquamarine." He inclined his head closer. Too close. "No, turquoise is nearer the color."

Her lids fluttered shut. His lips kissed one lid, then the other. The kisses had been softer than a down feather. Light. Lingering. Was that her sigh?

His hands, encompassing her waist, drew her slowly against him so that they were aligned from knee to chest. "Me thoughts turned to how I would like the honor of buckling the girdle around your waist. The girdle only. Set off by your fair skin."

"Aye," she gasped. Weak with this inexplicable wanting, her hands clung to his shoulders for support.

"Aye what, Mhorag?"

"Take me. Oh, God, do it now before the fear—" Her hands tore at her shirt, popping loose one button, before his hands captured hers.

"No. Not that way. I must love ye so the fear canna ever come again to torment ye."

Unaccountably, tears flooded her eyes. "Oh, Duncan, 'tis such a dark, flame-breathing, air-sucking dragon, this fear of mine."

His fingers gentled her trembling lips. "Sssh. Dinna speak like that. 'Tis not *your* fear. Ye dinna own it. It dinna own you."

Her shallow, rapid breathing gradually slowed. She lowered her eyes. "I feel foolish."

"I'm the dunce. Duncan the dunce. Seeking above his station, I am. Falling in love with the bonniest of lasses."

She glanced up at him to see if he were making fun of her. "Bonny? Me?"

His brow knit. "Ye dinna ken?"

She shook her head.

"Aye, that and more, me love." His fingers drew close the gaping shirt. "Why, Mhorag, ye are the sweetest-tempered—"

"Ohh! Ye swine!" She pushed him from her and began cursing all the Gaelic oaths she had ever heard.

"Yer hinge," he said, grinning and backing away. "'Tis ready for yer cabinet door."

"Come back here!" she sputtered. "Did ye hear me, Duncan?"

He grabbed up the hinge and his shirt and started for the doorway.

Furious beyond words, she snatched up the pitchfork and hurled it at his departing back. She missed. The pitchfork struck the wooden door, stuck, vibrated, then thudded on the ground. "Ye—ye—oh, ye!"

* * *

As the weeks moved into March, life for Enya had fallen into an almost peaceful pattern of rising early to kindle the kitchen fires. After cooking and cleaning, the afternoons were hers to fritter away as she chose—usually embroidering with her mother or engaging in philosophical discussions with Arch, whom she was coming to know on different terms.

Jamie she avoided for fear of the retribution Ranald would visit upon his cousin.

Duncan she should have avoided.

Regrettably, she didn't that morning.

The day began with sunlight that was brilliant that high in the mountains. Just a few patches of snow skirted the outer bailey. Townspeople streamed under the castle's iron-grated portcullis to partake in the first Highland games of the new year.

These games, the Wappinschaw, provided the opportunity to mingle, to demonstrate a swain's prowess, and to dissipate the winter's accumulation of lethargy, tension, and restlessness.

The Wappinschaw consisted of foot races, dancing, shinty, bagpipe competitions, and tossing the *caber*. The *caber* was a long log that weighed as much as a hefty yew trunk. The kilted contestants vied to see who could heave it the straightest, so that it landed in a precise way determined by the judge.

In this case the villagers selected Jamie as rightful judge. Not only was he a Cameron, but he was not athletic by nature. Ranald would have abstained, but the other men prodded him, albeit respectfully, to compete. Every male wanted the honor of being the one to defeat the mighty chief.

Many of the women found diversion in folk dances. Their partners were the men who did not compete in the games. Enya watched the beginning of the games. Their early stages revealed that the reluctant Ranald would be an outright winner, especially in the tossing of the *caber.* His brawn, his prowess, had no match.

Rather than watch them fawn over their laird at that final moment of his triumph, she forsook the sidelines to observe the dancing. Wooden clogs clapping against the hard-packed earth marked the staccato rhythm of the morris dance. Bagpipes skirled and skirts swirled. Even old Dame Margaret, clapping her hands in time to the music, managed a smile.

As Mhorag's bondservant, Duncan did not dare approach the chief's sister for a dance. Instead, he danced with first one maid and then another.

Enya delighted in seeing her childhood friend enjoying himself. With Duncan, one laughed at life. The woman who took Duncan to husband would be a lucky one, she mused. He might not be a valiant warrior, a skilled huntsman, or a towering intellect. But he valued people. He would make a woman feel treasured.

When he sauntered over to her and bowed with all the elegance of a court dandy she couldn't help but laugh and dip a curtsy.

That silly grin curved his lips. His eyes glinted with merriment. "Dance, m'lady?"

Her eyes reflected her buoyant feelings. "Aye, m'lord."

The steps weren't that difficult to master. After every round partners were circulated, until the original partner was regained. Several rapid rounds were enough to leave a dancer breathless.

Her auburn hair tumbling loose from its crown, Enya sashayed away from her last partner, a portly man whose stomach shook in time with the music, and fell into Duncan's arms.

Laughter gurgled on her lips. "Ah, but that was a grand time, me lad!" Without thinking, she bussed him on the cheek.

She was feeling marvelous. The dancing, she reasoned, was a reminder that she could not have changed, no matter how much her situation had. Alas, duty called her back to the kitchen, along with Flora and Annie. A hungry mass would clamor to be fed come mealtime.

Bridie-cakes, lamb's sweetbreads, tatties, venison pasties, and steak and kidney pudding would tease the palate. Whiskey, ale, beer, and hot tea would quench the thirst.

When Enya went below to the oak-beamed buttery, as was her practice before helping with the cooking, the entryway candle was missing from its sconce. In the dark, she felt her way along the cold, damp stone walls. As if blind, she let her feet carefully pick out each step.

She almost gained the mid-landing and the next candle sconce. Then her footing slipped on a step sweating with a thin coating of moisture that had iced over. She plummeted. At the same time her hand flailed for the rickety banister. Splinters gouged her palms and fingers. Her feet dangled over the dark abyss.

Her grip was slipping. The banister rung wobbled. She screamed again. Slivers of wood slid beneath her nails. The image of the twisted heap of barrel staves and cooper's bands mounded below her renewed her screams.

Above her a shaft of light penetrated the cold gloom. Someone had opened the door! "Help!"

A figure leaned over the balustrade. Tangled, tawny hair draped around a tortured countenance. Just as quickly, the light receded and was eclipsed with the shutting of the door.

Paralyzing fear robbed her blood and robbed her of coherent thought. Her fall was surely an accident, but then why hadn't—

With a crack, the rung to which she clung tilted outward.

From somewhere she drew upon a last burst of

energy. With a tremendous gathering of strength, she released her hold on the one banister railing and lunged for the next. It quivered—but didn't break off.

She didn't have the muscle to lever herself up, but she could lower herself, rung by rung . . . if she could ration her remaining stamina.

Her hands were slippery with sweat and blood. With each passing second her skirts weighed more heavily. She swung to another rung. Clung. Swung again to the next. Clutched it—for one brief instant—slipped—and plunged into the chasm of darkness and pain and, finally, oblivion.

"Mmmnnnhh."

"M'bairn? Ye are mending?"

Enya turned her gaze toward the voice and looked at Elspeth. It was as if peering through gauze. She blinked. Her cloudy vision coalesced.

"Ye got a braw egg-size lump on yer head, ye do." The old woman slipped her gnarled hand under her charge's head and held a pewter cup to her lips. "Here, drink this, we'an. 'T'will rid ye of yer drouthy tongue."

She swallowed the viscous green liquid. "Aggh! That is awful."

"Dinna be *carnaptious,* me bairn. Ye are lucky to be alive."

"How long . . . have I been unconscious?"

"Two days. 'Twas the laird who went looking for ye and found ye. For the past few minutes ye been talking dowfie-like. Sad moanings. I ken then ye were comin' round. Sent for yer mother. She's been *glaikit* with worry."

Glancing around, Enya realized she was in Ranald's room. "Did he—Ranald—sleep . . . here with me?"

Elspeth's hooked nose wrinkled. "Had he wanted to, do ye think I would ha' let him? Nae, he slept on yon rug." She nodded at the bearskin stretched before the fireplace. "If ye call *ain* eye on ye sleepin'."

The door opened, and Kathryn entered. "Enya! You are awake!"

"It appears that you and I are taking turns convalescing, Mother."

Her mother dropped a testing kiss on her forehead. "No fever." She straightened. Relief was reflected in her velvet-brown eyes. "You have visitors outside. Do you feel like seeing them?"

She nodded and managed a smile. Even that effort hurt. "Aye. Send them in."

Before the afternoon was over a steady stream of well-wishers had paraded through Ranald's room: Duncan, Arch, Annie, Mary Laurie, Jamie, Flora, Patric, and even Dame Margaret.

But not Ranald. Nor Mhorag.

Enya was certain Mhorag was the woman who had looked over the balustrade and ignored her plea for help. Just as Ranald's sister doubtlessly ignored Ruthven's pleas for help. For all that, Mhorag could have been the instigator of Ruthven's horrifying death!

Kathryn returned in the evening, bearing a tray of food and more evil-tasting medicine. The bowl of steaming stew assuaged Enya's hunger but not her hurt. Not the hurt in her heart. Ranald had not wanted to lose his precious captive—and not because she had succeeded in making him love her.

The medicine, or the stew, made her sleepy, and she welcomed the respite. Sometime during the night she awoke. Ranald knelt on one knee at the hearth. He was replenishing the fire that had languished. He must have heard her raise to one elbow because he glanced up. The anger blazing in his eyes was like a physical slap, and she recoiled.

Suddenly she lost all her determination, her resilience, her strength of will. "I yield. I lost. I canna make you love me. I dinna understand it, but you hate me something fierce. I canna make that go away."

He rose, brushed off his hands, and crossed to the bed. For once he was giving her a second and more attentive look. He had never seen her passive. She fell back onto the pillow, waiting.

He reached down and picked up a lock of her hair, pooled over the pillow like the Red Sea of his Bible. "You dinna try to rid yourself of our bairn?"

"What?" She felt a wee groggy and wasn't certain she had understood.

"The fall. You weren't carrying me we'an in you? You weren't trying to rid yourself of it?"

"My God, Ranald!" Gone was that moment of weakness. She sprang upright to a sitting position. Her head swam with the sudden action. She rubbed her temples and muttered hotly, "Damn ye, Ranald. How could I be carrying your child when I feel so—so barren?"

He turned away, began tugging off his shirt. She thought to bring up Mhorag's pitiless act, but what was the use?

He shucked his breeches. In the soft candlelight, his body was beautiful. Supremely male. Muscle plated his chest, knotted his shoulder blades, laddered his stomach, and roped his thighs and calves.

"Do you think I hate you so verra much," she asked, "that I would risk killing myself?"

He stretched out on his side on the rug, pillowed his head in his arm, and tugged one side of the rug over his shoulders. "I think ye do not care what you do."

The broad back presented to her told her that, in turn, he did not care what she did.

Chapter Sixteen

It couldn't be possible!

Enya swallowed the putrid taste and went in search of her mother. She was nowhere inside the castle. Outside, the drift of warmer air from the south had come so slowly that Enya was surprised to realized that spring was indeed here. Its drizzling rains had brought a drizzling overcast, but the air was raw and refreshingly penetrating.

She found her mother crossing the bailey. "You shouldn't be out in this weather, Mother."

"I was looking over the ponies."

"Looking over the ponies?" She fell in alongside her mother in returning to the great hall. "Why?"

"Arch believes Ranald has set some of his lackeys to watch him."

She lowered her voice. "Mother, the passes won't be clear of snow yet."

"Another couple of weeks they may be. Kincairn won't be expecting us to flee this soon. And we're not going down through the passes. Arch is taking the best of the horses for all of us and driving the rest with us into the woods. We'll wait out the thawing deep in the forest."

Enya had her doubts whether Ranald would let them go so easily. Especially if what she feared was true. "Mother . . . I was sick this morning. I threw up the oatmeal I had for breakfast."

"You have missed your monthly?"

She felt miserable. "Aye. I thought maybe the fall from the stairs had upset my bodily routine. But I am almost two months late now."

Her mother eyed her critically. "Daughter, I do not know what goes on in the privacy of Ranald's chamber between you two. But he seems, basically, a fair man. Highly intelligent, if not highly educated."

"Mother, his only interest is using me as an instrument of revenge. I am so bloody disgusted with him and his messianic sense of mission."

"Is that all you feel about him?"

She searched her feelings and replied honestly, "I . . . I am attracted to him."

Her mother was carefully keeping her expression bland. And her tone. "I see. But you don't love him?"

"I don't know. How can I? One moment I hate him for using me so callously. The next, when he touches me . . ." She broke off, embarrassed.

She was overwhelmed by one feeling these days: apathy. She behaved with a sickening helplessness. Day after day. Gone was her *joie de vivre,* her independent spirit. She let Ranald's moods act as a catalyst for her own actions. She was responding and reacting, rather than being her own person.

She was sinking fast into bottomless depths of shame as Ranald's captive—more appropriately, Ranald's whore—a shame from which there could be no faintest hope she might ever escape.

Should she manage to escape Lochaber Castle and Ranald Kincairn, she suspected that she would nonetheless feel that shame the rest of her life.

"That's not enough hot water."

Duncan lowered the empty pail and stared across the width of the copper tub at the wild Highland lass swathed in a linen towel. "Ye try me patience, Mhorag."

Her lids lowered. "You are insolent. Do you want another beating?"

"I want ye."

"Ye'll never have me!"

His stance relaxed. He grinned. "Ye know ye want me, too, Mhorag."

Her free hand knotted into a fist. "Like I want the plague!"

"I'll plague ye 'til ye give yerself to me."

He started around the tub toward her and she sidestepped the other way.

"Do you dare dream?" she sneered, but he noted the tinge of fear in her voice.

He laughed. "I'd climb Scotland's highest mountain, Ben Nevis, for ye—or swim Loch Morar." With that, he stepped into the knee-high water and latched an arm around her waist before she could retreat. "Mhorag, me mermaid, I want only to love ye."

She went rigid. Her lips quivered. Her eyes dilated. "I can't!"

"Sure ye can." He lifted her over the tub's rim and pulled her against him. The ends of her towel trailed in the steaming water. His gaze ran over her upturned oval face; those eyes closed and their long lashes lay like black lace fans over her high cheekbones. "Ye are verra beautiful."

Her lids snapped open. Her eyes were blue stones. "I'm ugly inside!"

"No. Only hurtin' inside." He took the towel from the clutch of her cold fingers and let it slide into the bathwater. "Dinna ye know ye're made for love?"

She did not try to cover her nakedness. "I have done things that have hurt other people."

"Fear drives us to do things we wished we hadn't. That doesn't make us ugly inside. Ye are formed so perfectly. Small waist. Breasts me hands could cup. A bum that begs to be—"

"A bum?"

He chuckled. "This." His hands slid down over her bare buttocks.

She trembled, but a hint of a smile touched her bow-shaped lips. "Something is prodding my stomach."

"Ach, he wants to be let out."

"He?"

"Look for yeself."

She eyed him doubtfully, and he said, "He willna hurt ye." His callused fingers played lazily with a nipple that hardened quickly. "He's quite tame. Just a wee insistent about making known his wants."

A flush the color of summer's wild roses tinted her cheeks. Her breathing was shallow and rapid. Her fingers drifted down to the fly of his breeches. She smiled shyly. "Mayhaps I'll make his acquaintance."

This time he was the one to close his eyes as she went on her knees in the water. "Take yer time. I want ye two to become intimate friends."

The onions Enya chopped for the pea soup not only made her teary-eyed but were making her nauseated. Gone was her sweet tooth. Not even black currant cake hot from the oven tempted her.

In a way, she reflected, the Lowlanders were all captives. She was Ranald's captive, Duncan was captivated by Mhorag, Mary Laurie's captor was a salter, even debonair Jamie had been taken by the country lass Annie Dubh.

Wiping away a tear with the back of her hand, she forced herself to think about another captive of sorts. Her mother had been Malcolm's captive. Then she had been forced to become his bride. Afterward, that descendant of wild Pictish princesses had become a captive of culture, doing what her head told her rather than her heart. Kathryn's love child by Arch had, also, become a captive of culture.

And her own love child?

She placed her hand on the flat of stomach, almost concave. Yet she knew life stirred there.

As for culture, was not Ranald's as impressive as her own? Gaelic was Europe's oldest vernacular literature, its manuscript illumination the finest flower of art, its harp music Europe's most advanced.

She could not meet Ranald's discerning gaze when she served him and his men that evening, for fear he might see her nervousness.

He barely glanced at her. He and Jamie and Ian were deep in discussion. "I rode down to

Corrieyarick Pass," Jamie was saying. "The snow there canna be more than a horse's wither high."

"But it could get deeper farther through the pass," Ian said.

"It could melt, also," Ranald said, and tore off a hunk of the hot, sweet bread and the hard and pungent goat cheese from the platter she set before him. "Murdock's regiments could be upon Lochaber before we know it."

Though she would have liked to linger, to hear more, she felt it best to move on so she would not arouse his suspicion. Besides, while Ranald and his men supped she had her own agenda, one which he was too preoccupied to take note.

Minutes later, she slipped into her mother's room. Arch stood behind her mother, who sat in a rocking chair with a woolen plaid thrown across her legs. Elspeth sat on a stool, and Mary Laurie leaned against one of the bed's four posters. Duncan perched a hip on the window seat. One booted ankle was crossed at his knee.

"A cache of supplies await us in the forest," Arch said without preamble. "The mounts will be saddled at the third hour two days hence."

"Already Ranald is discussing leaving Lochaber," Enya said.

"That settles it," he said. "We ride out just before dawn. Duncan and I shall divert the portcullis guard until everyone is safely on their way."

Kathryn leaned forward and addressed Enya. "Will there be any problem in escaping Ranald in the early-morning hours?"

Heat flushed her cheeks. "If he summons me to his chambers, I usually leave for the kitchens just before he rises at dawn."

Her mother nodded. "Then our plan remains as is. Who goes with us—and who stays? Duncan?"

He fingered the worn heel of his boot, then glanced up. "'Tis no secret I'm taken with Mhorag. But she'll never come away with a mere fisherman." He grinned unabashedly. "A smuggler at heart—and a Lowlander at that."

"Elspeth?" Kathryn asked.

That network of wrinkles webbing the old woman's face thickened. "Me soul is in the Lowlands. I go with Enya and ye."

"Mary Laurie?"

The plump maidservant focused an inordinate amount of attention on her folded hands. "I am loyal to the Clan Afton. Ye know that. But me heart is with Cyril the Salter. I willna be going with ye, but neither will I betray ye."

Kathryn nodded. "You two have my blessing. We'd best go our separate ways now."

"Until the third hour then," Arch said. "For now, go with God."

Enya felt as if she needed God and much more

to protect her, not from Ranald but from her own feelings.

Like a condemned prisoner, she walked the parameters of her quarters. Her stomach churned and knotted. At times she would rush to the window, throw open the shutters, and inhale the cold raw air until her nausea passed.

Her sorrow would not depart as easily. She had come to love the man. There was no denying he was respected by men, women, and children alike. And desired by any number of pretty young females.

So why would he love her? A woman whom most would not call beautiful or even pretty by any standard. A woman whom he associated with his greatest pain.

The mantle clock softly chimed the hour of midnight. She was so utterly exhausted these days. She paused before the mottled mirror. Her lips twisted in a grimace. With the mauve shadows that ringed her eyes she looked like a raccoon.

In the reflection of the mirror she saw the door open. Ranald appeared like her worst nightmare. "Not tonight," she told his reflection.

Those wondrously colored eyes scanned her face. "Ye are ill?"

"No." She rubbed her hands together, then thrust them behind her back. "Just tired."

He shut the door behind him and strode on

into her room to sprawl in its single chair.

"You look tired," she said, then regretted her outburst. It betrayed her concern. He had not shaven that day, and in the mirror the lines fanning either side of his eyes appeared more pronounced.

"Don't be thinking of leaving."

She whirled to face him. Her heart beat like a hummingbird's. "You know?"

He grimaced. "All of you vanished at the same time this evening. I may not be an Edinburgh engineer, but I can bloody well figure out something is afoot."

She sagged, slumped to the bed, and was barely able to remain in a sitting position. She braced a steadying hand on the mattress. Her head drooped. "Now what? What more can you do to me short of murdering me?" Slowly her gaze raised to meet his. She whispered, "Or is that, too, an alternative?"

He rubbed the bridge of his nose. "We ride out of here on the morrow. All of us. Except for Thane. He has a better chance of surviving if I leave him here. I shall miss him."

"You worry more for an animal than you do for me and my family and servants. You are a brute."

"I know. Ye have told me so often enough." He rose to his towering height. "The others have already been confined to their rooms. They will be released—unharmed—once we reach Loch Leven."

Her eyes widened. "I, also?"

"Aye."

His simple reply stung her pride, quenched her secret hope. "Why?"

"You will slow us down."

Somehow this was worse, this indifference. She almost welcomed his resentment if she couldn't have his love. "I see."

He strode to her door. "We ride out after breakfast. Be ready."

She didn't even go to bed that night. Like a sleepwalker she attended to her kitchen duties that morning. Flora and Annie looked as down at the mouth as she felt. The rank odor of frying bacon turned Enya's stomach. Even the porridge looked unappetizing. With enormous will she finished the last of her scullery tasks.

In the great room, the reivers' arms were loaded with assorted baggage, weapons, and gear. Like a stream of ants, they scurried out to the bailey and back.

She spotted Duncan and crossed to him. He toted a trunk, hers. Apparently, while she had been working, her belongings had been packed.

Duncan's mouth quirked in a lopsided smile. "Looks like our Grand Tour of the Highlands is over."

She put a hand on his arm. "You don't have

to go with us, Duncan," she whispered. "Stay."

"As I said, Mhorag wouldn't have me."

"How do you know? Have you asked her?"

His smile faded. "Aye. Half an hour ago. She said she liked having me in her bed, but that she could find plenty of men willing to warm her sheets."

Enya ached for her friend. She knew exactly how he felt. "I think the Cameron clan has separated the chaff from the wheat, and you and I are definitely in the former category."

"Milady?"

She turned. Jamie held out her fur-lined cloak for her. His gave her an encouraging smile. "Ranald is waiting for you."

Childishly, peevishly, she wanted to snap, "Let him wait!" She didn't. With a "Thank you, Jamie," she accepted the cloak he draped around her shoulders.

She didn't draw the hood. Partly because the day promised sunshine, and partly to flaunt her red hair. No mob cap covered it. Instead, she left it tumbling loose about her shoulders and down her back.

The bailey was filled with horses and riders, their breaths commingling to frost the morning air. The jingle of spur and surcingle and the creak of leather vied with the shouts and grumbling and yawning of the would-be sojourners. The village lasses who had worked for the reivers bade the men farewell with kisses and tears.

Enya hugged Mary Laurie and kissed her ruddy cheek. "You will make a lovely Highland bride."

This time the priggish lass didn't blush. "Me and Cyril will make good bairns."

"The best of the Lowlands and the Highlands," Enya predicted. The hope of Scotland lay in people like Cyril and Mary Laurie, who were willing to ignore regional differences.

Even crusty old Flora wept when Enya put her arms around her, but Annie was nowhere to be seen.

Enya noted that the fierce-looking Cameron chief was already astride his great horse. Next to Ranald, Mhorag sat in her saddle with the ease of a Cossack.

Mounted behind them and encompassed by riders armed with pistols and muskets, were her mother, Duncan, and Arch. One-eyed Robert was helping Elspeth into the saddle of a pony that had to be as old as she, and much more docile.

Enya approached the saddled Shetland waiting beside Ranald's mammoth horse, which danced in nervous impatience. With smug satisfaction she observed that Ranald took note of her unbound hair. She expected a reprimand for her rebellious act. She was disappointed when he switched his attention to one of his reivers, who had approached him for consultation.

She would have mounted her pony on her own, but Jamie appeared suddenly to assist her. Then he assisted Ian in mounting before doing so himself. Gradually the riders fell into a two-line formation, and Ranald gave the signal to move out.

The villagers gathered along the high road out of Lochaber to wave good-bye and cheer on the warriors. Ranald nodded solemnly at the shouts of encouragement. A girl of no more than five or six darted forward to press a sprig of holly into his hand.

Then, near the auld brig, Enya saw Annie standing, waiting. Her sloe eyes glistened with unshed tears. Enya glanced behind at Jamie. He, too, had seen the lone Lochaber lass. Would he leave her without saying a farewell?

As the horses' hooves clattered across the wooden bridge, Jamie leaned from the saddle and swept the buxom maiden into his saddle with all the gallantry of the knights of old. A round of cheers went up from the reivers.

"Well done, Jamie!" Ranald said.

Once the party was clear of town, she asked him, "What if the pass down is still snow-bound?"

"We're not going down."

"We're going by way of the Hidden Valley Trail?"

"Only partway. Then we go over. Over Buachaille Etive."

She shivered. She turned her face to the hazy sun, as if to absorb its warmth for storage against the arctic trek the party was preparing to make.

All that morning the double line traversed the same narrow path, the Hidden Valley Trail, by which Enya had arrived in Lochaber.

Bit by bit the conifer woods ceded the right of way to granite. Patches of snow began to glisten along the roadside. As the afternoon wore on, the snow mounded into curbs. Branches drooped with the weight of snow that thickly carpeted the ground beneath them. By late afternoon the cloud-streaked sun had disappeared behind the higher peaks. Fog settled lower. Moisture glistened on the path like a slick mirror.

A red squirrel darted in front of one of the horses, pot-bellied Macdonald's. His mount shied. Rearing, it danced precariously near the path's edge. Snow and dirt and stone crumbled beneath its hooves. With a valiant effort, Macdonald leaned forward in the saddle and goaded the horse to scramble to safety.

"Then 'tis over Buachaille Etive we go, after all?" Jamie asked.

"That means we won't be coming out at Loch Leven," Ian said.

Ranald fixed him with a gauging glance. "Is it important?"

The deep-set eyes beneath the grizzled brows looked troubled. "I thought we would be using the sloop for escape."

He shrugged. "If 'tis convenient, we shall. I'll worry about that after we get there."

"Relying on travel-weary mounts for escape could be hazardous," Ian said.

"Could be. So could a lot of things." As if dismissing any further consideration of the possibility, he nudged his mount into a trot and called over his shoulder, "We leave the road at Glen Corries."

At Glen Corries wilderness enveloped the party abruptly. Grouse exploded from the snow-crusted heather, startling Enya. Enormous red deer streaked between the white-shrouded pines and firs. A rising wind whistled through the branches. She felt a growing sense of oppression, a surfeit of desolation, a savage monotony. She huddled deeper in the folds of her cloak and blessed the heat rising off her plodding pony.

On and on the group traveled. Enya could never remember being so weary. When only eerie light floated amid the trees Ranald called for camp that night. The mounts were staked. A warming fire was built. Its orange tongues spit and crackled and drove back the demons of the dark.

Hunks of bread, cheese, and cold mutton were

distributed to Enya and the other silent travelers. Each knew the rigor that awaited on the morrow, when the more arduous part of the climb over the top would begin.

For her part, her toes and fingers and nose felt frostbitten. She wondered if she would ever know the sunlight of the Lowlands again.

Ranald moved among his men. An exchange here, a nod there.

Enya was reluctant to leave the reassurance of the fire and her mother, Duncan, and the other Lowlanders who found this land as hostile as she.

Duncan's lovelorn gaze was riveted on Mhorag. Apparently, she was determined to distance herself from him and had elected to sit among the reivers.

Too soon, Ranald returned to the circle of firelight. His hand touched her shoulder. "We turn in now." That one gesture told everyone she was still his property.

Arch made a movement, as if preparing to defend her, but he sank back down at her mother's touch at his forearm, calming yet restraining.

Enya wanted to respond that she wasn't ready, but, in truth, she welcomed the warmth of his massive body. Only a man built as he was could offer the kind of nurturing protection her own tall, solid body sought. She would sorely miss the security the big man's embrace and those powerful arms offered.

She stood up beside him. Enfolding her in the sheltering folds of his great cape, he drew her apart from the others to a bed of leaves and dirt he must have mounded himself when he was making his rounds.

Sinking into the bower, she tried to make light of her melancholy. "Did one of your trowies build our bed, my laird?"

He lay down alongside her and gathered her against his length, spoon fashion. His lips against her ear, he said, "Dinna jest about the wee folk. Like the monster of Loch Ness, they teach us to believe in something we canna see. You understand me?"

The wind howled. It tore at the travelers' clothing. Enya pulled her tartan scarf up over her nose and mouth. Worried for her mother, she glanced back. Kathryn was riding pillion with Arch, who was taking the brunt of the blizzard.

When the wind abated it left in its wake an intense cold that felt to Enya as if it were freezing her flesh to her bones. The very rocks seemed to groan. Limbs snapped. Bare branches scraped icy fingers against these intruders of Buachaille Etive's jagged summit. Then even the trees seemed to give up their precarious hold on the granite, brooding massif.

Now only the huge hump of rock, white-coated, opposed the travelers' descent to the other side. Her horse's hooves slipped and slid on the murderous rock. She noticed that the other mounts were blowing wind puffs up and down their forelegs.

Again the wind arose to hound the travelers. The blizzard drove sand and sleet and snow with stinging force. Despite Enya's gloves, her fingers would temporarily freeze in their clutched positions on the reins, and she would have to flex her hands to restore the circulation. She couldn't feel any sensation at all in her feet.

Ranald stood up in the stirrups and had to shout a halt to make himself understood above the wind's roar. When they paused in the lee of a rock wall she half fell into his arms. Her own and her legs were stiff and cramped from the agonizing cold. He peeled away the icy-wet tartan that covered her nose and mouth. " 'Tis doing more harm than good now."

He held her against him and chafed her arms and back and shoulders. For all too brief a moment it was a heavenly respite. Then he restored her to her saddle and called out for the march to resume. After that he called halts at one-hour intervals, with five-minute rests.

Seventeen hours passed in this way, with a little less than twenty kilometers transversed. Night came, yet the caravan continued its trek.

Toward dawn, Enya's pony was dying of exhaustion. She turned her back while Ranald disposed of the animal. Mercifully, the wind's shriek was loud enough that she just barely heard his pistol's retort.

Now, she, too, rode pillion, her arms wrapped around the steely strength of his body. By the time a gray dawn filtered through the denuded limbs of wind-twisted trees, the storm had blown past. Still, the air was bitter cold. Her lips were actually bleeding, and her face and hands were chapped and raw.

When Ranald called the first halt in the light of day she saw that the rest of the party had fared no better. It was a scraggly, weather-beaten bunch that had not the slightest semblance to the legendary Ranald's Reivers.

A serene loch, reedy around the edges, its surface frosted with mist, was the first indication to Enya that the worst of the weather was behind them. The horses cropped at the thin grass poking through soggy dunes, as she and the other riders, dazed, nibbled on the stores of food in their saddles and talked quietly among themselves, as if in awe that they had survived.

Duncan and Arch appeared to be tending the weary mount that had transported both the priest and her mother. Enya went to see about her mother and Elspeth, the frailest of the travelers. Both women looked like mummies but had proven themselves hardy. "Take more 'n a blizzard to do me in," Elspeth said.

Kathryn was comforting Annie, who trembled uncontrollably. "The journey will soon be over, lass."

"Give her whiskey," Mhorag suggested. "If it doesn't kill her, then the kirk's punishment will."

Enya almost smiled, but the movement of her cracked lips hurt too much. She sagged down atop a marshy knoll. She tried to remove one riding boot, but her hands wouldn't cooperate.

"Here, let me," Ranald said, coming to kneel before her and brush away her fumbling fingers. First one boot, then the other, then he peeled away her wet merino stockings. He cradled her foot in his large, callused hands and briskly massaged her blue-tinged flesh. "Knox should be showing sail sometime today."

She stared down at the indomitable, unyielding, and taciturn countenance. Could she believe in something she could not see?

Then, when she raised her gaze, what she did see shot horror through her heart.

Chapter Seventeen

The regiment commander astride the white stallion, Simon Murdock, knew the fifty-odd riders in Ranald's Reivers' party did not stand a chance against the surprise attack by the British patrol. Although only thirty-two strong, his own redcoated force crested the low-lying hills and rode down upon the dismounted, weather-whipped party.

At the burst of musket fire dozens of the frightened Highlanders plunged into the water. Those stragglers at the back of the group bounded onto their horses and fled back up the trail.

Their escape went hardly noticed. For one, the wind was so strong, Murdock's Lobsterbacks were blinded by their own gunsmoke. For another, his British patrol was drawn from the dregs of society and cared not a whit for military tactics.

Then, too, he, himself, had his sights on only one man in particular. The tall, brawny man could be no other than the legendary Ranald. The red-haired wench with him had to be the Lady Enya.

Just as Ian Cameron's message had warned—the reivers were headed for Loch Leven. Only earlier than spring thaw, as the message had indicated.

With just such a precaution in mind, Simon Murdock had forsaken the warmth of his office to ride patrol in the Loch Leven area. He dug his spurs into the flanks of his prized horse, gouging flesh. He wanted to be the first to reach the pair, to take Lady Enya from the reiver before he killed him.

Only then would he turn his attention to the Lowland lass, his tainted bride.

Ranald shoved Enya behind the nearest dune, a bracken-crested hill that afforded little concealment. He thrust a flintlock pistol into her hands. "Load it!"

Without pausing to think, she did as she was told. She was helping her sworn enemy—the love and passion of her life.

While he rammed grapeshot into his musket barrel and then fired, she jammed ammunition into his flintlock pistol. He exchanged the empty musket for the loaded flintlock and raised the sight to his eye to fire again. A redcoated rider somersaulted from his saddle.

Alternately, she continued to load the pistol and the musket. At the same time she darted anxious glances around, trying to locate her loved ones.

At another sand dune, Arch caught a pistol and ammunition pouch tossed by Patric. Kathryn and Elspeth crouched behind Arch and the young reiver. Concealed by another sand dune were Ian and Jamie, who had taken Annie under his wing.

Duncan? Her heart lurched.

Her gaze sped across the dunescape, past the sight of white sails, and encountered Mhorag. Ranald's sister stood upright to fire upon a Lobsterback riding full tilt toward her.

The musket misfired. The redcoated rider flung himself atop the breeches-clad woman. The pair tumbled, wrestled, grappled for supremacy. Sand spewed, making difficult the distinction between the two.

Then Enya spotted Duncan. He sprinted toward Mhorag and her assailant. He wrested the man from her and began pummeling him with his fists. As if dazed or blinded by the sand, Mhorag stumbled backwards.

Enya saw another mounted soldier charge

toward Mhorag. Saber drawn, the rider hurtled toward the woman who had made Enya's life such a misery at Lochaber Castle. Ranald's sister despised Enya and would have killed her had she had the courage. Now, within the space of seconds, Mhorag would join her parents and her infant son.

At that same moment, from the corner of her eye, Enya sighted a British officer galloping on a white stallion toward herself. "Lady Enya!" he called.

Ranald appeared distracted by a burst of musket fire off to his left. Escape was hers! Not an instant was left to spare.

Yet, instead of fleeing to the safety of the officer's outstretched arm, she raised the pistol she had just loaded and fired at Mhorag's attacker. With an ear-deafening retort the saber-wielding Redcoat was hurled backward.

In the next moment Enya whirled back to see Ian limp from the cover of the dune. He waved his arms to get the officer's attention. "Murdock! 'Tis Cameron. Ian Cameron."

The officer did not swerve his steed from the path of the Highlander. In horror, Enya watched the great animal trample Ian. The man bounced and rolled like a rag doll. With a soul-piercing shout, Jamie dashed toward his father and gathered the broken body in his arms.

The officer's frothing white horse stumbled

and broke stride. The man lost his balance and was pitched from his saddle, his highly polished Hessian boot catching in the stirrup. The frightened horse regained its footing and shot forward. It dragged the officer, as it would a plow, across the bracken and sand and rock.

At that, the remainder of the patrol reined in on their mounts and turned tail. Musket in hand, Ranald sprinted toward the loch's shoreline, where the white stallion had come to a panting halt. Its reins dangled in the foaming water.

She ran behind Ranald, caught up with him just as he knelt over Simon Murdock. His face was unrecognizable—a mass of torn flesh where lips and nose and eyes had once been. She felt like gagging.

Ranald reached into the vest pocket and withdrew a leather pouch. He balanced it in his palm, as if weighing it value.

"What is it? Is it important?"

His fingers closed over the pouch. A muscle in his jaw twitched. "I watched him take a knife to my brother's testicles and, holding aloft the skin, claim what a grand tobacco pouch it would make."

She shuddered, put her hand to her mouth. "No. No one can be that—"

"At that moment," he continued dispassionately, "I knew I would find a way to kill

Murdock. One day, some way, I would slay the monster."

"You didn't have to," she murmured. "His stallion did it for you."

Enya was heart-weary. Yesterday she had killed. How self-righteous she had been; how unfairly judgmental of Ranald, when she did not know the circumstances behind what had seemed brutal behavior. Once more she was in the ship's cabin. Once more her captor talked to her. Only this time she could see his face.

Ranald sat on the edge of the bunk. She stood. Waited to hear why he had summoned her. She had never seen him looking so tired. Elbow braced on one knee, he rubbed the bridge of his nose, a habit that was becoming dearly familiar to her.

"With Murdock dead . . . your rescue of Mhorag . . . there is no longer any need to hold you captive. The ship lies only fifteen knots off Ayrshire. By tomorrow ye and your companions will be returned to your home."

"You are . . . setting me free?"

He raised his head and gave her a dry grin that barely touched the pleats at either corner of his mouth. "Aye, the monster has recognized the insensitive brute for what he is."

Enya blinked back tears. *I have gone too far. It is I who have slain the wild beast. I have civilized him to the point he now no longer needs me.* Her hands ached to reach out, to smooth his disheveled hair where it fell across his forehead.

Instead, she clasped them before her in a semblance of perfect composure. "Where do you go from here?" Good. Her voice did not sound choked with the tears her heart were crying. In fact, she sounded quite composed. "Now, with Murdock dead, there will be no place safe for you. The Duke of Cumberland will not give up until you and your reivers are dead. Oh, don't you see, you can't continue to kill until the last British soldier is killed?"

Those incredibly wide shoulders seemed to sag. "I canna go on living under a government hostile to Highland ways."

"Then God speed," she whispered, and retreated from the cabin.

The Gulf's warm current blessed the morning with a clear, sunny day. Elspeth's hooked nose sniffled, as if she were suspiciously close to tears. "Good-bye and God bless," she told Ranald. The old woman had taken a liking to the Cameron chief, after all.

Enya couldn't look at him. Her averted gaze locked with that of Mhorag. The young woman held out Enya's tortoiseshell comb. "The comb couldn't make a woman of me. Ye did."

Enya took the comb and would have hugged

the young woman, but her eyes, glinting suspiciously with tears, warned her not to make the good-bye more difficult. "The lucky man who takes you to wife, Mhorag, will be getting all woman."

She turned quickly and descended the rope ladder to the waiting dinghy. Next to Jamie snuggled a beaming Annie. On the bench behind them a lone Duncan sat at the long oars. In another dinghy were her mother, Arch, and Elspeth.

"'Tis been a grand adventure," Duncan said, his gaze locked on Mhorag, who stood at the ship's railing, her expression grim and unyielding.

"Aye," Enya said, then added, "The Camerons, they be a proud clan."

"Too bloody proud," he said, not bothering to hide the heartache in his voice.

Despite Annie at his side, Jamie's own heartache was visible to see. He paused in rowing to glance back at the ship. The look in his eyes was bleak. With his father's death, some of the dash had gone out of the young man.

"My father's last words were not of his love for me but of his hatred for his nephew," he muttered. "Because of his hatred for Ranald, my father betrayed our clan. He was not the man I thought."

"I understand your father was once a remarkable leader," she said gently. "His infirmity must have eaten away at his heart and brain."

"Ye are certain this is what you want to do?" Duncan asked him. "To return to Edinburgh?"

"I go with Ranald's blessing. Resistance didn't gain us peace. Mayhaps cooperation will rescue for posterity our Scottish culture. Edinburgh is no longer a provincial backwater. Enough determined Scotsmen could make it an intellectual hub of Europe."

Peace was not waiting for Enya or her mother. Alistair met them at the door with joy at their return and grief weighing his tidings. "M'lord has passed away, Lady Kathryn."

Kathryn's composure shattered. Weeping wildly, she collapsed into Arch's arms. He hugged her and stroked her back. "Malcolm is released at last from his own captivity. Take solace in this, my love."

Since Enya had not expected to see her father alive again the news of his death was not such a blow. Though she was saddened, the life burdgeoning within her overrode her grief.

For more than a month the ever-present sickness plagued Enya. Then, just as quickly it passed, and she felt her swelling body to be life-giving. Renewed, even as spring renewed the earth.

Spring might have been evident in the flowering of the rhodendron and snapdragon and in the chorus of meadowlarks and robins, but she found no delight in the season for which she had once so longed.

Arch vanished, as was his wont. A man of missions, a man of mystery.

Duncan, too, took his leave, to return to the sea, whether it was to fish or smuggle he would never say. Only, "Things willna be the same in Ayrshire. The excitement is gone."

In those days of mourning, Elspeth and Alistair ran Afton House with quiet but brisk efficiency. Jamie and Annie stayed on, a comfort to both her mother and Enya. Indeed, his and Annie's comforting extended to Enya beyond the bounds of mere friendship.

He told her as the three of them sat one afternoon sunning on the terrace, "I know that you are with child, Enya."

Her head snapped in his direction. He sat on a low red brick wall that enclosed the terrace. "How do you know that?" Her hand, holding one of the rhodendron blooms, fluttered to her stomach. True, it was now nicely rounded, but she hadn't thought that condition was noticeable in the smocks and fuller gowns she had been wearing.

She glanced at Annie. Basking in the light of Jamie's love, she bloomed like spring's flowers. "You told him, Annie?"

"Nae, mistress." She smoothed the ruffles on

the sprigged muslin gown Kathryn had ordered refitted for her. "I didna ken. Mhorag did."

"Mhorag voiced her suspicion to me the morning we left ship," Jamie said. "She said that although she might not be able to bear children any longer, she knows when a woman is with child."

"I see." The young Highland woman must certainly suffer mixed feelings.

"Enya?"

She refocused on Jamie. He rubbed his palm, as if it were stained. "Aye?"

When he didn't speak Annie said, "The bairn will be needing a father. Jamie and me talked. We want you to know that he would be more than glad to stand in for the bairn's father."

She said carefully, gently, "I am touched more than you both realize by your offer. But Jamie's destiny is not mere fatherhood. 'Tis fatherhood of a dying nation. Scotland calls for your attention, Jamie."

Now he looked at her. "You are like your mother. A truly grand lady."

If her mother mourned the loss of Arch as well as her husband, she never expressed it. Gowned in black, she presided once more at the brilliant salons that had always been a hallmark of her rule of the Afton clan. However, her keen interest in the fashionable assemblage of notables was visibly lacking.

Jamie filled in the gaps in conversation admirably. "A school in every parish has become a reality in Lowland Scotland," he told their dinner companions one balmy May evening. "We must encourage our people to do the same for the Highlands."

"There has to be a social and intellectual balance in Scotland," said David Hume, a well-known philosopher and historian.

He spoke a Scots more broad than Ranald's, and Enya experienced such a painful yearning that she barely managed to keep a polite smile and mumble intelligible responses the remainder of the dinner.

None of the dinner guests made mention of her advanced condition. Had they dared, Annie would have been at their throats. With her blend of bawdiness and naiveté, she charmed these sophisticates.

Which was just as well. When the men adjourned to the Chinese Room for cigars and brandy Enya pleaded indigestion and escaped to her bedroom.

Sleep that night did not come easily, and when finally she succumbed it was to restive dreams of her months as a captive . . . dreams that too quickly became a reality once more.

The shadow-draped apparition leaning over her bed clamped a hand over her mouth. A handkerchief muffled her scream. Next, the blanket smothering her, enveloping her, brought her harshly awake.

Dreams didn't feel like this.

Trundled like Cleopatra in a rug, she kicked and tried to scream, but her flailing legs were ineffective against the strength of her captor, and her screams were only snorting noises.

She knew she was being taken down the stairs and out of the house by way of the terrace and the garden. The blanket's wool was rough against her bare legs. Her abductor loped easily with her over his shoulder. Bundled though she was, she could still perceive the direction her captor was taking—the cobblestone road that linked Afton House with Ayrshire.

Too soon, though, her abductor deserted the bumpy road for an incline of some kind. Then she heard the slap of breakers against shore. Next, she was dumped in what could only be a dinghy, if judged by its pitching. Just when she could feel dampness seeping through the blanket, she was transferred again. This time up, up, in a swaying fashion that harmonized with the wash of waves against something solid.

At last she was released and tossed onto something padded. The creak of timbers, the gentle rocking, told her she was aboard a boat of sorts.

When nothing further happened she struggled out of the blanket. Dazed, she stared around her. She was on the *Pelican* again. In Ranald's cabin again.

Encased in a jute sack, Duncan thrashed and pummeled his abductor. A resulting "Unnh" of pain gave him some satisfaction, but not liberation. To be impressed by the damned British Navy was one thing, but to be waylaid by a common brigand while he sat drinking fine Scots whiskey in his trawler was quite another.

If he had been a wee more clear in his head, he might have been able to determine where this seafaring highwayman was taking him. As it was, the floor came up beneath him with a solid thud.

"Damme, but if ye ain't picked a poor gent to hold hostage!" he sputtered, getting hairlike jute strands in his mouth.

He thought he heard a female say, "Ye can leave now, Patric—Colin."

He wriggled free of the blanket. On hands and knees, he was disoriented, and the lantern light momentarily blinded him. When he was able to focus he looked from the plank flooring upward.

Arms folded, a grinning Mhorag stood over him. "Me boots need polishing."

He fought against the sway of the ship to get his balance and stand upright. "Is that so? Well, ye just canna command me whenever ye feel like it, Mhorag! I've had enough of yer high-handed—"

"And me heart needs loving."

Now it was his turn to grin, that silly grin that revealed his crooked teeth and merry disposition. "Is that so?"

Panic swept over Kathryn. Her abductor had flung her over his shoulder, and her chest bumped painfully against his back with each rapid stride he took. Wrapped as she was in the blanket, breathing was next to impossible.

She didn't fear death, but she did fear torture. Her clansmen had always admired the wisdom and justice she dispensed as their ruler, but they knew nothing of her cowardice. As long as she was in control . . . Now, she wasn't.

Was she being abducted for reward, for retribution of some kind, or—for ravishment?

Ravishment. Strange, the word should mean both to take away by violence and to overcome with pleasure. She had never known real pleasure at the hands of her husband. And now never would.

Her lungs collapsed like bellows for want of air, and her rib cage hurt from the jostling. She grew dizzy, lost track of time and what was happening. It seemed to her that she was being carried aboard a ship.

Just as she felt as though she might faint, she was laid down. The blanket was peeled back from her face. She stared up into the dark, passionate eyes of Arch. "Dear, dear Arch. Did I give you permission to—"

He brushed the hair back from her face with tender hands. "You've always been in charge, my love. For the duration of our voyage I ask that you give over to me. If at its end you still wish to return to Afton and Ayrshire, then I will escort you back."

"Back?" she asked stupidly. "For where is this ship bound?"

"For the American colonies, the colony of North Carolina. I have taken out a grant of land on the upper Cape Fear River, near a village called Campbelltown. Governor Johnston has given asylum there to many of the Scottish chiefs."

Everything was spinning. Pleasantly spinning. Especially when she felt Arch's lips at her temple. He was stretched out beside her, pleasuring her love-starved body with his stroking hands. "What about Ayrshire? The Clan Afton?"

"Jamie has agreed to preside over matters there until you make up your mind."

She felt his hand follow the curve of her hip,

cup it, and rest there. "Make up my mind about what?"

"Whether you will marry me."

She put her arms around his neck. "Did you ever doubt my answer?" she murmured between kisses.

"It means leaving Scotland. Forever."

"My home is not in Scotland. 'Tis in your arms. 'Tis always been in your arms since that day in the stables, Arch, when I was but fifteen and you made me yours."

After all those years, more than twenty, he made her his again.

Enya tried the door. This time it gave. The companionway was dark. She found her way to its stairs. At the railing stood a moon-drenched apparition. She must have made a noise, because Ranald turned. That rough-hewn yet handsome face was as dispassionate as ever. She had never known what he was thinking. Or feeling.

He did not move to touch her, so she crossed to stand beside him. Staring out at the star-lit sea, she asked softly, "You've made me your captive again. Why?"

"Mhorag told me you carried our child. That I was a fool if I let you go. That you were one of a kind. The kind of woman I need."

"And that is why you came after me?"

"No." He looked down at her now. She saw the

anguish in his eyes. "You don't know why?"

She flung her arms around his neck. "Aye. I know. That you have to believe in what you canna see. Like the trowies and the monsters of the deep. Like love."

Chapter One

"Strip him! Strip him naked! Let's have a look at what we're bidding on!"

The strident female voice rose on the sweltering air, stirring a ripple of movement in the sullen, sweating crowd. All glanced in the woman's direction. Then, with a collective sigh, the people turned back to the huge, raised platform in the city square.

"She's right," another female cried. "These males come too highly priced as it is. He's pretty enough but we're not buying his looks. We're buying his breeding abilities. Strip him, I say!"

The auctioneer, a huge, hairy bear of a fellow, grumbled and mumbled to himself as he strode over to the bare-chested blond man pinned between two guards. "Damn them," he growled. "I'm a busy man and haven't the time to display each slave that passes through here."

He halted before the prisoner. Hard, dark brown eyes slammed into his. The auctioneer paused, startled by the savage look of warning. Then he grinned, his aterroot-stained teeth gleaming in the midday sun.

"You've only yourself to blame, you high-and-mighty off-worlder," he said to the man. "Strutting out here as cocky as you please, flaunting yourself before these women. You're lucky they don't swarm up here and tear you to pieces." His smile widened. "We had that happen once, you know."

The auctioneer's hands moved toward the prisoner's breeches. "Now, be sensible and don't give me any—"

A booted foot snapped out and upward, catching the auctioneer squarely in the groin. "Be damned!" Gage Bardwin snarled. "I'll not add to anyone's entertainment!"

With a whoosh of exhaled air, the big man clutched himself and sank to his knees. His face twisted in agony. For long seconds he knelt before Gage, breathing heavily. A stream of aterroot juice trickled down his chin to drip onto his shabby tunic.

Behind him, female voices rose to a wild shriek, a cacophony of primal excitement mixed with a growing bloodlust. "Strip him! Strip him! Teach the arrogant male a lesson!"

A small, scrawny man hurried over, nervous and perspiring profusely. He mopped his brow with the back of his sleeve, then grabbed at the auctioneer's arm, tugging him to his feet. "Get up, you fool! You should know better than to stand too close to a breeder."

He pulled the auctioneer out of harm's way, then motioned over four more guards. "Do whatever is necessary." He indicated the prisoner. "Just give the women what they ask. I want this one sold and out of here before he starts further trouble!"

They advanced on Gage, all eyes riveted warily on his legs. He fought against the two men who held him, struggling to break free.

Helpless frustration welled in Gage. Gods, what else could go wrong? Beryllium shackles bound his wrists and arms, he faced four other men and he was trapped on an unfriendly planet with no weapons or money.

Curse the lapse of vigilance in that tavern on Locare, the final transport station before Tenua! If he hadn't been so exhausted from a particularly long and difficult transport process, if he hadn't imbibed one mug of Moracan ale too many or been so overly attentive to that seductive little barmaid, he'd have seen those off-world bounty hunters coming. But none of that mattered now. He'd been careless. He must extricate himself as best he could.

There was only one consolation. He *had* arrived at his destination, the capital of Eremita on the planet Tenua. He just wasn't in any position to do anything about it right—

With a shout, the extra guards rushed Gage en masse. Two leaped simultaneously for a leg. Another slipped behind to snake an arm about his neck and throttle him.

Gage fought wildly. He threw the full weight of his heavily muscled body first into one guard, then another. He managed to fling one man free of his right leg, then lashed out, kicking him full in the chest. The guard snapped backward, the wind knocked out of him.

Pivoting on his still encumbered leg, Gage kicked at the other man. Something flashed in his peripheral vision. A fist slammed into his jaw, then his gut.

The fourth guard.

Gage staggered backward, his knees buckling. Bright light exploded in his skull. Pain engulfed him. He battled past the agony, shaking his head to scatter the stars dancing before his eyes.

It was too late. The six men wrestled Gage to the platform, encasing him in a body lock he could only jerk against in impotent fury. His upper torso pinned, his legs held down in a spread-eagle position, Gage fought with all the strength left in him. Finally, as oxygen-starved limbs weakened, his powerful body could give no more. He lay there, panting in exhaustion, his face and chest sheened with sweat.

The sun beat down, its radiance blinding him. Gods, but it was hot on this hellish planet. So very hot. So draining . . . desolate.

A huge form moved to stand over him. "Proud, stupid off-worlder," the auctioneer snarled. "You'll pay dearly for your defiance before I'm done and satisfied, but first we'll give the women what they want."

He knelt between his prisoner's outspread legs.

With a smirking grin, the man grasped the front of Gage's breeches and ripped them apart.

"No, damn you!" Gage roared. With a superhuman effort he reared up, sinews taut, muscles straining.

The guards' grips tightened, strangling the life from him. A swirling gray mist swallowed Gage. He fell back. At the sudden lack of resistance the guards' holds loosened.

Gage dragged in great gulps of air, fighting past the loss of consciousness, sick to the very marrow of his bones. Sick with his sense of helplessness, of defeat.

It didn't matter that they'd bared his body. What mattered was the implied submission of the act—the utter *subservience*. And he'd never, ever, allowed another to use him without his express consent. Never, since that sol he'd confronted his mother . . . .

Rage swelled, white hot and searing. In a sudden, unexpected movement, Gage twisted to the side, dragging all six guards with him.

"Let . . . me . . . go!"

The endeavor took all he had. They quickly wrestled him back to the floor, slamming him down, crushing his head into the rough, splintered wood. Gage tasted his own blood, then his despair, bitter as gall.

"Damn you all! Let me go!" he cried again, choking the words past his sudden surge of nausea.

"Do as he says," a new voice, rich with authority, commanded. "Free him. Now."

The guards paused, looking up in surprise. The

auctioneer glanced over his shoulder. With a strangled sound he released Gage, then climbed to his feet.

"Domina Magna," the man murmured, bowing low to the woman who was Queen and ruler of the planet. "I-I am honored that the royal family chose to attend my humble sale."

"And why not?" the Queen's voice came again. "Haven't you some of the finest breeders in the Imperium? Now, get out of my way. Let us have a closer look at the male."

"As you wish, Domina Magna." The auctioneer stepped aside.

For a moment all Gage saw was color, a bright, vibrant swirl of crimsons, blues and greens. Then the hues solidified into folds of shimmering, ultralight fabric, and the fabric into gowns. Gage levered himself to one elbow and glared up at the two women.

One was young with glossy black hair tucked under a sheer veil and striking, deep violet eyes. She was dressed in a loose, bulky gown that completely disguised whatever figure she might have. At his direct scrutiny her lashes lowered. A becoming flush darkened her cheeks.

A maiden, Gage thought wryly, and as shy as they came.

He shifted to the other woman. She was equally striking—her ripe femininity blatantly accentuated by the voluptuous bosom thrusting from her low-cut, snugly molded dress. There was no doubt as to the quality of her figure.

She met his hard-eyed gaze and held it for a long moment before turning to her younger companion.

"Well, daughter? Are you certain he's the one for you?" Her bold glance lowered to Gage's groin. "Your maiden's flesh will be sorely tried by a man such as he. And he strikes me as none too gentle, if his antics a few seconds ago are any indication."

"Mother, please." The girl bit her lip, turning nearly as crimson as her gown. Her hesitant gaze lifted, meeting Gage's for an instant before skittering away to slide down the tautly sculpted, hair-roughened planes of his body.

The girl's eyes halted at the gaping vee of his breeches. A river of dark hair arrowed straight down from his flat belly to a much denser nest and hint of a large, thick organ before disappearing beneath the torn cloth. She swallowed hard, dragging her gaze back to her mother's.

"H-he couldn't help it. His pride was at stake. He had to fight them."

A slender brow arched in amusement. "Did he now? I think the sisters at our royal nunnery filled your head with too many tales of days long past. Days when men still possessed some shred of gentleness and integrity. And I think," the Queen said as she took her daughter's arm and began to lead her away, "that I called you back to your royal duties none too soon."

"Mother. Wait." The girl dug in her heels.

"Yes, child?"

"May I have him or not? You said it was my choice."

The Queen eyed her daughter, then sighed. "Yes, you may have him if your heart is set. The law dictates that you take a breeder before commencing a royal life mating. But heed my words. You'll regret it. He's not the male for you."

She glanced at the auctioneer. "We'll take him," she said, indicating Gage. "Have him sent to the palace immediately."

"Er, pardon, Domina Magna." The small, scrawny man stepped forward.

"Yes?"

"This is an especially high-quality breeder. He'll cost extra."

The Queen's lips tightened. "How much extra?"

"Five thousand imperials."

Her nostrils flared. "No breeder, not even one for a Royal Princess of Corba, is worth that much! I'll give you two thousand and not an imperial more!"

"But Domina Magna—"

"Enough!" The woman held up a silencing hand. "Another word and I'll forget I'm your queen and simply confiscate the male." She smiled thinly. "And everything else you possess as well."

"As you wish, Domina Magna," the little man croaked, bowing and backing away. "The breeder will be delivered immediately."

Triumph gleamed in the Queen's eyes. "Good. See that he is."

"You will mate with my daughter and impregnate her. An easy task, I'm sure, for a breeder of your quality," Queen Kadra proclaimed, leaning back with an air of finality in her ornately gilded throne.

"Indeed?" Gage Bardwin drawled.

The woman glared down at the prisoner, her patience at an end. Though still bound and ensconced between two burly guards, the man was as defiant as he'd been on the auctioneer's platform. Obviously, more drastic measures were needed to ensure his cooperation.

She motioned to the guards. "Leave us."

At the order, Gage arched a dark brow. His lips twisted in cynical amusement.

Kadra waited until they were alone. "Have you had an opportunity to observe my palace?" She indicated the room with a regal sweep of her bejeweled hand.

Gage shrugged. "It appears adequate."

"*Adequate?*" Kadra nearly choked on the word. "It's *impregnable*, both from within and from without." Her smoldering gaze met his. "There is no hope of escape."

He eyed her, knowing there was more to come.

"You will service my daughter and impregnate her, or you will die. It's that simple."

"Is it now?"

Gage slowly surveyed the room. She was right. This chamber was just as heavily fortified as was the rest of the palace. The doors and windows were barricaded by a sturdy grillwork of what looked to be a beryllium-impregnated alloy. Not even a laser gun could cut through that metal. The exterior walls were of solid rock and several feet thick. Add to that the highly complex video monitoring system Gage had noticed in his journey through the palace, and escape seemed a near impossibility.

He clamped down on a surge of angry frustration and turned back to the queen. "And what's wrong with your own men that you must turn to an off-worlder for breeding purposes—especially for your own daughter?"

The Queen's grip on her chair tightened. "Tenuan men are not the issue here. I have given you a command. The consequences are clear. What is your decision?"

Gage's eyes narrowed. Damn her. She held the advantage—at least for now—and she knew it.

He was on a mission of vital importance. The issue of his pride, no matter how dearly cherished, paled in light of the threat of Volan infiltration. And there *were* potential benefits to stalling for time, for being in the Tenuan Royal Palace. Information could be gleaned, conversations overheard . . . .

"She's a pretty one, your daughter," Gage said, conceding the Queen a temporary victory. "What's her name?"

A smile glimmered on Kadra's lips. "Meriel. Do I take this to mean you accept my terms?"

"A mating with your lovely daughter in exchange for my freedom?" Gage nodded. "In reality, I win all the way around. How soon do you require my services?"

"My daughter's fertile time spans this very day. You will be bathed, dressed more appropriately, then taken to her. I expect several matings to assure your seed is properly planted. Do you understand me?"

Gods, there went his opportunity for leisure to explore the palace. Well, the girl herself might be the best source of information anyway. He nodded. "Yes. And on the morrow I am free to go?"

"But of course. There will be no further need for you."

"No, I'd imagine not." Gage paused. "Is there anything I need to know about your daughter? To ease the 'wooing', as it were?"

Kadra bristled at the barely veiled sarcasm. The insolent bastard! But why should she be surprised? Bellatorians were all alike—arrogant, unfeeling and endlessly belittling of Tenua and all things Tenuan. It was exactly that attitude that had finally prodded her to cut her planet off from the rest of the Imperium. She'd be damned if she'd grovel and beg for the few crumbs of support that the Bellatorian-led, exalted organization of planets deigned to toss her way.

Meanwhile, she'd deal with this particular Bellatorian as she saw fit, the only possible outcome his death. Kadra smiled grimly. She'd take great pleasure in seeing this breeder died as painfully as possible. She had enough problems without being forced to tolerate his arrogance.

"Meriel is gently reared, having just completed her girlhood training at the royal nunnery. She knows little of men. You will treat her with care and not subject her to any crudities. And you will be constantly monitored, so don't think I won't know what you do or say."

"Even to our mating?" Gage inquired dryly. "Will you be privy to that as well?"

The Queen's eyes narrowed. "I owe you no explanation of what I will or will not do. You're a breeder, not a compatriot. Use your body and use it well. That's what I bought you for."